"In all the many-colored worlds of the universe no single ethical code shows a universal force. The good citizen on Almanatz would be executed on Judith IV. Commonplace conduct of Medellin excites the wildest revulsion on Earth and on Moritaba a deft thief commands the highest respect. I am convinced that virtue is but a reflection of good intent."
—Magnus Ridolph

As a professional trouble-shooter in the varied worlds and vari-shaped populations of the galaxy, such a philosophy was vital. In this book, the first complete collection of all the recorded cases of Magnus Ridolph, interstellar operative, readers will find the unique qualities of Jack Vance at their best.

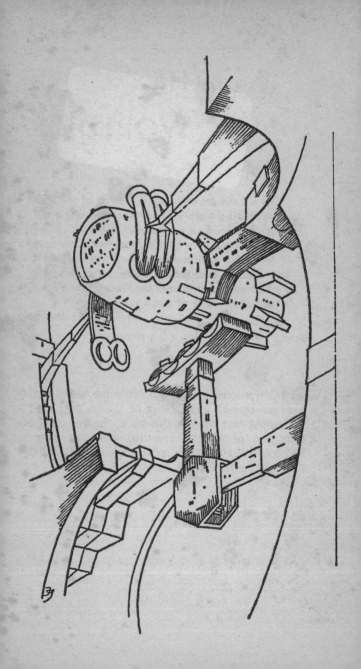

THE
MANY WORLDS
OF
MAGNUS RIDOLPH

JACK VANCE

DAW BOOKS, INC.
DONALD A. WOLLHEIM, PUBLISHER

1633 Broadway
New York, N.Y.   10019

FIRST PRINTING, APRIL 1980

1 2 3 4 5 6 7 8 9

 DAW TRADEMARK REGISTERED
U.S. PAT. OFF. MARCA
REGISTRADA. HECHO EN U.S.A.

PRINTED IN U.S.A.

TABLE OF CONTENTS

THE KOKOD WARRIORS

I

MAGNUS RIDOLPH sat on the Glass Jetty at Providencia, fingering a quarti-quartino of Blue Ruin. At his back rose Granatee Head; before him spread Milles-Iles Ocean and the myriad little islands, each with its trees and neo-classic villa. A magnificent blue sky extended overhead; and beneath his feet, under the glass floor of the jetty, lay Coral Canyon, with schools of sea-moths flashing and flickering like metal snowflakes. Magnus Ridolph sipped his liqueur and considered a memorandum from his bank describing a condition barely distinguishable from poverty.

He had been perhaps too trusting with his money. A few months previously, the Outer Empire Investment and Realty Society, to which he had entrusted a considerable sum, had been found to be bankrupt. The Chairman of the Board and the General Manager, a Mr. See and a Mr. Holpers, had been paying each other unexpectedly large salaries, most of which had been derived from Magnus Ridolph's capital investment.

Magnus Ridolph sighed, glanced at his liqueur. This would be the last of these; hereafter he must drink *vin ordinaire*, a fluid rather like tarragon vinegar, prepared from the fermented rind of a local cactus.

A waiter approached. "A lady wishes to speak to you, sir."

Magnus Ridolph preened his neat white beard. "Show her over, by all means."

The waiter returned; Magnus Ridolph's eyebrows went S-shape as he saw his guest: a woman of commanding presence, with an air of militant and dignified virtue. Her interest in Magnus Ridolph was clearly professional.

She came to an abrupt halt. "You are Mr. Magnus Ridolph?"

He bowed. "Will you sit down?"

The woman rather hesitantly took a seat. "Somehow, Mr. Ridolph, I expected someone more—well . . ."

Magnus Ridolph's reply was urbane. "A younger man, perhaps? With conspicuous biceps, a gun on his hip, a space helmet on his head? Or perhaps my beard alarms you?"

"Well, not exactly that, but my business—"

"Ah, you came to me in a professional capacity?"

"Well, yes. I would say so."

In spite of the memorandum from his bank—which now he folded and tucked into his pocket—Magnus Ridolph spoke with decision. "If your business requires feats of physical prowess, I beg you hire elsewhere. My janitor might satisfy your needs: an excellent chap who engages his spare time moving bar-bells from one elevation to another."

"No, no," said the woman hastily. "I'm sure you misunderstand; I merely pictured a different sort of individual. . . ."

Magnus Ridolph cleared his throat. "What is your problem?"

"Well—I am Martha Chickering, secretary of the Women's League Committee for the Preservation of Moral Values. We are fighting a particularly disgraceful condition that the law refuses to abate. We have appealed to the better nature of the persons involved, but I'm afraid that financial gain means more to them than decency."

"Be so kind as to state your problem."

"Are you acquainted with the world"—she spoke it as if it were a social disease—"Kokod?"

Magnus Ridolph nodded gravely, stroked his neat white beard. "Your problem assumes form."

"Can you help us, then? Every right-thinking person condemns the goings-on—brutal, undignified, nauseous . . ."

Magnus Ridolph nodded. "The exploitation of the Kokod natives is hardly commendable."

"Hardly commendable!" cried Martha Chickering. "It's despicable! It's trafficking in blood! We execrate the sadistic beasts who patronize bull-fights—but we condone, even encourage the terrible things that take place on Kokod while Holpers and See daily grow wealthier."

"Ha, ha!" exclaimed Magnus Ridolph. "Bruce Holpers and Julius See?"

"Why, yes." She looked at him questioningly. "Perhaps you know them?"

Magnus Ridolph sat back in his chair, turned the liqueur down his throat. "To some slight extent. We had what I be-

8

lieve is called a business connection. But no matter, please continue. Your problem has acquired a new dimension, and beyond question the situation is deplorable."

"Then you agree that the Kokod Syndicate should be broken up? You will help us?"

Magnus Ridolph spread his arms in a fluent gesture. "Mrs. Chickering my good wishes are freely at your disposal; active participation in the crusade is another matter and will be determined by the fee your organization is prepared to invest."

Mrs. Chickering spoke stiffly. "Well, we assume that a man of principle might be willing to make certain sacrifices—"

Magnus Ridolph sighed. "You touch me upon a sensitive spot, Mrs. Chickering. I shall indeed make a sacrifice. Rather than the extended rest I had promised myself, I will devote my abilities to your problem . . . Now let us discuss my fee—no, first, what do you require?"

"We insist that the gaming at Shadow Valley Inn be halted. We want Bruce Holpers and Julius See prosecuted and punished. We want an end put to the Kokod wars."

Magnus Ridolph looked off into the distance and for a moment was silent. When at last he spoke, his voice was grave. "You list your requirements on a descending level of feasibility."

"I don't understand you, Mr. Ridolph."

"Shadow Valley Inn might well be rendered inoperative by means of a bomb or an epidemic of Mayerheim's Bloat. To punish Holpers and See, we must demonstrate that a nonexistent law has been criminally violated. And to halt the Kokod wars, it will be necessary to alter the genetic heritage, glandular makeup, training, instinct, and general outlook on life of each of the countless Kokod warriors."

Mrs. Chickering blinked and stammered; Magnus Ridolph held up a courteous hand. "However, that which is never attempted never transpires; I will bend my best efforts to your requirements. My fee—well, in view of the altruistic ends in prospect, I will be modest; a thousand munits a week and expenses. Payable, if you please, in advance."

Magnus Ridolph left the jetty, mounted Granatee Head by steps cut into the green-veined limestone. On top, he paused by the wrought-iron balustrade to catch his breath and enjoy the vista over the ocean. Then he turned and entered the blue lace and silver filigree lobby of the Hotel des Mille Iles.

Presenting a bland face to the scrutiny of the desk clerk he sauntered into the library, where he selected a cubicle, settled

9

himself before the mnemiphot. Consulting the index for Kokod, he punched the appropriate keys.

The screen came to life. Magnus Ridolph inspected first a series of charts which established that Kokod was an exceedingly small world of high specific gravity.

Next appeared a projection of the surface, accompanied by a slow-moving strip of descriptive matter:

Although a small world, Kokod's gravity and atmosphere make it uniquely habitable for men. It has never been settled, due to an already numerous population of autochthones and a lack of valuable minerals.

Tourists are welcomed at Shadow Valley Inn, a resort hotel at Shadow Valley. Weekly packets connect Shadow Valley Inn with Starport.

Kokod's most interesting feature is its population.

The chart disappeared, to be replaced by a picture entitled, "Typical Kokod Warrior (from Rock River Tumble)," and displaying a man-like creature two feet tall. The head was narrow and peaked; the torso was that of a bee—long, pointed, covered with yellow down. Scrawny arms gripped a four-foot lance; a stone knife hung at the belt. The chitinous legs were shod with barbs. The creature's expression was mild, almost reproachful.

A voice said, "You will now hear the voice of Sam 192 Rock River."

The Kokod warrior inhaled deeply; wattles beside his chin quivered. From the mnemiphot screen issued a high-pitched stridency. Interpretation appeared on a panel to the right.

"I am Sam 192, squadronite, Company 14 of the Advance Force, in the service of Rock River Tumble. Our valor is a source of wonder to all; our magnificent stele is rooted deep, and exceeded in girth only by the steles of Rose Slope Tumble and crafty Shell Strand Tumble.

"This day I have come at the invitation of the (untranslatable) of Small Square Tumble, to tell of our victories and immensely effective strategies."

Another sound made itself heard: a man speaking falsetto in the Kokod language. The interpretation read:

Question: Tell us about life in Rock River Tumble.

Sam 192: It is very companionable.

Q: What is the first thing you do in the morning?

A: We march past the matrons, to assure ourselves of a properly martial fecundity.

Q: What do you eat?

A: We are nourished in the fields. (Note: The Kokod metabolism is not entirely understood; apparently they ferment organic material in a crop, and oxidize the resultant alcohols.)

Q: Tell us about your daily life.

A: We practice various disciplines, deploy in the basic formations, hurl weapons, train the kinderlings, elevate the veterans.

Q: How often do you engage in battle?

A: When it is our time: when the challenge has issued and the appropriate Code of Combat agreed upon with the enemy.

Q: You mean you fight in various styles?

A: There are 97 conventions of battle which may be employed: for instance, Code 48, by which we overcame strong Black Glass Tumble, allows the lance to be grasped only by the left hand and permits no severing of the leg tendons with the dagger. Code 69, however, insists that the tendons must be cut before the kill is made and the lances are used thwart-wise, as bumpers.

Q: Why do you fight? Why are there wars?

A: Because the steles of the other tumbles would surpass ours in size, did we not fight and win victories.

(Note: the stele is a composite tree growing in each tumble. Each victory is celebrated by the addition of a shoot, which joins and augments the main body of the stele. The Rock River Stele is 17 feet in diameter, and is estimated to be 4,000 years old. The Rose Slope Stele is 18 feet in diameter, and the Shell Strand Stele is almost 20 feet in diameter.)

Q: What would happen if warriors from Frog Pond Tumble cut down Rock River Stele?

Sam 192 made no sound. His wattles blew out; his head bobbed. After a moment he turned, marched out of view.

Into the screen came a man wearing shoulder tabs of Commonwealth Control. He looked after Sam 192 with an expression of patronizing good humor that Magnus Ridolph considered insufferable.

"The Kokod warriors are well known through the numerous sociological studies published on Earth, of which the most authoritative is perhaps the Carlisle Foundation's *Kokod: A Militaristic Society*, mnemiphot code AK-SK-RD-BP.

"To summarize, let me state that there are 81 tumbles, or castles, on Kokod, each engaged in highly formalized warfare with all the others. The evolutionary function of this warfare is the prevention of overpopulation on a small world. The Tumble Matrons are prolific, and only these rather protean measures assure a balanced ecology.

"I have been asked repeatedly whether the Kokod warriors fear death. My belief is that identification with the home tumble is so intense that the warriors have small sense of individuality. Their sole ambition is winning battles, swelling the girth of their stele and so glorifying their tumble."

The man spoke on. Magnus Ridolph reached out, speeded up the sequence.

On the screen appeared Shadow Valley Inn—a luxurious building under six tall parasol trees. The commentary read: "At Shadow Valley Inn, genial co-owners Julius See and Bruce Holpers greet tourists from all over the universe."

Two cuts appeared—a dark man with a lowering broad face, a mouth uncomfortably twisted in a grin; the other, lanky, with a long head sparsely thatched with red excelsior. "See" and "Holpers" read the sub-headings.

Magnus Ridolph halted the progression of the program, studied the faces for a few seconds, then allowed the sequence to continue.

"Mr. See and Mr. Holpers," ran the script, "have ingeniously made use of the incessant wars as a means of diverting their guests. A sheet quotes odds on each day's battle—a pastime which arouses enthusiasm among sporting visitors."

Magnus Ridolph turned off the mnemiphot, sat back in the chair, stroked his beard reflectively. "Where odds exist," he said to himself, "there likewise exists the possibility of upsetting the odds. . . . Luckily, my obligation to Mrs. Chickering will in no way interfere with a certain measure of subsidiary profits. Or better, let us say, recompense."

II

ALIGHTING FROM the Phoenix Line packet, the *Hesperornis*, Ridolph was startled momentarily by the close horizons of Kokod. The sky seemed to begin almost at his feet.

Waiting to transfer the passengers to the inn was an over-decorated charabanc. Magnus Ridolph gingerly took a seat, and when the vehicle lurched forward a heavy woman

12

scented with musk was thrust against him. "Really!" complained the woman.

"A thousand apologies," replied Magnus Ridolph, adjusting his position. "Next time I will take care to move out of your way."

The woman brushed him with a contemptuous glance and turned to her companion, a woman with the small head and robust contour of a peacock.

"Attendant!" the second woman called presently.

"Yes, Madame."

"Tell us about these native wars; we've heard so much about them."

"They're extremely interesting, Madame. The little fellows are quite savage."

"I hope there's no danger for the onlookers?"

"None whatever; they reserve their unfriendliness for each other."

"What time are the excursions?"

"I believe the Ivory Dune and the Eastern Shield Tumbles march tomorrow; the scene of battle no doubt will center around Muscadine Meadow, so there should be three excursions. To catch the deployments, you leave the inn at 5:00 A.M.; for the onslaught, at 6:00 A.M.; and 7:00 or 8:00 for the battle proper."

"It's ungodly early," the matron commented. "Is nothing else going on?"

"I'm not certain, Madame. The Green Ball and the Shell Strand might possibly war tomorrow, but they would engage according to Convention 4, which is hardly spectacular."

"Isn't there anything close by the inn?"

"No, Madame. Shadow Valley Tumble only just finished a campaign against Marble Arch, and are occupied now in repairing their weapons."

"What are the odds on the first of these—the Ivory Dune and the Eastern Shield?"

"I believe eight gets you five on Ivory Dune, and five gets you four on Eastern Shield."

"That's strange. Why aren't the odds the same both ways?"

"All bets must be placed through the inn management, Madame."

The carry-all rattled into the courtyard of the inn. Magnus Ridolph leaned forward. "Kindly brace yourself, Madame; the vehicle is about to stop, and I do not care to be held responsible for a second unpleasant incident."

The woman made no reply. The charabanc halted; Magnus

13

Ridolph climbed to the ground. Before him was the inn and behind a mountainside, dappled with succulent green flowers on lush violet bushes. Along the ridge grew tall, slender trees like poplars, vivid black and red. A most colorful world, decided Magnus Ridolph, and, turning, inspected the view down the valley. There were bands and layers of colors—pink, violet, yellow, green, graying into a distant dove color. Where the mouth of the valley gave on the river peneplain, Magnus Ridolph glimpsed a tall conical edifice. "One of the tumbles?" he inquired of the charabanc attendant.

"Yes sir—the Meadow View Tumble. Shadow Valley Tumble is further up the valley, behind the inn."

Magnus Ridolph turned to enter the inn. His eyes met those of a man in a severe black suit—a short man with a dumpy face that looked as if it had been compressed in a vise. Ridolph recognized the countenance of Julius See. "Well, well, this is a surprise indeed," said Magnus.

See nodded grimly. "Quite a coincidence. . . ."

"After the unhappy collapse of Outer Empire Realty and Investment I feared—indeed, I dreaded—that I should never see you again." And Magnus Ridolph watched Julius See with mild blue eyes blank as a lizard's.

"No such luck," said See. "As a matter of fact, I run this place. Er, may I speak to you a moment inside?"

"Certainly, by all means."

Ridolph followed his host through the well-appointed lobby into an office. A thin-faced man with thin red hair and squirrel teeth rose quickly to his feet. "You'll remember my partner, Bruce Holpers," said See with no expression in his voice.

"Of course," said Ridolph. "I am flattered that you honor me with your personal attention."

See cut the air with his hand—a small petulant gesture. "Forget the smart talk, Ridolph. . . . What's your game?"

Magnus Ridolph laughed easily. "Gentlemen, gentlemen—"

"Gentlemen my foot! Let's get down to brass tacks. If you've got any ideas left over from that Outer Empire deal, put them away."

"I assure you—"

"I've heard stories about you, Ridolph, and what I brought you in to tell you was that we're running a nice quiet place here, and we don't want any disturbance."

"Of course not," agreed Ridolph.

"Maybe you came for a little clean fun, betting on these native chipmunks; maybe you came on a party that we won't like."

14

Ridolph held out his hands guilelessly. "I can hardly say I'm flattered. I appear at your inn, an accredited guest; instantly you take me aside and admonish me."

"Ridolph," said See, "you have a funny reputation, and a normal sharpshooter never knows what side you're working on."

"Enough of this," said Magnus sternly. "Open the door, or I shall institute a strong protest."

"Look," said See ominously, "we own this hotel. If we don't like your looks, you'll camp out and rustle your own grub until the next packet—which is a week away."

Magnus Ridolph said coldly, "You will become liable to extensive damages if you seek to carry out your threat; in fact, I defy you, put me out if you dare!"

The lanky red-haired Holpers laid a nervous hand on See's arm. "He's right, Julie. We can't refuse service or the Control yanks our charter."

"If he misbehaves or performs, we can put him out."

"You have evidence, then, that I am a source of annoyance?"

See stood back, hands behind him. "Call this little talk a warning, Ridolph. You've just had your warning."

Returning to the lobby, Magnus Ridolph ordered his luggage sent to his room, and inquired the whereabouts of the Commonwealth Control officer.

"He's established on the edge of Black Bog, sir; you'll have to take an air-car unless you care for an all-night hike."

"You may order out an air-car," said Magnus Ridolph.

Seated in the well-upholstered tonneau, Ridolph watched Shadow Valley Inn dwindle below. The sun, Pi Sagittarius, which had already set, once more came into view as the car rose to clear Basalt Mountain, then sank in a welter of purples, greens and reds—a phoenix dying in its many-colored blood. Kokod twilight fell across the planet.

Below passed a wonderfully various landscape: lakes and parks, meadows, cliffs, crags, sweeping hillside slopes, river valleys. Here and there Ridolph sensed shapes in the fading light—the hive-like tumbles. As evening deepened into dove-colored night, the tumbles flickered with dancing orange sparks of illumination.

The air-car slanted down, slid under a copse of trees shaped like featherdusters. Magnus Ridolph alighted, stepped around to the pilot's compartment.

"Who is the Control officer?"

15

"His name is Clark, sir, Everley Clark."

Magnus Ridolph nodded. "I'll be no more than twenty minutes. Will you wait, please?"

"Yes, sir. Very well, sir."

Magnus Ridolph glanced sharply at the man: a suggestion of insolence behind the formal courtesy? . . . He strode to the frame building. The upper half of the door hung wide; cheerful yellow light poured out into the Kokod night. Within, Magnus Ridolph glimpsed a tall pink man in neat tan chord of memory; where had he seen this round pink face before? He rapped smartly on the door; the man turned his gabardines. Something in the man's physiognomy struck a head and rather glumly arose. Magnus Ridolph saw the man to be he of the mnemiphot presentation on Kokod, the man who had interviewed the warrior, Sam 192.

Everley Clark came to the door. "Yes? What can I do for you?"

"I had hoped for the privilege of a few words with you," replied Magnus Ridolph.

Clark blew out his cheeks, fumbled with the door fastenings. "By all means," he said hollowly. "Come in, sir." He motioned Magnus Ridolph to a chair. "Won't you sit down? My name is Everley Clark."

"I am Magnus Ridolph."

Clark evinced no flicker of recognition, responding with only a blank stare of inquiry.

Ridolph continued a trifle frostily. "I assume that our conversation can be considered confidential?"

"Entirely, sir. By all means." Clark showed a degree of animation, went to the fireplace, stood warming his hands at an imaginary blaze.

Ridolph chose his words for their maximum weight. "I have been employed by an important organization which I am not at liberty to name. The members of this organization—who I may say exert a not negligible political influence—feel that Control's management of Kokod business has been grossly inefficient and incorrect."

"Indeed!" Clark's official affability vanished as if a pink spotlight had been turned off.

Magnus Ridolph continued soberly. "In view of these charges, I thought it my duty to confer with you and learn your opinions."

Clark said grimly. "What do you mean—'charges'?"

"First, it is claimed that the gambling operations at

16

Shadow Valley Inn are—if not illegal—explicitly, shamelessly and flagrantly unmoral."

"Well?" said Clark bitterly. "What do you expect me to do? Run out waving a Bible? I can't interfere with tourist morals. They can play merry hell, run around naked, beat their dogs, forge checks—as long as they leave the natives alone, they're out of my jurisdiction."

Magnus Ridolph nodded sagely. "I see your position clearly. But a second and more serious allegation is that in allowing the Kokod wars to continue day in and day out, Control condones and tacitly encourages a type of brutality which would not be allowed on any other world of the Commonwealth."

Clark seated himself, sighed deeply. "If you'll forgive me for saying so, you sound for all the world like one of the form letters I get every day from women's clubs, religious institutes and anti-vivisectionist societies." He shook his round pink face with sober emphasis. "Mr. Ridolph, you just don't know the facts. You come up here in a lather of indignation, you shoot off your mouth and sit back with a pleased expression—good deed for the day. Well, it's not right! Do you think I enjoy seeing these little creatures tearing each other apart? Of course not—although I admit I've become used to it. When Kokod was first visited, we tried to stop the wars. The natives considered us damn fools, and went on fighting. We enforced peace, by threatening to cut down the steles. This meant something to them; they gave up the wars. And you never saw a sadder set of creatures in your life. They sat around in the dirt; they contracted a kind of roup and died by the droves. None of them cared enough to drag the corpses away. Four tumbles were wiped out; Cloud Crag, Yellow Bush, Sunset Ridge and Vinegrass. You can see them today, colonies thousands of years old, destroyed in a few months. And all this time the Tumble-matrons were producing young. No one had the spirit to feed them, and they starved or ran whimpering around the planet like naked little rats."

"Ahem," said Magnus Ridolph. "A pity."

"Fred Exman was adjutant here then. On his own authority he ordered the ban removed, told them to fight till they were blue in the face. The wars began half an hour later, and the natives have been happy and healthy ever since."

"If what you say is true," Magnus Ridolph remarked mildly, "I have fallen into the common fault of wishing to

17

impose my personal tenor of living upon creatures constitutionally disposed to another."

Clark said emphatically, "I don't like to see those sadistic bounders at the hotel capitalizing on the wars, but what can I do about it? And the tourists are no better: morbid unhealthy jackals, enjoying the sight of death. . . ."

Magnus Ridolph suggested cautiously, "Then it would be safe to say that, as a private individual, you would not be averse to a cessation of the gambling at Shadow Valley Inn?"

"Not at all," said Everley Clark. "As a private citizen, I've always thought that Julius See, Bruce Holpers and their guests represented mankind at its worst."

"One more detail," said Magnus Ridolph. "I believe you speak and understand the Kokod language?"

"After a fashion—yes." Clark grimaced in apprehension. "You realize I can't compromise Control officially?"

"I understand that very well."

"Just what do you plan, then?"

"I'll know better after I witness one or two of these campaigns."

III

Soft chimes roused Magnus Ridolph; he opened his eyes into the violet gloom of a Kokod dawn. "Yes?"

The hotel circuit said, "Five o'clock, Mr. Ridolph. The first party for today's battle leaves in one hour."

"Thank you." Ridolph swung his bony legs over the edge of the air-cushion, sat a reflective moment. He gained his feet, gingerly performed a set of calisthenic exercises.

In the bathroom he rinsed his mouth with tooth-cleanser, rubbed depilatory on his cheeks, splashed his face with cold water, applied tonic to his trim white beard.

Returning to the bedroom, he selected a quiet gray and blue outfit, with a rather dashing cap.

His room opened upon a terrace facing the mountainside; as he strolled forth, the two women whom he had encountered in the charabanc the day previously came past. Magnus Ridolph bowed, but the women passed without even a side glance.

"Cut me dead, by thunder," said Magnus Ridolph to himself. "Well, well." And he adjusted his cap to an even more rakish angle.

In the lobby a placard announced the event of the day:

18

All bets must be placed with the attendant.

Odds against Ivory Dune:	8:13
Odds against Eastern Shield:	5:4

In the last hundred battles Ivory Dune has won 41 engagements, Eastern Shield has won 59.

Excursions leave as follows:

For deployment:	6:00 A.M.
For onslaught:	7:00 A.M.
For battle proper:	8:00 A.M.

It is necessary that no interference be performed in the vicinity of the battle. Any guest infringing on this rule will be barred from further wagering. There will be no exceptions.

At a booth nearby, two personable young women were issuing betting vouchers. Magnus Ridolph passed quietly into the restaurant, where he breakfasted lightly on fruit juice, rolls and coffee, finishing in ample time to secure a place with the first excursion.

The observation vehicle was of that peculiar variety used in conveying a large number of people across a rough terrain. The car proper was suspended by a pair of cables from a kite-copter which flew five hundred feet overhead. The operator, seated in the nose of the car, worked pitch and attack by remote control, and so could skim quietly five feet over the ground, hover over waterfalls, ridges, ponds, other areas of scenic beauty with neither noise nor the thrash of driven air to disturb the passengers.

Muscadine Meadow was no small distance away; the operator lofted the ship rather abruptly over Basalt Mountain, then slid on a long slant into the northeast. Pi Sagittarius rolled up into the sky like a melon, and the grays, greens, reds, purples of the Kokod countryside shone up from below, rich as Circassian tapestry.

"We are near the Eastern Shield," the attendant announced in a mellifluous baritone. "The tumble is a trifle to the right, beside that bold face of granite whence it derives its name. If you look closely you will observe the Eastern Shield armies already on the march."

Bending forward studiously, Magnus Ridolph noticed a brown and yellow column winding across the mountainside.

To their rear he saw first the tall stele, rising two hundred feet, spraying over at the top into a fountain of pink, black and light green foliage; then below, the conical tumble.

The car sank slowly, drifted over a wooded patch of broken ground, halted ten feet above a smooth green meadow.

"This is the Muscadine," announced the guide. "At the far end you can see Muscadine Tumble and Stele, currently warring against Opal Grotto, odds 9 to 7 both ways. . . . If you will observe along the line of bamboo trees you will see the green caps of the Ivory Dune warriors. We can only guess their strategy, but they seem to be preparing a rather intricate offensive pattern—"

A woman's voice said peevishly, "Can't you take the car up higher so we can see everything?"

"Certainly, if you wish, Mrs. Chaim."

Five hundred feet above, copter blades slashed the air; the car wafted up like thistledown.

The guide continued, "The Eastern Shield warriors can be seen coming over the hill. . . . It seems as if they surmise the Ivory Dune strategy and will attempt to attack the flank. . . . There!" His voice rose animatedly. "By the bronze tree! The scouts have made a brush. . . . Eastern Shield lures the Ivory Dune scouts into ambush. . . . They're gone. Apparently today's code is 4, or possibly 36, allowing all weapons to be used freely, without restriction."

An old man with a nose like a raspberry said, "Put us down, driver. From up here we might as well be back at the inn."

"Certainly, Mr. Pilby."

The car sank low. Mrs. Chaim sniffed and glared.

The meadow rose from below; the car grounded gently on glossy dark green creepers. The guide said, "Anyone who wishes may go further on foot. For safety's sake, do not approach the battle more closely than three hundred feet; in any event the inn assumes no responsibility of any sort whatever."

"Hurry," said Mr. Pilby sharply. "The onslaught will be over before we're in place."

The guide good-naturedly shook his head. "They're still sparring for position, Mr. Pilby. They'll be dodging and feinting half an hour yet; that's the basis of their strategy—neither side wants to fight until they're assured of the best possible advantage." He opened the door. With Pilby in the lead, several dozen of the spectators stepped down on Muscadine Meadow, among them Magnus Ridolph, Mrs. Chaim

20

and her peacock-shaped friend whom she addressed as "Mrs. Borgage."

"Careful, ladies and gentlemen," called the guide, "Not too close to the battle."

"I've got my money on Eastern Shield," said Mrs. Borgage with heavy archness. "I'm going to make sure there's no funny business."

Magnus Ridolph inspected the scene of battle. "I'm afraid you are doomed to disappointment, Mrs. Borgage. In my opinion, Ivory Dune has selected the stronger position; if they hold on their right flank, give a trifle at the center, and catch the Eastern Shield forces on two sides when they close in, there should be small doubt as to the outcome of today's encounter."

"It must be wonderful to be so penetrating," said Mrs. Borgage in a sarcastic undertone to Mrs. Chaim.

Mr. Pilby said, "I don't think you see the battleground in its entire perspective, sir. The Eastern Shield merely needs to come in around that line of trees to catch the whole rear of the Ivory Dune line—"

"But by so doing," Magnus Ridolph pointed out, "they leave their rear unguarded; clearly Ivory Dune has the advantage of maneuver."

To the rear a second excursion boat landed. The doors opened, there was a hurrying group of people. "Has anything happened yet?" "Who's winning?"

"The situation is fluid," declared Pilby.

"Look, they're closing in!" came the cry. "It's the onslaught!"

Now rose the piping of Kokod war hymns: from Ivory Dune throats the chant sacred and long-beloved at Ivory Dune Tumble, and countering, the traditional paean of the Eastern Shield.

Down the hill came the Eastern Shield warriors, half-bent forward.

A thud and clatter—battle. The shock of small bodies, the dry whisper of knife against lance, the hoarse orders of leg-leaders and squadronites.

Forward and backward, green and black mingled with orange and white. Small bodies were hacked apart, dryly dismembered; small black eyes went dead and dim; a hundred souls raced all together, pell-mell, for the Tumble Beyond the Sky.

Forward and backward moved the standard-bearers—those

21

who carried the sapling from the sacred stele, whose capture would mean defeat for one and victory for the other.

On the trip back to the inn, Mrs. Chaim and Mrs. Borgage sat glum and solitary while Mr. Pilby glowered from the window.

Magnus Ridolph said affably to Pilby, "In a sense, an amateur strategist, such as myself, finds these battles a trifle tedious. He needs no more than a glance at the situation, and his training indicates the logical outcome. Naturally, none of us are infallible, but given equal forces and equal leadership, we can only assume that the forces in the better position will win."

Pilby lowered his head, chewed the corners of his mustache. Mrs. Chaim and Mrs. Borgage studied the landscape with fascinated absorption.

"Personally," said Ridolph, "I never gamble. I admire a dynamic attack on destiny, rather than the suppliance and passivity of the typical gambler; nevertheless, I feel for you all in your losses, which I hope were not too considerable?"

There was no reply. Magnus Ridolph might have been talking to empty air. After a moment Mrs. Chaim muttered inaudibly to the peacock-shaped Mrs. Borgage, and Mr. Pilby slouched even deeper in his seat. The remainder of the trip was passed in silence.

After a modest dinner of cultivated Bylandia protein, a green salad, and cheese, Magnus Ridolph strolled into the lobby, inspected the morrow's scratch sheet.

The announcement read:

TOMORROW'S FEATURED BATTLE:
VINE HILL TUMBLE
vs
ROARING CAPE TUMBLE
near Pink Stone Table.

Odds against Vine Hill Tumble: 1:3
Odds against Roaring Cape Tumble: 4:1
All bets must be placed with the attendant.

In the last hundred engagements Vine Hill Tumble has won 77, Roaring Cape has won 23.

Turning away, Magnus Ridolph bumped into Julius See, who was standing, rocking on his heels, his hands behind his back.

22

"Well, Ridolph, think you'll maybe take a flyer?"

Magnus Ridolph nodded. "A wager on Roaring Cape Tumble might prove profitable."

"That's right."

"On the other hand, Vine Hill is a strong favorite."

"That's what the screamer says."

"What would be your own preference, Mr. See?" asked Magnus Ridolph ingenuously.

"I don't have any preference. I work 23 to 77."

"Ah, you're not a gambling man, then?"

"Not any way you look at it."

Ridolph rubbed his beard and looked reflectively toward the ceiling. "Normally I should say the same of myself. But the wars offer an amateur strategist an unprecedented opportunity to test his abilities, and I may abandon the principles of a lifetime to back my theories."

Julius See turned away. "That's what we're here for."

"Do you impose a limit on the bets?"

See paused, looked over his shoulder. "We usually call a hundred thousand munits our maximum pay-off."

Manus Ridolph nodded. "Thank you." He crossed the lobby, entered the library. On one wall was a map of the planet, with red discs indicating the location of each tumble.

Magnus Ridolph located Vine Hill and Roaring Cape Tumbles, and found Pink Stone Table, the latter near an arm of Drago Bay. Magnus Ridolph went to a rack, found a large scale physiographic map of the area under his consideration. He took it to a table and spent half an hour in deep concentration.

He rose, replaced the map, sauntered through the lobby and out the side entrance. The pilot who had flown him the previous evening rose to his feet smartly. "Good evening, Mr. Ridolph. Intending another ride?"

"As a matter of fact, I am," Magnus Ridolph admitted. "Are you free?"

"In a moment, as soon as I turn in my day's report."

Ridolph looked thoughtfully after the pilot's hurrying figure. He quietly stepped around to the front entrance. From the vantage of the open door he watched the pilot approach Bruce Holpers and speak hastily.

Holpers ran a lank white hand through his red hair, gave a series of nervous instructions. The pilot nodded sagely, turned away. Magnus Ridolph returned by the route he had come.

He found the pilot waiting beside the ship. "I thought I had better notify Clark that I was coming," said Ridolph

23

breezily. "In case the car broke down, or there were any accident, he would understand the situation and know where to look for me."

The pilot's hands hesitated on the controls. Magnus Ridolph said, "Is there game of any sort on Kokod?"

"No, sir, none whatever."

"A pity. I am carrying with me a small target pistol with which I had hoped to bag a trophy or two. . . . Perhaps I'll be able to acquire one or two of the native weapons."

"That's quite unlikely, sir."

"In any case," said Magnus Ridolph cheerily, "you might be mistaken, so I will hold my weapon ready?"

The pilot looked straight ahead.

Magnus Ridolph climbed into the back seat. "To the Control office, then."

"Yes, Mr. Ridolph."

IV

EVERLEY CLARK greeted his visitor cautiously; when Ridolph sat back in a basket chair, Clark's eyes went everywhere in the room but to those of his guest.

Magnus Ridolph lit an *aromatique*. "Those shields on the wall are native artifacts, I presume?"

"Yes," said Clark quickly. "Each tumble has its distinct colors and insignia."

"To Earthly eyes, the patterns seem fortuitous, but naturally and inevitably Kokod symbology is unique. . . . A magnificent display. Does the collection have a price?"

Clark looked doubtfully at the shields. "I'd hate to let them go—although I suppose I could get others. These shields are hard to come by; each requires many thousand hours of work. They make the lacquer by a rather painstaking method, grinding pigment into a vehicle prepared from the boiled-down dead."

Ridolph nodded. "So that's how they dispose of the corpses."

"Yes; it's quite a ritual."

"About those shields—would you take ten thousand munits?"

Clark's face mirrored indecision. Abruptly he lit a cigarette. "Yes, I'd have to take ten thousand munits; I couldn't afford to refuse."

"It would be a shame to deprive you of a possession you obviously value so highly," said Magnus Ridolph. He exam-

24

ined the backs of his hands critically. "If ten thousand munits means so much to you, why do you not gamble at the inn? Surely with your knowledge of Kokod ways, your special information . . ."

Clark shook his head. "You can't beat that kind of odds. It's a sucker's game, betting at the inn."

"Hmm." Magnus Ridolph frowned. "It might be possible to influence the course of a battle. Tomorrow, for instance, the Vine Hill and Roaring Cape Tumbles engage each other, on Pink Stone Table, and the odds against Roaring Cape seem quite attractive."

Clark shook his head. "You'd lose your shirt betting on Roaring Cape. All their veterans went in the Pyrite campaign."

Magnus Ridolph said thoughtfully, "The Roaring Cape might win, if they received a small measure of assistance."

Clark's pink face expanded in alarm like a trick mask. "I'm an officer of the Commonwealth! I couldn't be party to a thing like that! It's unthinkable!"

Magnus Ridolph said judiciously, "Certainly the proposal is not one to enter upon hastily; it must be carefully considered. In a sense, the Commonwealth might be best served by the ousting of Shadow Valley Inn from the planet, or at least the present management. Financial depletion is as good a weapon as any. If, incidentally, we were to profit, not an eyebrow in the universe could be justifiably raised. Especially since the part that you might play in the achievement would be carefully veiled. . . ."

Clark shoved his hands deep in his pockets, stared a long moment at Magnus Ridolph. "I could not conceivably put myself in the position of siding with one tumble against another. If I did so, what little influence I have on Kokod would go up in smoke."

Magnus Ridolph shook his head indulgently. "I fear you imagine the two of us carrying lances, marching in step with the warriors, fighting in the first ranks. No, no, my friend, I assure you I intend nothing quite so broad."

"Well," snapped Clark, "just what do you intend?"

"It occurred to me that if we set out a few pellets of a sensitive explosive, such as fulminate of mercury, no one could hold us responsible if tomorrow the Vine Hill armies blundered upon them, and were thereby thrown into confusion."

"How would we know where to set out these pellets? I should think—"

Magnus Ridolph made an easy gesture. "I profess an

amateur's interest in military strategy; I will assume responsibility for that phase of the plan."

"But I have no fulminate of mercury," cried Clark, "no explosive of any kind!"

"But you do have a laboratory?"

Clark assented reluctantly. "Rather a makeshift affair."

"Your reagents possibly include fuming nitric acid and iodine?"

"Well—yes."

"Then to work. Nothing could suit our purpose better than nitrogen iodide."

The following afternoon Magnus Ridolph sat in the outdoor café overlooking the vista of Shadow Valley. His right hand clasped an eggshell goblet of Methedeon wine; his left held a mild cigar. Turning his head, he observed the approach of Julius See, and, a few steps behind, like a gaunt red-headed ghost, his partner, Bruce Holpers.

See's face was compressed into layers: a smear of black hair, creased forehead, barred eyebrows, eyes like a single dark slit, pale upper lip, mouth, wide sallow chin. Magnus Ridolph nodded affably. "Good evening, gentlemen."

See came to a halt, as, two steps later, did Bruce Holpers.

"Perhaps you can tell me the outcome of today's battle?" asked Magnus Ridolph. "I indulged myself in a small wager, breaking the habit of many years, but so far I have not learned whether the gods of chance have favored me."

"Well, well," said See throatily. " 'The gods of chance' you call yourself."

Magnus Ridolph turned him a glance of limpid inquiry. "Mr. See, you appear disturbed; I hope nothing is wrong?"

"Nothing special, Ridolph. We had a middling bad day— but they average out with the good ones."

"Unfortunate. . . . I take it, then, that the favorite won? If so, my little wager has been wiped out."

"Your little 25,000 munit wager, eh? And half a dozen other 25,000 munit wagers placed at your suggestion?"

Magnus Ridolph stroked his beard soberly. "I believe I did mention that I thought the odds against Roaring Cape interesting, but now you tell me that Vine Hill has swept the field."

Bruce Holpers uttered a dry cackle. See said harshly, "Come off it, Ridolph. I suppose you're completely unaware that a series of mysterious explosions" ("Land mines," interrupted Holpers, "that's what they were.") "threw Vine Hill

26

enough off stride so that Roaring Cape mopped up Pink Stone Table with them."

Magnus Ridolph sat up.

"Is that right, indeed? Then I have won after all!"

Julius See became suddenly silky, and Bruce Holpers, teetering on heel and toe, glanced skyward. "Unfortunately, Mr. Ridolph, so many persons had placed large bets on Roaring Cape that on meeting the odds, we find ourselves short on cash. We'll have to ask you to take your winnings out in board and room."

"But gentlemen!" protested Magnus Ridolph. "A hundred thousand munits! I'll be here until doomsday!"

See shook his head. "Not at our special Ridolph rates. The next packet is due in five days. Your bill comes to 20,000 munits a day. Exactly 100,000 munits."

"I'm afraid I find your humor a trifle heavy," said Magnus Ridolph frostily.

"It wasn't intended to make you laugh," said See. "Only us. I'm getting quite a kick out of it. How about you, Bruce?"

"Ha, ha, ha," laughed Holpers.

Magnus Ridolph rose to his feet. "There remains to me the classical recourse. I shall leave your exorbitant premises."

See permitted a grin to widen his lips. "Where are you going to leave to?"

"He's going to Roaring Cape Tumble," snickered Holpers. "They owe him a lot."

"In connection with the hundred thousand munits owed me, I'll take a note, an IOU. Oddly enough, a hundred thousand munits is almost exactly what I lost in the Outer Empire Realty and Investment failure."

See grinned sourly. "Forget it, Ridolph, give it up—an angle that didn't pay off."

Magnus Ridolph bowed, marched away. See and Holpers stood looking after him. Holpers made an adenoidal sound. "Think he'll move out?"

See grunted. "There's no reason why he should. He's not getting the hundred thousand anyway; he'd be smarter sitting tight."

"I hope he does go; he makes me nervous. Another deal like today would wipe us out. Six hundred thousand munits—a lot of scratch to go in ten minutes."

"We'll get it back. . . . Maybe we can rig a battle or two ourselves."

Holpers' long face dropped, and his teeth showed. "I'm not

27

so sure that's a good idea. First thing you know Commonwealth Control would be—"

"Pah!" spat See. "What's Control going to do about it?
Clark has all the fire and guts of a Leghorn pullet."

"Yes, but—"

"Just leave it to me."

They returned to the lobby. The desk clerk made an urgent
motion. "Mr. Ridolph has just checked out! I don't understand where—"

See cut him off with a brusque motion. "He can camp under a stele for all I care."

Magnus Ridolph sat back in the most comfortable of Everley Clark's armchairs and lit a cigarette. Clark watched him
with an expression at once wary and obstinate. "We have
gained a tactical victory," said Magnus Ridolph, "and suffered a strategic defeat."

Everley Clark knit his brows uneasily. "I don't quite follow
you. I should think—"

"We have diminished the financial power of Shadow Valley Inn, and hence, done serious damage. But the blow was
not decisive and the syndicate is still viable. I was unable to
collect my hundred thousand munits, and also have been
forced from the scene of maximum engagement. By this token we may fairly consider that our minimum objectives have
not been gained."

"Well," said Clark, "I know it hurts to have to admit defeat, but we've done our best and no one can do more. Considering my position, perhaps it's just as well that—"

"If conditions were to be allowed to rest on the present
basis," said Magnus Ridolph, "there might be reason for
some slight relaxation. But I fear that See and Holpers have
been too thoroughly agitated by their losses to let the matter
drop."

Everley Clark eyed Magnus Ridolph in perturbation. "But
what can they do? Surely I never—"

Magnus Ridolph shook his head gravely. "I must admit
that both See and Holpers accused me of setting off the explosions which routed the Vine Hill Tumble. Admission of
guilt would have been ingenuous; naturally I maintained that
I had done nothing of the sort. I claimed that I had no opportunity to do so, and further, that the Ecologic Examiner
aboard the *Hesperornis* who checked my luggage would
swear that I had no chemicals whatsoever among my effects.
I believe that I made a convincing protestation."

28

Everley Clark clenched his fists in alarm, hissed through his teeth.

Magnus Ridolph, looking thoughtfully across the room, went on. "I fear that they will ask themselves the obvious questions. 'Who has Magnus Ridolph most intimately consorted with, since his arrival on Kokod?' 'Who, besides Ridolph, has expressed disapproval of Shadow Valley Inn?' "

Everley Clark rose to his feet, paced back and forth. Ridolph continued in a dispassionate voice: "I fear that they will include these questions and whatever answers come to their minds in the complaint which they are preparing for the Chief Inspector at Methedeon."

Clark slumped into a chair, sat staring glassily at Magnus Ridolph. "Why did I let you talk me into this?" he asked hollowly.

Magnus Ridolph rose to his feet in his turn, paced slowly, tugging at his beard. "Certainly, events have not taken the trend we would have chosen, but strategists, amateur or otherwise, must expect occasional setbacks."

"Setbacks!" bawled Clark. "I'll be ruined! Disgraced! Drummed out of the Control!"

"A good strategist is necessarily flexible," mused Magnus Ridolph. "Beyond question, we now must alter our thinking; our primary objective becomes saving you from disgrace, expulsion, and possible prosecution."

Clark ran his hands across his face. "But—what can we do?"

"Very little, I fear," Magnus Ridolph said frankly. He puffed a moment on his cigarette, shook his head doubtfully. "There is one line of attack which might prove fruitful. . . . Yes, I think I see a ray of light."

"How? In what way? Your'e not planning to confess?"

"No," said Magnus Ridolph. "We gain little, if anything, by that ruse. Our only hope is to discredit Shadow Valley Inn. If we can demonstrate that they do not have the best interests of the Kokod natives at heart, I think we can go a long way toward weakening their allegations."

"That might well be, but—"

"If we could obtain iron-clad proof, for instance, that Holpers and See are callously using their position to wreak physical harm upon the natives, I think you might consider yourself vindicated."

"I suppose so. But doesn't the idea seem—well, impractical? See and Holpers have always fallen over backwards to avoid anything of that sort."

29

"So I would imagine. Er, what is the native term for Shadow Valley Inn?"

"Big Square Tumble, they call it."

"As the idea suggests itself to me, we must arrange that a war is conducted on the premises of Shadow Valley Inn, that Holpers and See are required to take forcible measures against the warriors!"

V

EVERLEY CLARK shook his head. "Devilish hard. You don't quite get the psychology of these tribes. They'll fight till they fall apart to capture the rallying standard of another tumble—that's a sapling from the sacred stele, of course—they won't be dictated to, or led or otherwise influenced."

"Well, well," said Magnus Ridolph. "In that case, your position is hopeless." He came to a halt before Clark's collection of shields. "Let us talk of pleasanter matters."

Everley Clark gave no sign that he had heard.

Magnus Ridolph stroked one of the shields with reverent fingertips. "Remarkable technique, absolutely unique in my experience. I assume that this rusty orange is one of the ochers?"

Everley Clark made an ambiguous sound.

"A truly beautiful display," said Magnus Ridolph. "I suppose there's no doubt that—if worse comes to worst in our little business—you will be allowed to decorate your cell at the Regional Penitentiary as you desire."

Everley Clark said in a thick voice, "Do you think they'll go that far?"

Ridolph considered. "I sincerely hope not. I don't see how we can prevent it unless"—he held up a finger—"unless—"

"What?" croaked Clark.

"It is farcically simple; I wonder at our own obtuseness."

"What? What? For Heaven's sake, man—"

"I conceive one certain means by which the warriors can be persuaded to fight at Shadow Valley Inn."

Everley Clark's face fell. "Oh. Well, how, then?"

"Shadow Valley Inn or Big Square Tumble, if you like, must challenge the Kokod warriors to a contest of arms."

Everley Clark's expression became more bewildered than ever. "But that's out of the question. Certainly Holpers and See would never . . ."

Magnus Ridolph rose to his feet. "Come," he said, with decision. "We will act on their behalf."

30

Clark and Magnus Ridolph walked down Shell Strand. On their right the placid blue-black ocean transformed itself into surf or mingled meringue and whipped-cream; on the left bulked the Hidden Hills. Behind towered the magnificent stele of the Shell Strand Tumble; ahead soared the almost equally impressive stele of the Sea Stone Tumble, toward which they bent their steps. Corps of young warriors drilled along the beach; veterans of a hundred battles who had grown stiff, hard and knobby came down from the forest bearing faggots of lance-stock. At the door to the tumble, infant warriors scampered in the dirt like rats.

Clark said huskily, "I don't like this, I don't like it a bit. . . . If it ever gets out—"

"Is such a supposition logically tenable?" asked Magnus Ridolph. "You are the only living man who speaks the Kokod language."

"Suppose there is killing—slaughter?"

"I hardly think it likely."

"It's not impossible. And think of these little warriors—they'll be bearing the brunt—"

Magnus Ridolph said patiently, "We have discussed these points at length."

Clark muttered, "I'll go through with it . . . but God forgive us both if—"

"Come, come," exclaimed Magnus Ridolph. "Let us approach the matter with confidence; apologizing in advance to your deity hardly maximizes our morale. . . . Now, what is protocol at arranging a war?"

Clark pointed out a dangling wooden plate painted with one of the traditional Kokod patterns. "That's the Charter Board: all I need to do is—well, watch me."

He strode up to the board, took a lance from the hands of a blinking warrior, smartly struck the object. It resonated a dull musical note.

Clark stepped back, and through his nose passed the bagpipe syllables of the Kokod language.

From the door of the tumble stepped a dozen blank-faced warriors, listening attentively.

Clark wound up his speech, turned, scuffed dirt toward the magnificent Sea Stone stele.

The warriors watched impassively. From within the stele came a torrent of syllables. Clark replied at length, then turned on his heel and rejoined Magnus Ridolph. His forehead was damp. "Well, that's that. It's all set. Tomorrow morning at Big Square Tumble."

31

"Excellent," said Magnus Ridolph briskly. "Now to Shell Strand Tumble, then Rock River, and next Rainbow Cleft."

Clark groaned. "You'll have the entire planet at odds."

"Exactly," said Magnus Ridolph. "After our visit to Rainbow Cleft, you can drop me off near Shadow Valley Inn, where I have some small business."

Clark darted him a suspicious sideglance. "What kind of business?"

"We must be practical," said Magnus Ridolph. "One of the necessary appurtenances to a party at war on Kokod is a rallying standard, a sacred sapling, a focus of effort for the opposing force. Since we can expect neither Holpers nor See to provide one, I must see to the matter myself."

Ridolph strolled up Shadow Valley, approached the hangar where the inn's aircraft were housed. From the shadow of one of the fantastic Kokod trees, he counted six vehicles: three carry-alls, two air-cars like the one which had conveyed him originally to the Control station, and a sleek red sportster evidently the personal property of either See or Holpers.

Neither the hangar-men nor the pilots were in evidence; it might well be their dinner hour. Magnus Ridolph sauntered carelessly forward, whistling an air currently being heard along far-off boulevards.

He cut his whistle off sharply, moved at an accelerated rate. Fastidiously protecting his hands with a bit of rag, he snapped the repair panels from each of the observation cars, made a swift abstraction from each, did likewise for the air-cars. At the sleek sportster he paused, inspected the lines critically.

"An attractive vehicle," he said to himself, "one which might creditably serve the purposes for which I intend it."

He slid back the door, looked inside. The starter key was absent.

Steps sounded behind him. "Hey," said a rough voice, "what are you doing with Mr. See's car?"

Magnus Ridolph withdrew without haste.

"Offhand," he said, "what would you estimate the value of this vehicle?"

The hangarman paused, glowering and suspicious. "Too much not to be taken care of."

Magnus Ridolph nodded. "Thirty thousand munits, possibly."

"Thirty thousand on Earth. This is Kokod."

"I'm thinking of offering See a hundred thousand munits."

32

The hangarman blinked. "He'd be crazy not to take it."

"I suppose so," sighed Magnus Ridolph. "But first, I wanted to satisfy myself as to the craft's mechanical condition. I fear it has been neglected."

The hangarman snorted in indignation. "Not on your life."

Magnus Ridolph frowned. "That tube is certainly spitting. I can tell by the patina along the enamel."

"No such thing!" roared the hangarman. "That tube flows like a dream."

Ridolph shook his head. "I can't offer See good money for a defective vehicle. . . . He'll be angry to lose the sale."

The hangarman's tone changed. "I tell you, that tube's good as gold. . . . Wait, I'll show you"

He pulled a key-ring from his pocket, plugged it into the starter socket. The car quivered free of the ground, eager for flight. "See? Just what I told you?"

Magnus Ridolph said doubtfully. "It seems to be working fairly well now. . . . You get on the telephone and tell Mr. See that I am taking his car for a trial spin, a final check. . . ."

The mechanic looked dumbly at Magnus Ridolph, slowly turned to the speaker on the wall.

Magnus Ridolph jumped into the seat. The mechanic's voice was loud. "The gentleman that's buying your boat is giving it the once-over. Don't let him feed you no line about a bum tube; the ship is running like oil down a four mile bore. Don't take nothing else . . . What? . . . Sure he's here; he said so himself . . A little schoolteacher guy with a white beard like a nanny-goat . . ." The sound from the telephone caused him to jump back sharply. Anxiously, he turned to look where he had left Magnus Ridolph and Julius See's sleek red air-car.

Both had disappeared.

Mrs. Chaim roused her peacock-shaped friend Mrs. Borgage rather earlier than usual. "Hurry, Altamira; we've been so late these last few mornings, we've missed the best seats in the observation car."

Mrs. Borgage obliged by hastening her toilet; in short order the two ladies appeared in the lobby. By a peculiar coincidence both wore costumes of dark green, a color which each thought suited the other not at all. They paused by the announcement of the day's war in order to check the odds, then turned into the dining room.

They ate a hurried breakfast, set out for the loading platform. Mrs. Borgage, pausing to catch her breath and enjoy the freshness of the morning, glanced toward the roof of the inn. Mrs. Chaim rather impatiently looked over her shoulder. "Whatever are you staring at, Altamira?"

Mrs. Borgage pointed. "It's that unpleasant little man Ridolph . . . I can't fathom what he's up to. He seems to be fixing some sort of branch to the roof."

Mrs. Chaim sniffed. "I thought the management had turned him out."

"Isn't that Mr. See's air-car on the roof behind him?"

"I really couldn't say," replied Mrs. Chaim. "I know very little of such things." She turned away toward the loading platform, and Mrs. Borgage followed.

Once more they met interruption; this time in the form of the pilot. His clothes were disarranged; his face had suffered scratching and contusion. Running wild-eyed, he careened into the two green-clad ladies, disengaged himself and continued without apology.

Mrs. Chaim bridled in outrage. "Well, I never!" She turned to look after the pilot. "Has the man gone mad?"

Mrs. Borgage, peering ahead to learn the source of the pilot's alarm, uttered a sharp cry.

"What is it?" asked Mrs. Chaim irritatedly.

Mrs. Borgage clasped her arm with bony fingers. "Look."

VI

DURING THE subsequent official investigation, Commonwealth Control Agent Everley Clark transcribed the following eyewitness account:

"I am Joe 234, Leg-leader of the Fifteenth Brigade, the Fanatics, in the service of the indomitable Shell Strand Tumble.

"We are accustomed to the ruses of Topaz Tumble and the desperate subleties of Star Throne; hence the ambush prepared by the giant warriors of Big Square Tumble took us not at all by surprise.

"Approaching by Primary Formation 17, we circled the flat space occupied by several flying contrivances, where we flushed out a patrol spy. We thrashed him with our lances, and he fled back toward his own forces.

"Continuing, we encountered a first line of defense consisting of two rather ineffectual warriors accoutred in garments of green cloth. These we beat, also, according to Convention 22, in force during the day. Uttering terrible cries, the two warriors retreated, luring us toward prepared positions inside the tumble itself. High on the roof the standard of Big Square Tumble rose, plain to see. No deception there, at least! Our strategic problem assumed a clear form; how best to beat down resistance and win to the roof.

"Frontal assault was decided upon; the signal to advance was given. We of the Fifteenth were first past the outer defense—a double panel of thick glass which we broke with rocks. Inside we met a spirited defense which momentarily threw us back.

"At this juncture occurred a diversion in the form of troops from the Rock River Tumble, which, as we now know, the warriors of the Big Square Tumble had rashly challenged for the same day. The Rock River warriors entered by a row of flimsy doors facing the mountain, and at this time the Big Square defenders violated Convention 22, which requires that the enemy be subdued by blows of the lance. Flagrantly they hurled glass cups and goblets, and by immemorial usage we were allowed to retaliate in kind.

"At the failure of this tactic, the defending warriors withdrew to an inner bastion, voicing their war-cries.

"The siege began in earnest; and now the Big Square warriors began to pay the price of their arrogance. Not only had they pitted themselves against Shell Strand and Rock River, but they likewise had challenged the redoubtable Rainbow Cleft and Sea Stone, conquerors of Rose Slope and Dark Fissure. The Sea Stone warriors, led by their Throw-away Legion, poured through a secret rear-entrance, while the Rainbow Cleft Special Vanguard occupied the Big Square main council hall.

"A terrible battle raged for several minutes in a room designed for the preparations of nourishments, and again the Big Square warriors broke code by throwing fluids, pastes, and powders—a remission which the alert Shell Strand warriors swiftly copied.

"I led the Fanatic Fifteenth outside, hoping to gain exterior access to the roof, and thereby win the Big Square standard. The armies of Shell Strand, Sea Stone, Rock River and Rainbow Cleft now completely surrounded Big Square Tumble, a magnificent sight which shall live in my memory till at last I lay down my lance.

"In spite of our efforts, the honor of gaining the enemy standard went to a daredevil squad from Sea Stone, which scaled a tree to the roof and so bore away the trophy. The defenders, ignorant of, or ignoring the fact that the standard had been taken, broke the code yet again, this time by using

35

tremendous blasts of water. The next time Shell Strand wars with Big Square Tumble we shall insist on one of the Conventions allowing any and all weapons; otherwise we place ourselves at a disadvantage.

"Victorious, our army, together with the troops of Sea Stone, Rock River and Rainbow Cleft, assembled in the proper formations and marched off to our home tumbles. Even as we departed, the great Black Comet Tumble dropped from the sky to vomit further warriors for Big Square. However, there was no pursuit, and unmolested we returned to the victory rituals."

Captain Bussey of the Phoenix Line packet *Archaeornix*, which had arrived as the Kokod warriors marched away, surveyed the wreckage with utter astonishment. "What in God's name happened to you?"

Julius See stood panting, his forehead clammy with sweat. "Get me guns," he cried hoarsely. "Get me a blaster; I'll wipe out every damn hive on the planet. . . ."

Holpers came loping up, arms flapping the air. "They've completely demolished us; you should see the lobby, the kitchen, the day rooms! A shambles—"

Captain Bussey shook his head in bewilderment. "Why in the world should they attack you? They're supposed to be a peaceable race . . . except toward each other, of course."

"Well, something got into them," said See, still breathing hard. "They came at us like tigers—beating us with their damn little sticks. . . . I finally washed them out with firehoses."

"What about your guests?" asked Captain Bussey in sudden curiosity.

See shrugged. "I don't know what happened to them. A bunch ran off up the valley, smack into another army. I understand they got beat up as good as those that stayed."

"We couldn't even escape in our aircraft," complained Holpers. "Not one of them would start. . . ."

A mild voice interrupted. "Mr. See, I have decided against purchasing your air-car, and have returned it to the hangar."

See slowly turned, the baleful aura of his thoughts almost tangible. "You, Ridolph. . . . I'm beginning to see daylight. . . ."

"I beg your pardon?"

"Come on, spill it!" See took a threatening step forward.

Captain Bussey said, "Careful, See, watch your temper."

See ignored him. "What's your part in all this, Ridolph?"

36

Magnus Ridolph shook his head in bewilderment. "I'm completely at a loss. I rather imagine that the natives learned of your gambling on events they considered important, and decided to take punitive steps."

The ornamental charabanc from the ship rolled up; among the passengers was a woman of notable bust, correctly tinted, massaged, coiffed, scented and decorated. "Ah!" said Magnus Ridolph. "Mrs. Chickering! Charming!"

"I could stay away no longer," said Mrs. Chickering. "I had to know how—our business was proceeding."

Julius See leaned forward curiously. "What kind of business do you mean?"

Mrs. Chickering turned him a swift contemptuous glance; then her attention was attracted by two women who came hobbling from the direction of the inn. She gasped, "Olga! Altamira! What on Earth—"

"Don't stand there gasping," snapped Mrs. Chaim. "Get us clothes. Those frightful savages tore us to shreds."

Mrs. Chickering turned in confusion to Magnus Ridolph. "Just what has happened! Surely you can't have—"

Magnus Ridolph cleared his throat. "Mrs. Chickering, a word with you aside." He drew her out of earshot of the others. "Mrs. Chaim and Mrs. Borgage—they are friends of yours?"

Mrs. Chickering cast an anxious glance over her shoulder. "I can't understand the situation at all," she muttered feverishly. "Mrs. Chaim is the president of the Woman's League and Mrs. Borgage is treasurer. I can't understand them running around with their clothing in shreds. . . ."

Magnus Ridolph said candidly, "Well, Mrs. Chickering, in carrying out your instructions, I allowed scope to the natural combativeness of the natives, and perhaps they—"

"Martha," came Mrs. Chaim's grating voice close at hand, "what is your connection with this man? I have reason to suspect that he is mixed up in this terrible attack. Look at him!" Her voice rose furiously. "They haven't laid a finger on him! And the rest of us—"

Martha Chickering licked her lips. "Well, Olga, dear, this is Magnus Ridolph. In accordance with last month's resolution, we hired him to close down the gambling here at the inn."

Magnus Ridolph said in his suavest tones, "Following which, Mrs. Chaim and Mrs. Borgage naturally thought it best to come out and study the situation at first hand; am I right?"

Mrs. Chaim and Mrs. Borgage glared. Mrs. Chaim said, "If you think, Martha Chickering, that the Woman's League will in any way recognize this rogue—"

"My dear Mrs. Chaim," protested Magnus Ridolph.

"But, Olga—I promised him a thousand munits a week!"

Magnus Ridolph waved his hand airily. "My dear Mrs. Chickering, I prefer that any sums due me be distributed among worthy charities. I have profited during my short stay here—"

"*See!*" came Captain Bussey's voice. "For God's sake, man, control yourself!"

Magnus Ridolph, turning, found See struggling in the grasp of Captain Bussey. "Try and collect!" See cried out to Magnus Ridolph. He angrily thrust Captain Bussey's arms aside, stood with hands clenching and unclenching. "Just try and collect!"

"My dear Mr. See, I have already collected."

"You've done nothing of the sort—and if I catch you in my boat again, I'll break your scrawny little neck!"

Magnus Ridolph held up his hand. "The hundred thousand munits I wrote off immediately; however, there were six other bets which I placed by proxy; these were paid, and my share of the winnings came to well over three hundred thousand munits. Actually, I regard this sum as return of the capital which I placed with the Outer Empire Investment and Realty Society, plus a reasonable profit. Everything considered, it was a remunerative as well as instructive investment."

"Ridolph," muttered See, "one of these days—"

Mrs. Chaim shouldered forward. "Did I hear you say 'Outer Empire Realty and Investment Society'?"

Magnus Ridolph nodded. "I believe that Mr. See and Mr. Holpers were responsible officials of the concern."

Mrs. Chaim took two steps forward. See frowned uneasily; Bruce Holpers began to edge away. "Come back here!" cried Mrs. Chaim. "I have a few words to say before I have you arrested."

Magnus Ridolph turned to Captain Bussey. "You return to Methedeon on schedule, I assume?"

"Yes," said Captain Bussey dryly.

Magnus Ridolph nodded. "I think I will go aboard at once, since there will be considerable demand for passage."

"As you wish," said Captain Bussey.

"I believe No. 12 is your best cabin?"

"I believe so," said Captain Bussey.

"Then kindly regard Cabin No. 12 as booked."

"Very well, Mr. Ridolph."

Magnus Ridolph looked up the mountainside. "I noticed Mr. Pilby running along the ridge a few minutes ago. I think it would be a real kindness if he were notified that the war is over."

"I think so too," said Captain Bussey. They looked around the group. Mrs. Chaim was still engaged with Julius See and Bruce Holpers. Mrs. Borgage was displaying her bruises to Mrs. Chickering. No one seemed disposed to act on Magnus Ridolph's suggestion.

Magnus Ridolph shrugged, climbed the gangway into the *Archaeornyx*. "Well, no matter. In due course he will very likely come by himself."

THE UNSPEAKABLE McINCH

"MYSTERY is a word with no objective pertinence, merely describing the limitations of a mind. In fact, a mind may be classified by the order of the phenomena it considers mysterious. . . . The mystery is resolved, the solution made known. "Of course, it is obvious!" comes the chorus. A word about the obvious: it is always obvious. . . . The common mind transposes the sequence, letting the mystery generate the solution. This is logic in reverse; actually the mystery relates to the solution as the foam relates to the beer. . . .
                                                —*Magnus Ridolph*.

The Uni-Culture Mission had said simply, "His name's McInch; he's a murderer. That's all we know."

Magnus Ridolph would have refused the commission had his credit balance stood at its usual level. But the collapse of an advertising venture—sky-writing with luminescent gases across interplanetary space—had left the white-bearded philosopher in near-destitution.

A first impression of Sclerotto Planet reinforced his distaste for the job. The light from the two suns—red and blue—struck discordantly at his eyes. The sluggish ocean, the crazy clutter of a slab-sided rock suggested no repose, and Sclerotto City, a wretched maze of cabins and shacks, promised no en-

39

tertainment. Finally, his host, Klemmer Boek, chaplain-in-charge of the Uni-Culture Mission, greeted him with little warmth—in fact seemed to resent his presence, as if it were due to some private officiousness of Magnus Ridolph's own.

They rode in a battered old car up to the Mission, perched high on a shoulder of naked stone, and the dim interior was refreshingly cool after the dust and dazzle of the ride.

Magnus Ridolph took a folded handkerchief from his pocket, patted his forehead, his distinguished nose, his neat, white beard. To his host he turned a quizzical glance.

"I'm afraid I find the illumination disturbing. Blue, red—three different shadows for every stick and stone."

"I'm used to it," said Klemmer Boek tonelessly. He was a short man, with a melon-sized paunch pressing out the front of his tunic. His face was pink and glazed, like cheap china-ware, with round blue eyes and a short lumpy nose. "I hardly remember what Earth looks like."

"The tourist guide," said Magnus Ridolph, replacing the handkerchief, "describes the effect as 'stimulating and exotic.' It must be that I am unperceptive."

Boek snorted. "The tourist guide? It calls Sclerotto City 'colorful, fascinating, a commonwealth-in-miniature, a con-crete example of interplanetary democracy in action.' I wish the man who wrote that eyewash had to live here as long as I have!"

He pulled out a rattan chair for Magnus Ridolph, poured ice-water into a glass. Magnus Ridolph settled himself into the chair and Boek sank into another opposite.

"Now then," said Magnus Ridolph, "who or what is McInch?"

Boek smiled bitterly. "That's what you're here for."

Magnus Ridolph airily glanced across the room, lit a cigar, said nothing.

"After six years," said Boek presently, "all I know about McInch I can tell you in six seconds. First—he's boss over that entire stinking welter out there." He gestured at the city. "Second, he's a murderer, a self-seeking scoundrel. Third, no one but McInch knows who McInch is."

Magnus Ridolph arose, walked to the window, depolarized it, looked out over the ramshackle roofs, stretching like a tattered Persian rug to Magnetic Bay. His gaze wandered to the shark-tooth crags stabbing the sky opposite, down the bay to where it opened into the tideless ocean, out to a horizon shrouded in lavender haze.

40

"Unprepossessing. I fail to understand how it attracts visitors."

Boek joined him at the window. "Well—it's a strange world, certainly." He nodded at the roofs below. "Down in that confusion live at least a dozen different types of intelligent creatures—expatriates, exiles, fugitives—all crowded together cheek by jowl. Unquestionably it's amazing, the adjustments they've made to each other."

"Hm . . ." said Magnus Ridolph noncommittally. Then: "This McInch—is he a man?"

Boek shrugged. "No one knows. And anyone who finds out dies almost at once. Twice Headquarters has sent out key men to investigate. Both of them dropped dead in the middle of town—one by the Export Warehouse, the other in the Mayor's office."

Magnus Ridolph coughed slightly.

"And the cause of their deaths?"

"Unclassified disease." Boek stared down at the roofs, the walls, lanes, arcades below. "The Mission tries to stand apart from local politics, though naturally in rubbing alien noses into Earth culture we're propagandizing our own system of life. And sometimes"—he grinned sourly—"circumstances like McInch arise."

"Of course," said Magnus Ridolph. "Just what form do McInch's depredations take?"

"Graft," said Boek. "Graft, pure and simple. Old-fashioned Earth-style civic corruption. I should have mentioned"—another sour grin for Magnus Ridolph—"that Sclerotto City has a duly elected mayor, and a group of civic officers. There's a fire department, a postal service, a garbage disposal unit, police force—wait till you see 'em!" He chuckled, a noise like a bucket scraping on a stone floor. "That's actually what brings the tourists—the way these creatures go about making a living Earth-style."

Magnus Ridolph bent forward slightly, a furrow appearing in his forehead. "There seems to be no ostentation, no buildings of pretension—other than that one there by the bay."

"That's the tourist hotel," said Boek. "The Pondicherry House."

"Ah, I see," said Magnus Ridolph abstractedly. "I admit that at first sight Sclerotto City's form of government seems improbable."

"It becomes more sensible when you think of the city's history," said Boek. "Fifty years ago, a colony of Ordinationalists was founded here—the only flat spot on the planet.

41

Gradually—Sclerotto hangs just about outside the Commonwealth and no questions asked—misfits from everywhere in the cluster accumulated, and one way or another found means to survive. Those who failed"—he waved his hand—"merely didn't survive.

"When you come upon it fresh, like the tourists, it's astounding. The first time I walked down the main street, I thought I was having a nightmare. The Kmaush, in tanks, secreting pearls in their gizzards . . . centipedes from Portmar's Planet, the Tau Geminis, the Armadillos from Carnegie Twelve . . . Yellowbirds, Zeeks, even a few Aldebaranese—not to mention several types of anthropoids. How they get along without tearing each other to pieces still bothers me once in a while."

"This difficulty is perhaps more apparent than real," said Magnus Ridolph, his voice taking on a certain resonance.

Boek glanced sidewise at his guest, curled his lip. "You haven't lived here as long as I have." He turned his eyes back down to Sclerotto City. "With that dust, that smell, that . . ." He struggled for a word.

"In any event," said Magnus Ridolph, "these are all intelligent creatures. . . . Just a few more questions. First, how does McInch collect his graft?"

Boek returned to his own chair, leaned back heavily. "Apparently he helps himself outright to city funds. The municipal taxes are collected in cash, taken to the city hall and locked in a safe. McInch merely opens the safe when he finds himself short, takes what he needs, closes the safe again."

"And the citizens do not object?"

"Indignation is an emotion," said Boek with heavy sarcasm. "The bulk of the population are non-human, and don't have emotions."

"And those of the population that are men, and therefore can know indignation?"

"Being men—they're afraid."

Magnus Ridolph stroked his beard gently. "Let me put it this way. Do the citizens show any reluctance toward paying their taxes?"

"They have no choice," said Boek. "All the imports and exports are handled by a municipal cooperative. Taxes are assessed there."

"Why isn't the safe moved, or guarded?"

"That's been tried—by our late mayor. The guards he posted were also found dead. Unclassifiable disease."

"In all probability," said Magnus Ridolph, "McInch is one

42

of the city officials. They would be the first to be exposed to temptation."

"I agree with you," said Boek. "But which one?"

"How many are there?"

"Well—there's the postmaster, a Portmar multipede. There's the fire-chief, a man; the chief of police, a Sirius Fifth; the garbage collector, he's a—a—I can't think of the name. From 1012 Aurigae."

"A Golespod?"

"That's right. He's the only one of them in the city. Then there's the manager of the municipal warehouse, who is also the tax collector—one of the Tau Gemini ant-things—and last but not least, there's the Mayor. His name is Juju Jeejee—that's what it sounds like to me. He's a Yellowbird."

"I see. . . ."

After a pause Boek said, "Well, what do you think?"

"The problem has points of interest," admitted Magnus Ridolph. "Naturally I want to look around the city."

Boek looked at his watch. "When would you like to go?"

"I'll change my linen," said Magnus Ridolph, rising to his feet. "Then, if it's convenient to you, we'll look around at once."

"You understand, now," said Boek gruffly, "the minute you start asking questions about McInch, McInch knows it and he'll try to kill you."

"The Uni-Culture Mission is paying me a large fee to take that chance," declared Magnus Ridolph. "I am, so to speak, a latter-day gladiator. Logic is my sword, vigilance is my shield. And also"—he touched his short well-tended beard—"I will wear air-filters up my nostrils, and will spray myself with antiseptic. To complete my precautions, I'll carry a small germicidal radiator."

"Gladiator, eh?" snorted Boek. "You're more like a turtle. Well, how long before you'll be ready?"

"If you'll show me my quarters," said Magnus Ridolph, "I'll be with you in half an hour."

In gloomy triumph Boek said, "There's all that's left of the Ordinationalists."

Magnus Ridolph looked at the cubical stone building. Small dunes of gray dust lay piled against the walls; the door gaped into blankness.

"And that, it's the solidest building in Sclerotto," said Boek.

"A wonder McInch hasn't moved in," observed Magnus Ridolph.

"It's now the municipal dump. The garbage collector has his offices behind. I'll show you, if you like. It's one of the sights. Er—by the way, are you incognito?"

"No," said Magnus Ridolph. "I think not. I see no special need for subterfuge."

"Just as you like," said Boek, jumping out of the car. He watched with pursed lips as Magnus Ridolph soberly donned a gleaming sun-helmet, adjusted his nasal air-filters and dark glasses.

They plowed through fine gray dust, which, disturbed by their steps, rose into the dual sunlight in whorls of red, blue and a hundred intermediate shades.

Magnus Ridolph suddenly tilted his head. Boek grinned. "Quite a smell, isn't it? Almost call it a stink, wouldn't you?"

"I would indeed," assented Magnus Ridolph. "What in the name of Pluto are we approaching?"

"It's the garbage collector, the Golespod. Actually, he doesn't collect the garbage—the citizens bring it here and throw it on him. He absorbs it."

They circled the ancient Ordinationalist church, and Magnus Ridolph now saw that the back wall had been battered open, permitting the occupant light and air, but shading him from the two suns. This, the Golespod, was a wide rubbery creature, somewhat like a giant ray, though blockier, thicker in cross-section. It had a number of pale short legs on its underside, a blank milk-blue eye on its front, a row of pliant tendrils dangling under the eye. It crouched half-submerged in semi-solid rottenness—scraps of food, fish entrails, organic refuse of every sort.

"He gets paid for it," said Boek. "The pay is all velvet, as his board and room are thrown in with the job."

A rhythmic shuffling sound came to their ears. Around the corner of the old stone church came a snakelike creature suspended on thirty skinny jointed legs.

"That's one of the mail carriers," said Boek. "They're all multipedes—and pretty good at it, too."

The creature was long, wiry, and his body shone a burnished copper-red. He had a flat caterpillar face, four black shiny eyes, a small horny beak. A tray hung under his body containing letters and small parcels. One of these latter he seized with a foot, whistled shrilly. The Golespod grunted, flung back its front, tossing the trailing tentacles away from a black maw underneath.

44

The multipede tossed the little parcel into the mouth, and with a bright blank stare at Boek and Magnus Ridolph, turned in a supple arc and trundled around the building. The Golespod grunted, honked, burrowed deeper into the filth, where it lay staring at Boek and Magnus Ridolph—these two returning the scrutiny with much the same detached, faintly contemptuous curiosity.

"Does he understand human speech?" inquired Magnus Ridolph.

Boek nodded. "But don't go too near him. He's an irascible brute."

Magnus Ridolph took a cautious step or two forward, looked into the milky blue eye.

"I'm trying to identify a criminal named McInch. Can you help me?"

The black body moved in sudden agitation, and a furious honking came from the pale under-body. The eye distended, swelled. Boek cocked an ear.

"It's saying, 'Go away, go away.' "

Magnus Ridolph said, "You are unable to help me, then?"

The creature redoubled its angry demonstrations, suddenly lurched back, flung up its head, spewed a gout of vile-smelling fluid. Magnus Ridolph jumped nimbly back, but a few drops struck his tunic, inundated him with a choking fetor.

Boek watched with an undisguised smile as Magnus Ridolph scrubbed at the spot with his handkerchief. "It'll wear off after a while."

"Umph," said Magnus Ridolph.

They returned through the dust to the car.

"I'll take you to the Export Warehouse," said Boek. "That's about the center of town, and we can go on foot from there. You can see more on foot."

To either side of the street, now, the shacks and small shops, built of slate and split dried seaweed stalks, pressed ever closer, and life clotted more thickly about them. Human children, grimed and ragged, played in the street with near-featureless Capella-anthropoids, young, immature Carnegie Twelve Armadillos, Martian frog-children.

Hundreds of small Portman multipedes darted underfoot like lizards; most of them would be killed by their parents for reasons never quite understood by men. Yellowbirds—ostrich-like bipeds with soft yellow scales—strode quietly through the crowd, heads raised high, eyes rolled up. Like a parade of monsters in a dipsomaniac's delirium passed the population of Sclerotto City.

45

Stalls at either side of the street displayed simple goods—baskets, pans, a thousand utensils whose use only the seller and the buyer knew. Other shops sold what loosely might be termed food—fruits and canned goods for men, hard brown capsules for the Yellowbirds, squirming red worm-things for the Aldebaranese. And Magnus Ridolph noticed here and there little knots of tourists, for the most part natives of Earth, peering, talking, laughing, pointing.

Boek pulled his car up to a long corrugated-metal shed, and again they stepped out into the dust.

The warehouse was full of a hushed murmur. Scores of tourists walked about, buying trinkets—carved rock, elaborately patterned fabrics, nacreous jewels that were secreted in the bellies of the Kmaush, perfumes pressed from seaweed, statuttes, tiny aquaria in sealed globes, with a microscopic lens through which could be seen weirdly beautiful seascapes peopled with infusoria, tiny sponges, corals, darting squids, infinitesimal fish. Behind loomed bales of the planet's staple exports; seaweed resin, split dried seaweed for surfacing veneer, sacks of rare metallic salts.

"There's the warehouse manager," said Boek, nodding toward an antlike creature standing waist high on six legs. It had dog-like eyes, a pelt of satiny gray fur, a relatively short thick thorax. "Do you want to meet him? He can talk, understand you. Mind like an adding-machine."

Interpreting Magnus Ridolph's silence as assent, Boek threaded the aisles to the Tau Gemini insect-thing.

"I can't introduce you," said Boek jovially—Magnus Ridolph noticed that he assumed affability like a cloak in the presence of the town's citizens—"because the manager here has no name."

"On my planet," said the insect in a droning accentless voice, "we are marked by chords, as you call them. Mine is—" A quick series of tones came from the two flaps near the base of his head.

"This is Magnus Ridolph, representing the Mission Headquarters."

"I'm interested," said Magnus Ridolph, "in identifying the criminal known as McInch. Can you help me?"

"I'm sorry," came the ant-creature's even vibrations. "I have heard the name. I am aware of his thefts. I do not know who he is."

Magnus Ridolph bowed.

"I'll take you to the fire-chief," said Boek.

The fire-chief was a tall blue-eyed Negro with dull bronze hair, wearing only a pair of knee-length scarlet trousers. Boek and Magnus Ridolph found him at an observation tower near the central square, with one foot on the bottom rung of the ladder. He nodded to Boek.

"Joe, a friend of mine from home," said Boek. "Mr. Magnus Ridolph, Mr. Joe Bertrand, our fire-chief."

The fire-chief darted a swift surprised glance at Magnus Ridolph, at Boek, and back again. "How do you do," he said as they shook hands. "I think I've heard your name somewhere before."

"It's an uncommon name," said Magnus Ridolph, "but I presume there are other Ridolphs in the Commonwealth."

Boek looked from one to the other, shifted his weight on his short legs, sighed, looked off down the street.

"Not many Magnus Ridolphs, though," said the fire-chief.

"Very few," agreed the white-bearded sage.

"I suppose you're after McInch."

"I am. Can you help me?"

"I know nothing about him. I don't want to. It's healthier."

Magnus Ridolph nodded. "I see. Thank you, in any event."

Boek jerked his plump thumb at a tall building built of woven seaweed panels between bleached bone-white poles. "That's the city hall," he said. "The Mayor lives upstairs, where he can, *ha, ha,* guard the city funds."

"Just what are his other ditues?" Magnus Ridolph asked, gently beating the dust from the front of his tunic.

"He meets all the tourist ships, walks around town wearing a red fez. He's the local magistrate, and then he's in charge of town funds and pays the municipal salaries. Personally, I don't think he's got the brains to be McInch."

"I'd like to see the safe that McInch is so free with," said Magnus Ridolph.

They pushed through a flimsy creaking door, into a long low room. The seaweed paneling of the walls was old, worn, shot with cracks, and each crack admitted twin rays of light, these painting twin red and blue images on the floor. The safe bulked against the opposite side of the room, an antique steel box with button combination.

A long yellow-scaled neck pushed down through a hole in the ceiling, and a flat head topped by a ridiculous little red fez turned a purple eye at them. A sleek yellow body followed the head, landing on thin flexible legs.

"Hello there, Mayor," said Boek heartily. "A man from

47

Mission Headquarters—Mr. Ridolph, our Mayor, Juju Jeejee."

"Pleased-to-meet-you," said the Mayor shrilly. "Would you like my autograph?"

"Certainly," said Magnus Ridolph. "I'd be delighted."

The Mayor ducked his head between his legs, plucked a card from a body pouch. The characters were unintelligible to Magnus Ridolph.

"That is my name in the script of my native planet. The translation is roughly 'Enchanting Vibration.'"

"Thank you," said Magnus Ridolph. "I'll treasure this memento of Sclerotto. By the way, I'm here to apprehend the creature known as McInch"—the Mayor gave a sharp squawk, darted its head back and forth—"and thought that perhaps you might be able to assist me."

The Mayor wove his neck in a series of S's. "No, no, no," he piped, "I know nothing, I am the Mayor."

Boek glanced at Magnus Ridolph, who nodded.

"Well, we'll be leaving, Mayor," said Boek. "I wanted my friend to meet you."

"Delighted," rasped the Mayor, and tensing his legs, hopped up through the hole in the ceiling.

A hundred yards through the red and blue shimmer brought them to the jail, a long barracks built of slate. The cells faced directly out on the street. Visible were the disconsolate head of a Yellowbird, the blank face of a Capella anthropoid, a man who stared as Boek and Magnus Ridolph passed, and spit speculatively into the dust.

"And what are their sins?" inquired Magnus Ridolph.

"The man stole some roofing; the Yellowbird assaulted a young Portmar centipede; the Capellan, I don't know. The chief of police—a Sirius Fifth—has his office behind."

The office was a tentlike lean-to, the chief of police an enormous torpedo-shaped amphibian. His flippers ended in long maniples, his skin was black and shiny, he smelled sickly-sweet. A ring of beady deep-sunk eyes completely circled his head.

When Boek and Magnus Ridolph—both perspiring, dirty and tired—appeared around the corner of the lean-to, he rose quivering and swaying on spring foot-flippers, drew one of his flippers across his barrel. Where the fingers had passed words sprang out on the black hide in startling white.

"Good-day, Mr. Boek. Good-day, sir."

48

"Hello, Fritz," said Boek. "Just passing through, showing my friend the town."

The amphibian lay back in his trough-shaped seat. The flippers passed along his barrel, the first message having faded.

"Anything I can show you?"

"I'm trying to find McInch," said Magnus Ridolph. "Can you help me?"

The flippers hesitated, fluttered across the barrel. "I know nothing. I will assist you in every official manner."

Magnus Ridolph nodded, turned slowly away. "I'll let you know when and if I discover anything."

"Now," said Boek, coughing, clearing his throat of dust, "there's the post-office." He turned, looked back toward the Export Warehouse. "I think it's about as short to walk as it is to return for the car."

Magnus Ridolph glanced up at the two suns in the sea-green sky. "Does it cool off during the evening?"

"To some extent," said Boek, stepping forward doggedly. "We want to be back at the Mission by sunset. I never feel quite easy out after dark. Especially now, with McInch." He pursed his plump mouth.

Their path took them between the rickety shacks toward the waterfront. Life swarmed everywhere, life of the most disparate sorts. Through the windows and doors they saw quiet unnamed bulks, other shapes, agile and quick. Eyes of a dozen different kinds watched them, sounds never heard on Earth met their ears, smells never intended for earthly nostrils drifted across the roadway.

The scene around them gradually assumed a redder tone, as the blue sun sank lower toward the horizon. As they reached the post-office—a slate shed adjacent to the spaceport—it dropped below the horizon and vanished.

If Magnus Ridolph expected interest and enthusiasm for his mission from the Postmaster, a Portmar centipede, he was disappointed. They found him sorting mail—standing on half his legs, rhythmically pigeonholing letters with those remaining.

He paused in his work, while Boek introduced Magnus Ridolph, stared at the detective with the impersonal uninterested gaze to which Magnus Ridolph was becoming accustomed and disavowed any knowledge of McInch.

Magnus Ridolph glanced at Boek, said, "Excuse me, Mr

49

Boek, I'd like to ask the Postmaster one or two confidential questions."

"Certainly," sniffed Boek, and moved away.

Magnus Ridolph presently rejoined him.

"I wanted to find out what type of mail the civic officers received, and also any other circumstances he might have noted which would help me."

"And did he help you?"

"Very much," said Magnus Ridolph.

The two men skirted the waterfront, where giant seaweed barges loomed dark at their moorings, then back toward the Export Warehouse. The red sun was close to the horizon when they finally reached the car, and blood-colored light gave the town an aspect of fabled antiquity, softening the clutter and squalor. Silently they drove up the bumpy road to the Mission at the top of the ridge.

As they alighted, Magnus Ridolph turned to Boek.

"Have you a microscope conveniently at hand?"

"Three," said Boek shortly. "Visual, electronic, gamma-beta."

"I'd like to use one of them tonight," said Magnus Ridolph.

"As you wish."

"Tomorrow I believe that, one way or another, we shall clear up the affair."

Boek stared at him curiously. "You think you know who McInch is?"

"It was immediately obvious," said Magnus Ridolph, "in the light of my special knowledge."

Boek clamped his jaw. "I'd bolt my door tonight, if I were you. Whoever he is—he's a murderer."

Magnus Ridolph nodded. "I believe you're right."

Sclerotto night was long at this season—fourteen hours— and Magnus Ridolph arose, bathed, dressed himself in a clean white and blue tunic, all before dawn.

From the windows of the reception hall he stood watching for the sunrise, the sky as yet holding only a blue electric glare, when he heard a tread behind him.

Turning, he found Klemmer Boek watching him, the round head twisted to one side, the blue eyes full of brittle speculation.

"Sleep well?" said Boek's greeting.

"Indeed I did," said Magnus Ridolph. "I hope you slept as soundly."

50

Boek grunted. "Ready for breakfast?"

"Quite ready," said Magnus Ridolph. They passed into the dining room, and Boek ordered breakfast from his lone servant.

They ate silently, the blue pre-dawn light growing ever stronger. Only after coffee did Magnus Ridolph lean back, expansively light a small cigar.

"Still think you can settle the case today?" asked Boek.

"Yes," said Magnus Ridolph. "I think it's very possible."

"Er—you know who McInch is?"

"Beyond a doubt."

"And you can prove it?"

Magnus Ridolph let a plume of cigar smoke curl up through his fingers into the first watery ray from the sapphire-blue sun. "After a fashion—yes."

"You don't sound very assured."

"Well—I have a strategem in mind which will save a great deal of time."

"Yes?" Boek said, with heavy sarcasm, drumming his fingers.

"I would like you to have Mayor—ah, Juju? . . . call a meeting this afternoon of the city officials. The city hall would be a satisfactory place. And at the meeting we will discuss McInch."

As they plowed through the dust to the city hall, Boek snapped, "This seems a little melodramatic."

"Possibly, possibly," said Magnus Ridolph. "Possibly dangerous also."

Boek hesitated in midstride. "Are you sure—"

"Nothing is a certainty," said Magnus Ridolph. "Not even the continued rotation of this planet on its axis. And the least predictable phenomena I know of is the duration of life."

Boek looked straight ahead, said nothing.

They entered the city hall, paused in the ante-room a moment to let their eyes adapt to the dimness. Ahead of them to right and left, bulks of different masses and shapes began to form, splotched here and there by the rays of red and blue which entered through the matting.

"The garage collector is here," said Magnus Ridolph behind his hand to Boek. "I can smell him."

They had advanced into the central room. The Mayor had been pacing solemnly back and forth, red fez perched slantwise, in the center of a rough circle formed by the Golespod garbage-collector, the multipede postmaster, Joe Bertrand the

51

fire-chief, the Tau Gemini warehouse manager, and the amphibian Chief of Police.

"Gentlemen," said Magnus Ridolph, "I won't take up much of your time. As you all know, I have been investigating that entity known as McInch."

There was a movement about the room—a twinkling of the multipede postmaster's legs, a quiver on the police-chief's rubbery hide, a twist of the Mayor's neck. There were slight nervous sounds—a soft hiss from the skatelike Golespod, the Negro fire-chief clearing his throat.

The warehouse manager—the ant-like creature of Tau Gemini—spoke in his toneless voice. "Exactly why are we here? Make your purpose clear."

Magnus Ridolph serenely stroked his beard, glanced from creature to creature. "I have learned McInch's identity. I have estimated the sum he costs Sclerotto every day. I can prove that this creature is a murderer, or at the very least that he attempted to murder me. Yes, me—Magnus Ridolph!" And Magnus Ridolph stood stiff and stern as he spoke.

Again there was the guarded movement, the near-silent eddy of sound, as each of the creatures took itself into the familiar places of its own brain.

Magnus Ridolph said gravely, "As the governing body of the community I would value your advice on what course of action I should follow. Mr. Mayor, have you a suggestion?"

The Yellowbird wove its neck in a series of quick darts and plunges, piped a shrill series of excited unintelligible tones. The head came to a stand-still; the purple eye stared craftily at Magnus Ridolph. "McInch might kill us all."

Boek cleared his throat, muttered uncomfortably, "Do you think it's a good idea for us to . . ."

Fire-chief Joe Bertrand said, "I'm sick of all this pussy-footing. We have a jail. We have a legal code. Let's judge McInch by what he's done. If he's a thief, put him in jail. If he's a murderer, and if he can take mental surgery, let's give it to him. If he can't, let's execute him!"

Magnus Ridolph nodded. "I can prove McInch is a thief. Several years in jail might prove a salutary experience. You have a clean sanitary jail, with germicidal air-filters, compulsory bathing, pure, sanitary food—"

"Why do you emphasize the wholesomeness of the jail?" buzzed the warehouse manager.

"Because McInch will be exposed to it," said Magnus Ridolph solemnly. "He'll be vaccinated and immunized, and

52

live in a completely germ-free environment. And this will hurt McInch more than death. Now"—and he looked at the metal-tense figures around him—"who is McInch?"

The garbage-collector reared amazingly erect, leaning far back, revealing its pale under-body, it's double row of pale short legs. It writhed, hunched. "Duck!" yelled Boek as the Golespod spat a stinking wash of liquid to all quarters of the room. From the depths of its body came a rumbling voice. "Now all die, all die . . ."

"Quiet!" said Magnus Ridolph sharply. "Quiet everyone! Mayor, quiet please!"

The Yellowbird's crazed piping diminished. "There is no danger for anyone," said Magnus Ridolph, coolly wiping his face, eyes upon the Golespod, who still reared back. "An ultra-sonic vibrator below the floor, a Hecthmann irradiator in the ceiling have been operating ever since we entered the room. The bacteria in McInch's serum were dead as soon as they left his mouth, if not before."

The Golespod hissed, lowered himself, plunged for the door, little legs pumping like pistons. The chief of police lunged like a porpoise from a wave, landed on the Golespod's flat writhing back. His clawed flippers hooked in the flesh, tore. The Golespod screamed, turned on its back, scraped the amphibian between its legs, folded itself around him, squeezed. Joe Bertrand sprang forward, kicking at the milk-blue eye. The Portmar centipede ripped into the melée, and with each of his slender feet seized one of the Golespod's, strained to pull them aside from the constricted chief of police. The Mayor hopped up through the hole in the ceiling, hopped back with a skewer, stabbed, stabbed, stabbed. . . .

Boek staggered out to the car. Magnus Ridolph, throwing his stinking white and blue tunic into a ditch, joined him.

Boek clung to the wheel, his pink face clabbered.

"They—they tore him to pieces," he whispered.

"An unnerving spectacle," said Magnus Ridolph, testing his clotted beard. "A sordid adventure in every respect."

Boek turned a round accusing eye at him. "I believe you planned it like that!"

Magnus Ridolph said, gently, "My friend, may I suggest that we return to the Mission and bathe ourselves? I believe clean clothes would help restore our perspectives."

A sober Klemmer Boek sat across from Magnus Ridolph at the dinner table, a Klemmer Boek who barely looked at his

53

food. Magnus Ridolph ate fastidiously, though substantially. Once again he wore crisp linen, and his white beard was soft, expertly trimmed.

"But how," blurted Boek, "did you know the garbage-collector was McInch?"

"A simple process," said Magnus Ridolph, gesturing with his fork. "A perfectly straightforward sequence of logic; a framework of theory, the consulting of references—"

"Yes, yes, yes," muttered Boek. "Logic this, intelligence that. . . ."

Magnus Ridolph's mouth twitched slightly. "Here, in the concrete, is my chain of thought. McInch is a grafter, a thief, stealing large sums of money. What does he do with his loot? Nothing very conspicuous, otherwise his identity would be common knowledge. Assuming that McInch spent some or all of his money—an assumption by no means sure—I considered each of the civic officials, the most likely suspects, from the viewpoint of one of his own race.

"There was Joe Bertrand, the fire-chief. By this test, he was innocent. He lived frugally in an uncongenial environment.

"I considered the Mayor. What was a Yellowbird's definition of delight? I found it would include a field of a certain type of flower, the scent of which drugs and exalts the Yellowbirds. Nothing of this sort was evident on Sclerotto. The Mayor, in his own eyes, lived a meager life.

"Next the warehouse manager, the Tau Gemini ant-creature. The wants of these individuals are very modest. The words 'luxury' and 'leisure' have no equivalents in their language. If for this reason alone I was tempted to drop him. I learned from the postmaster that he purchased a number of books every month—these were his only conspicuous indulgence—but their value was commensurate with his salary. Temporarily, at least, I dismissed the warehouse manager.

"The chief of police—a decisive case. By nature he is an amphibian, accustomed to a diet of mollusks. His planet is marshy and dank. Contrast all this to his life here on Sclerotto. A wonder he is able to survive.

"I wondered about the postmaster—the multipede from Portmar's Planet. His concept of luxury is a deep tank of warm oil, massage by little animals captured and trained for that purpose. This treatment bleaches the skin to a sandy beige. The postmaster's skin is horny and brick-red, a sign of poverty and neglect.

"Consider the garbage-collector. The human reaction to his way of life is disgust, contempt. We cannot believe that a

54

creature wallowing in filth possesses subtle discriminations. However, I knew that the Golespods possess an internal sense of the most delicate precision. They exist by ingesting organic matter, allowing it to ferment under the action of bacteria in a series of stomachs, and the ensuing alcohol they oxidize for energy.

"Now the composition or quality of the organic raw materials is of no concern to the Golespod—garbage, protein waste, carrion, it's all one, just as we ignore slight variations in the air we breathe. They derive their enjoyment not from these raw materials, but from the internal products—and to these ends, the variety and blends of bacteria in their stomachs is all-important.

"Over the course of thousands of years, the Golespods have become bacteriologists of an extremely high order. They have isolated millions of various types, created new strains, each invoking in them a different sensual response. The most prized strains are difficult to isolate and hence are expensive.

"When I learned this, I knew that the garbage-collector was McInch. In his own mind he was in a supremely enviable position—surrounded by unlimited quantities of organic materials, able to afford the rarest, most enticing blends of bacteria.

"I learned from the postmaster that the Golespod indeed received a small parcel from every incoming mail-ship—these of course the bacteria he imported from his home planet, some fantastically expensive."

Magnus Ridolph leaned back now, sipped his coffee, watching his wan host over the rim. Boek stirred. "How—how did he kill the two investigators, then?" he asked. "And you said he tried to kill you."

"Do you recall how he spat at me yesterday? When I returned to the Mission I examined the stain under your microscope. It was a thick blanket of dead bacteria. I could not identify them, but luckily my precautions had killed them." He sipped his coffee, puffed his cigar. "Now, as for my fee, I believe you received instructions in that connection."

Boek rose heavily, walked to his desk, returned with a check.

"Thank you," said Magnus Ridolph, gazing at the figure. He tapped his fingers musingly on the table. "So Sclerotto City finds itself without a garbage-collector. . . ."

Boek scowled. "And no prospect of finding one. The city'll stink worse than ever."

Magnus Ridolph had been languidly stroking his beard,

gazing throughfully into space. "No . . . I fancy that the profit would hardly repay the effort."

"How's that?" inquired Boek, blinking.

Magnus Ridolph roused himself from his reverie, dispassionately considered Boek, who was chewing his fingernails.

"Your dilemma aroused a train of thought."

"Well?"

"In order to make money," said Magnus Ridolph, "you must provide something that someone is willing to pay for. A self-evident statement? Not so. A surprising number of people are occupied selling objects and services no one wants. Very few are successful."

"Yes," said Boek patiently. "What's that got to do with collecting garbage? Do you want the job? If you do, say so, and I'll recommend you to the Mayor."

Magnus Ridolph turned him a glance of mild reproach. "It occurred to me that 1012 Aurigae teems with Golespods any one of whom would pay for the privilege of filling the job." He sighed, shook his head. "The profit of a single transaction would hardly justify the effort . . . A Commonwealth-wide employment service? It might be a venture of considerable profit."

THE HOWLING BOUNDERS

My brain, otherwise a sound instrument, has a serious defect—a hypertrophied lobe of curiosity.
—*Magnus Ridolph.*

THE AFTERNOON BREEZE off Irremedial Ocean ruffling his beard, yellow Naos-light burnishing the side of his face, Magnus Ridolph gazed glumly across his newly-acquired plantation. So far, so good; in fact, too good to be true.

He shook his head, frowned. All Blantham's representations had been corroborated by the evidence of his own eyes; three thousand acres of prime ticholama, ready for harvest; a small cottage, native-style, but furnished adequately; the ocean at his doorstep, the mountains in his back-yard. Why had the price been so low?

"Is it possible," mused Magnus Ridolph, "that Blantham is the philanthropist his acts suggest? Or does the ointment conceal a fly?" And Magnus Ridolph pulled at his beard with petulant fingers.

Now Naos slipped into Irremedial Ocean and lime-green evening flowed like syrup down out of the badlands which formed the northern boundary of the plantation. Magnus Ridolph half-turned in the doorway, glanced within. Chook, his dwarfish servant, was sweeping out the kitchen, grunting softly with each stroke of the broom.

Magnus Ridolph stepped out into the green twilight, strolled down past the copter landing to the first of the knee-high ticholama bushes.

He froze in his tracks, cocked his head.

"*Ow-ow-ow-ow-ow-ow-ow*," in a yelping chorus, wild and strange, drifted from across the field. Magnus Ridolph strained, squinted through the dusk. He could not be sure. . . . It seemed that a tumult of dark shapes came boiling down from the badlands, vague sprawling things. Olive-green darkness settled across the land. Magnus Ridolph turned on his heel, stalked back to the cottage.

Magnus Ridolph had been resting quietly in his hotel—the Piedmont Inn of New Napoli, on Naos V—with no slightest inclination toward or prospect of an agricultural life. Then Blantham knocked and Magnus Ridolph opened the door.

Blantham's appearance in itself was enough to excite interest. He was of early middle-age, of medium height, plump at the waist, wide at the hips, narrow at the shoulders.

His forehead was pale and narrow, with eyes set fish-like, wide apart under the temples, the skin between them taut, barely dented by the bridge of his nose. He had wide jowls, a sparse black mustache, a fine white skin, the cheeks meshed, however, with minute pink lines.

He wore loose maroon corduroy trousers, in the "Praesepe Ranger" style, a turquoise blouse with a diamond clasp, a dark blue cape, and beside Magnus Ridolph's simple white and blue tunic he appeared somewhat overripe.

Magnus Ridolph blinked, like a delicate and urbane owl. "Ah, yes?"

"I'm Blantham," said his visitor bluffly. "Gerard Blantham. We haven't met before."

Watching under his fine white eyebrows, Magnus Ridolph

57

gestured courteously. "I believe not. Will you come in, have a seat?"

Blantham stepped into the room, flung back his cape.

"Thank you," he said. He seated himself on the edge of a chair, extended a case. "Cigarette?"

"Thank you." Magnus Ridolph gravely helped himself. He inhaled, frowned, took the cigarette from his lips, examined it.

"Excuse me," said Blantham, producing a lighter. "I sometimes forget. I never smoke self-igniters; I can detect the flavor of the chemical instantly, and it annoys me."

"Unfortunate," said Magnus Ridolph, after his cigarette was aglow. "My senses are not so precisely adjusted, and I find them extremely convenient. Now, what can I do for you?"

Blantham hitched at his trousers. "I understand," he said looking archly upward, "that you're interested in sound investment."

"To a certain extent," said Magnus Ridolph, inspecting Blantham through the smoke of his cigarette. "What have you to offer?"

"This." Blantham reached in his pocket, produced a small white box. Magnus Ridolph, snapping back the top, found within a cluster of inch-long purple tubes, twisting and curling away from a central node. They were glossy, flexible, and interspersed with long pink fibers. He shook his head politely.

"I'm afraid I can't identify the object."

"It's ticholama," said Blantham. "Resilian in its natural state."

"Indeed!" And Magnus Ridolph examined the purple cluster with new interest.

"Each of those tubes," said Blantham, "is built of countless spirals of resilian molecules, each running the entire length of the tube. That's the property, naturally, which gives resilian its tremendous elasticity and tensile strength."

Magnus Ridolph touched the tubes, which quivered under his fingers. "And?"

Blantham paused impressively. "I'm selling an entire plantation, three thousand acres of prime ticholama ready to harvest."

Magnus Ridolph blinked, handed back the box. "Indeed?" He rubbed his beard thoughtfully. "The holding is evidently on Naos Six."

"Correct, sir. The only location which supports the growth of the ticholama."

58

"And what is your price?"

"A hundred and thirty thousand munits."

Magnus Ridolph continued to pull at his beard. "Is that a bargain? I know little of agriculture in general, ticholama in specific."

Blantham moved his head solemnly. "It's a giveaway. An acre produces a ton of ticholama. The selling price, delivered at Starport, is fifty-two munits a ton, current quotation. Freight, including all handling, runs about twenty-one munits a ton. And harvesting costs you about eight munits a ton. Expenses twenty-nine munits a ton, net profits, twenty-three munits a ton. On three thousand acres that's sixty-nine thousand munits. Next year you've paid the land off, and after that you're enjoying sheer profit."

Magnus Ridolph eyed his visitor with new interest, the hyper-developed lobe in his brain making its influence felt. Was it possible that Blantham intended to play him—Magnus Ridolph—for a sucker? Could he conceivably be so optimistic, so ill-advised?

"Your proposition," said Magnus Ridolph aloud, "sounds almost too good to be true."

Blantham blinked, stretching the skin across his nose even tauter. "Well, you see, I own another thirty-five hundred acres. The plantation I'm offering for sale is half the Hourglass Peninsula, the half against the mainland. Taking care of the seaward half keeps me more than busy.

"And then, frankly, I need money quick. I had a judgment against me—copter crash, my young son driving. My wife's eyes went bad. I had to pay for an expensive graft. Wasn't covered by Med service, worse luck. And then my daughter's away at school on Earth—St. Brigida's, London. Terrible expense all around. I simply need quick money."

Magnus Ridolph stared keenly at the man from beneath shaggy brows, and nodded.

"I see," he said. "You certainly have suffered an unfortunate succession of events. One hundred thirty thousand munits. A reasonable figure, if conditions are as you state?"

"They are indeed," was Blantham's emphatic reply.

"The ticholama is not all of first quality?" inquired Magnus Ridolph.

"On the contrary," declared Blantham. "Every plant is in prime condition."

"*Hm-m!*" Magnus Ridolph chewed his lower lip. "I assume there are no living quarters."

Blantham chortled, his lips rounded to a curious red O. "I

forgot to mention the cottage. A fine little place, native-style, of course, but in A-One condition. Absolutely livable. I believe I have a photograph. Yes, here it is."

Magnus Ridolph took the paper, saw a long building of gray and green slate—convex-gabled, with concave end-walls, a row of Gothic-arch openings. The field behind stretched rich purple out to the first crags of the badlands.

"Behind you'll see part of the plantation," said Blantham. "Notice the color? Deep dark purple—the best."

"*Humph*," said Magnus Ridolph. "Well, I'd have to furnish the cottage. That would run into considerable money."

Blantham smilingly shook his head. "Not unless you're the most sybaritic of sybarites. But I must guard against misrepresentation. The cottage is primitive in some respects. There is no telescreen, no germicide, no autolume. The power plant is small, there's no cold cell, no laundromat. And unless you fly out a rado-cooker, you'd have to cook in pots over heating elements."

Magnus Ridolph frowned, glanced sharply at Blantham. "I'd naturally hire a servant. The water? What arrangements, if any, exist?"

"An excellent still. Two hundred gallons a day."

"That certainly seems adequate," said Magnus Ridolph. He returned to the photograph. "What is this?" He indicated a patch in the field where one of the spurs from the badlands entered the field.

Blantham examined the photograph. "I really can't say. Evidently a small area where the soil is poor. It seems to be minor in extent."

Magnus Ridolph studied the photograph a minute longer, returned it. "You paint an arresting picture. I admit the possibility of doubling my principal almost immediately is one which I encounter rarely. If you'll tick off your address on my transview, I'll notify you tomorrow of my decision."

Blantham rose. "I've a suite right here in the hotel, Mr. Ridolph. You can call me any time. I imagine that the further you look into my proposition, the more attractive you'll find it."

To Magnus Ridolph's puzzlement, Blantham's prediction was correct. When he mentioned the matter to Sam Quien, a friend in the brokerage business, Quien whistled, shook his head.

"Sounds like a steal. I'll contract right now for the entire crop."

Magnus Ridolph next obtained a quotation on freight rates from Naos VI to Starport, and frowned when the rate proved a half munit less per ton than Blantham's estimate. By the laws of logic, somewhere there must be a flaw in the bargain. But where?

In the Labor Office he approached a window behind which stood a Fomalhaut V Rhodopian.

"Suppose I want to harvest a field of ticholama on Naos Six," said Magnus Ridolph. "What would be my procedure?"

The Rhodopian bobbed his head as he spoke. "You make arrangements on Naos Six," he lisped. "In Garswan. Contractor, he fix all harvest. Very cheap, on Naos Six. Contractor he use many pickers, very cheap."

"I see," said Magnus Ridolph. "Thank you."

He slowly returned to the hotel. At the mnemiphot in the reading room he verified Blantham's statement that an acre of land yielded a ton of ticholama, which, when processed and the binding gums dissolved, yielded about five hundred pounds of resilian. He found further that the demand for resilian exceeded by far the supply.

He returned to his room, lay down on his bed, considered an hour. At last he stood up, called Blantham on the transview. "Mr. Blantham, I've provisionally decided to accept your offer."

"Good, good!" came Blantham's voice.

"Naturally, before finally consummating the sale, I wish to inspect the property."

"Of course," came the hearty response. "An interplanet ship leaves day after tomorrow. Will that suit you?"

"Very well indeed," was Magnus Ridolph's reply. . . .

Blantham pointed, "That's your plantation, there ahead, the entire first half of the peninsula. Mine is the second half, just over that cliff."

Magnus Ridolph said nothing, peered through the copter windows. Below them the badlands—arid crags, crevasses, rock-jumble—fell astern, and they flew out over Hourglass Peninsula. Beyond lay Irremedial Ocean, streaked and mottled red, blue, green, yellow by vast colonies of colored plankton.

They put down at the cottage. Magnus Ridolph alighted, walked to the edge of the field, bent over. The plants were thick, luxuriant, amply covered with clusters of purple tubes. Magnus Ridolph straightened, looked sidelong at Blantham, who had come up behind him.

"Beautiful, isn't it?" said Blantham mildly.

Magnus Ridolph was forced to agree. Everything was beautiful. Blantham's title was clear, so Magnus Ridolph had verified in Garswan. The harvester agreed to a figure of eight munits a ton, the work to begin immediately after he had finished Blantham's field. In short, the property at the price seemed an excellent buy. And yet—

Magnus Ridolph took another look across the field. "That patch of poor soil seems larger than it appeared in the photograph."

Blantham made a deprecatory noise in his nose. "I can hardly see how that is possible."

Magnus Ridolph stood quietly a moment, the nostrils of his long distinguished nose slightly distended. Abruptly he pulled out his checkbook.

"Your check, sir."

"Thank you. I have the deed and the release in my pocket. I'll just sign it and the property's yours."

Blantham politely took his leave in the copter and Magnus Ridolph was left on the plantation in the gathering dusk. And then—the wild yelling from across the field, the vaguely seen shapes, pelting against the afterglow. Magnus Ridolph returned into the cottage.

He looked into the kitchen, to become acquainted with his servant Chook, a barrel-shaped anthropoid from the Garswan Highlands. Chook had gray lumpy skin, boneless rope-like arms, eyes round and bottle-green, a mouth hidden somewhere behind flabby folds of skin. Magnus Ridolph found him standing with head cocked to the distant yelping.

"Ah, Chook," said Magnus Ridolph. "What have you prepared for our dinner?"

Chook gestured to a steaming pot. "Stew." His voice came from his stomach, a heavy rumble. "Stew is good." A gust of wind brought the yelping closer. Chook's arms twitched.

"What causes that outcry, Chook?" demanded Magnus Ridolph, turning a curious ear toward the disturbance.

Chook looked at him quizzically. "Them the Howling Bounders. Very bad. Kill you, kill me. Kill everything. Eat up ticholama."

Magnus Ridolph seated himself. "Now—I see." He smiled without humor. "I see! . . . *Hmph.*"

"Like stew?" inquired Chook, pot ready. . . .

Next morning Magnus Ridolph arose early, as was his habit, strolled into the kitchen. Chook lay on the floor, curled into a gray leathery ball. At Magnus Ridolph's tread he raised his head, showed an eye, rumbled from deep inside his body.

"I'm going for a walk," said Magnus Ridolph. "I intend to be gone an hour. When I return we shall have our breakfast."

Chook slowly lowered his head and Magnus Ridolph stepped out into the cool silence, full into the horizontal light of Naos. just rising from the ocean like a red-hot stove-lid. The air from the ticholama fields seemed very fresh and rich in oxygen, and Magnus Ridolph set off with a feeling of well-being.

A half-hour's walk through the knee-high bushes brought him to the base of the outlying spur and to the patch of land which Blantham had termed poor soil.

Magnus Ridolph shook his head sadly at the devastation. Ticholama plants had been stripped of the purple tubes, ripped up, thrown into heaps.

The line of ruin roughly paralleled the edge of the spur. Once again Magnus Ridolph shook his head.

"A hundred and thirty thousand munits poorer. I wonder if my increment of wisdom may be valued at that figure?"

He returned to the cottage. Chook was busy at the stove, and greeted him with a grunt.

"Ha, Chook," said Magnus Ridolph, "and what have we for breakfast?"

"Is stew," said Chook.

Magnus Ridolph compressed his lips. "No doubt an excellent dish. But do you consider it, so to speak, a staple of diet?"

"Stew is good," was the stolid reply.

"As you wish," said Magnus Ridolph impassively.

After breakfast he retired to the study and called into Garswan on the antiquated old radiophone.

"Connect me with the T.C.I. office."

A hum, a buzz. "Terrestrial Corps of Intelligence," said a brisk male voice. "Captain Solinsky speaking."

"Captain Solinsky," said Magnus Ridolph, "I wonder if you can give me any information concerning the creatures known as the Howling Bounders."

A slight pause. "Certainly, sir. May I ask who is speaking?"

"My name is Magnus Ridolph; I recently acquired a ticholama plantation here, on the Hourglass Peninsula. Now I find that it is in the process of despoilation by these same Howling Bounders."

The voice had taken a sharper pitch. "Did you say—Magnus Ridolph?"

"That is my name."

"Just a moment, Mr. Ridolph! I'll get everything we have."

After a pause the voice returned. "What we have isn't much. No one knows much about 'em. They live in the Bouro Badlands, nobody knows how many. There's apparently only a single tribe, as they're never reported in two places at the same time. They seem to be semi-intelligent simians or anthropoids—no one knows exactly."

"These creatures have never been examined at close hand?" asked Magnus Ridolph in some surprise.

"Never." After a second's pause Solinsky said: "The weird things can't be caught. They're elastic—live off ticholama, eat it just before it's ready to harvest. In the day time they disappear, nobody knows where, and at night they're like locusts, black phantoms. A party from Carnegie Tech tried to trap them, but they tore the traps to pieces. They can't be poisoned, a bullet bounces off their hides, they dodge out of heat-beams, deltas don't phase them. We've never got close enough to use supersonics, but they probably wouldn't even notice."

"They would seem almost invulnerable, then—to the usual methods of destruction," was Magnus Ridolph's comment.

"That's about it," said Solinsky brightly. "I suppose a meson grenade would do the trick, but there wouldn't be much specimen left for you to examine."

"My interest in these creatures is not wholly impersonal," said Magnus Ridolph. "They are devouring my ticholama; I want to halt this activity."

"Well—" Solinsky hesitated. "I don't like to say it, Mr. Ridolph, but I'm afraid there's very little you can do—except next year don't raise so tempting a crop. They only go after the choicest fields. Another thing, they're dangerous. Any poor devil they chance upon, they tear him to pieces. So don't go out with a shotgun to scare 'em away."

"No," said Magnus Ridolph. "I shall have to devise other means."

"Hope you succeed," said Solinsky. "No one ever has before."

Magnus Ridolph returned to the kitchen, where Chook was peeling starchy blue bush-apples.

"I see you are preparing lunch," said Magnus Ridolph. "Is it—?" He raised his eybrows interrogatively.

64

Chook rumbled an affirmative. Magnus Ridolph came over beside him, watched a moment.

"Have you ever seen one of these Howling Bounders close at hand?"

"No," said Chook. "When I hear noise, I sleep, stay quiet."

"What do they look like?"

"Very tall, long arms. Ugly—like men." He turned a lambent bottle-green eye at Magnus Ridolph's beard. "But no hair."

"I see," said Magnus Ridolph, stroking the beard. He wandered outside, seated himself on a bench, and relaxed in the warm light of Naos. He found a piece of paper, scribbled. A buzz reached his ears, grew louder, and presently Blantham's copter dropped into his front yard. Blantham hopped out, brisk, cleanly-shaven, his wide-set eyes bright, his jowls pink with health. When he saw Magnus Ridolph, he shaped his features into a frame of grave solicitude.

"Mr. Ridolph, a distressing report has reached me. I understand—I just learned this morning—that those devilish Bounders have been on your plantation."

Magnus Ridolph nodded. "Yes, something of that nature has been called to my attention."

"Words can't convey my sense of guilt," said Blantham. "Naturally I'd never have saddled you with the property if I'd known . . ."

"Naturally," agreed Magnus Ridolph siccatively.

"As soon as I heard, I came over to make what amends I could, but I fear they can only be nominal. You see, last night, as soon as I banked your check, I paid off a number of outstanding debts and I only have about fifty thousand munits left. If you'd like me to take over the burden of coping with those beasts . . ." He paused, coughed.

Magnus Ridolph looked mildly upward. "That's exceedingly generous of you, Mr. Blantham—a gesture few men would make. However, I think I may be able to salvage something from the property. I am not completely discouraged."

"Good, good," was Blantham's hasty comment. "Never say die; I always admire courage. But I'd better warn you that once those pestiferous Bounders start on a field they never stop till they've run through the whole works. When they reach the cottage you'll be in extreme danger. Many, many men and women they've killed."

"Perhaps," Magnus Ridolph suggested, "you will permit the harvester to gather such of my crop as he is able before starting with yours?"

Blantham's face became long and doleful. "Mr. Ridolph, nothing could please me more than to say yes to your request, but you don't know these Garswan contractors. They're stubborn, inflexible. If I were to suggest any change in our contract, he'd probably cancel the entire thing. And naturally, I must protect my wife, my family. In the second place, there is probably little of your ticholama ripe enough to harvest. The Bounders, you know, attack the plant just before its maturity." He shook his head. "With the best of intentions, I can't see how to help you, unless it's by the method I suggested a moment ago."

Magnus Ridolph raised his eyebrows. "Sell you back the property for fifty thousand munits?"

Blantham coughed. "I'd hardly call it selling. I merely wish—"

"Naturally, naturally," agreed Magnus Ridolph. "However, let us view the matter from a different aspect. Let us momentarily forget that we are friends, neighbors, almost business associates, each acting only through motives of the highest integrity. Let us assume that we are strangers, unmoral, predatory."

Blantham blew out his cheeks, eyed Magnus Ridolph doubtfully. "Far-fetched, of course. But go on."

"On the latter assumption, let us come to a new agreement"

"Such as?"

"Let us make a wager," mused Magnus Ridolph. "The plantation here against—say, a hundred thirty thousand munits—but I forgot. You have spent your money."

"What would be the terms of the wager?" inquired Blantham, inspecting his finger-tips.

"A profit of sixty-nine thousand munits was mentioned in connection with the sale of the property. The advent of the—ah!—Howling Bounders made this figure possibly over-optimistic."

Blantham murmured sympathetically.

"However," continued Magnus Ridolph, "I believe that a profit of sixty-nine thousand munits is not beyond reason, and I would like to wager the plantation against 130,000 munits on those terms."

Blantham gave Magnus Ridolph a long bright stare. "From the sale of ticholama?"

Magnus Ridolph eloquently held his arms out from his sides. "What else is there to yield a profit?"

"There's no mineral on the property, that's certain," muttered Blantham. "No oil, no magnoflux vortex." He looked across the field to the devastated area. "When those Bounders start on a field, they don't stop, you know."

Magnus Ridolph shrugged. "Protecting my land from intrusion is a problem to which a number of solutions must exist."

Blantham eyed him curiously. "You're very confident."

Magnus Ridolph pursed his lips. "I believe in an aggressive attitude toward difficulties."

Blantham turned once more toward the blighted area, looked boldly back at Magnus Ridolph. "I'll take that bet."

"Good," said Magnus Ridolf. Let us take your copter to Garswan and cast the wager into a legal form."

In the street below the notary's office later, Magnus Ridolph tucked his copy of the agreement into the microfilm compartment of his wallet.

"I think," he told Blantham, who was watching him covertly with an air of sly amusement, "that I'll remain in Garswan the remainder of the day. I want to find a copter, perhaps take back a few supplies."

"Very well, Mr. Ridolph." Blantham inclined his head courteously, swung his dark blue cape jauntily across his shoulders. "I wish you the best of luck with your plantation."

"Thank you," said Magnus Ridolph, equally punctilious, "and may you likewise enjoy the returns to which you are entitled."

Blantham departed; Magnus Ridolph turned up the main street. Garswan owed its place as Naos VI's first city only to a level field of rock-hard clay, orginally the site of native fire-dances. There was little else to commend Garswan, certainly no scenic beauty.

The main street started at the space-port, wound under a great raw bluff of red shale, plunged into a jungle of snake-vine, inch-moss, hammock tree. The shops and dwellings were half of native-style, of slate slabs with curving gables and hollow end-walls; half dingy frame buildings. There was a warehouse, a local of the space-men's union, a Rhodopian social hall, an Earth-style drug-store, a side street given to a native market, a copter yard.

At the copter yard, Magnus Ridolph found a choice of six or seven vehicles, all weatherbeaten and over-priced. He ruefully selected a six-jet Spur, and closing his ears to the whine of the bearings, flew it away to a garage, where he ordered it fueled and lubricated.

He stepped into the TCI office, where he was received with courtesy. He requested and was permitted use of the mnemiphot. Seating himself comfortably, he found the code for resilian, ticked it into the selector, attentively pursued the facts, pictures, formulae, statistics drifting across the screen. He noted the tensile strength, about the same as mild steel, and saw with interest that resilian dampened with hessopenthol welded instantly into another pience of resilian.

He leaned back in his chair, tapped his pencil thoughtfully against his notebook. He returned to the mnemiphot, dialed ahead to the preparation of resilian from the raw ticholama. The purple tubes, he found, were frozen in liquid air, passed through a macerator, which pulverized the binding gums, soaked in hesso-hexylic acid, then alcohol, dried in a centrifuge, a process which left the fibres in a felt-like mat. This mat was combed until the fibers lay parallel, impregnated with hesso-penthol and compressed into a homogeneous substance—resilian.

Again Magnus Ridolph sat back, his mild blue eyes focused on space. Presently he arose, left the office, crossed the street to the headquarters of the local construction company. Here he spent almost an hour; then, returning to the garage, he picked up his copter and, rising high over the jungle, headed south. The jumble of the Bouro Badlands passed below. Hourglass Peninsula spread before him, with his plantation filling the landward half, that of Blantham the remainder.

Naos hung low over the sea when he landed. Chook was standing in the pointed doorway, eyes fixed vacantly across the ticholama field, arms dangling almost to the ground.

"Good evening, Chook," said Magnus Ridolph, handing his servant a parcel. "A bottle of wine to aid your digestion."

"R-r-r-r."

Magnus Ridolph glanced into the kitchen. "I see that you have dinner prepared. Well, let us eat our stew, and then the evening will be free for intellectual exercises."

The blurred green twilight drifted down from the badlands, and, dinner over, Magnus Ridolph stepped outside into the evening quiet. Under different circumstances he would have enjoyed the vista—the olive-dark *massif* to his left, the fields black in the greenish light, the blue-green sky with a few lavender and orange clouds over the ocean. A faint yelp came to his ears—far, far distant, mournful, lonely as a ghost-cry. Then there came a quick far chorus: "*Ow-ow-ow-ow.*"

Magnus Ridolph entered the cottage, emerged with a pair of infra-red-sensitive binoculars. Down from the mountains came the Bounders, leaping pell-mell high in the air, hopping like monstrous fleas, and the suggestion of humanity in their motion sent a chill along Magnus Ridolph's usually imperturbable spine.

"*Ow-ow-ow-ow*," came the far chorus, as the Bounders flung themselves upon Magnus Ridolph's ticholama.

Magnus Ridolph nodded grimly. "Tomorrow night, my destructive guests, you shall sing a different song."

The construction crew arrived from Garswan the next morning in a great copter which carried below a bulldozer. They came while Magnus Ridolph was still at breakfast. Swallowing the last of his stew, he took them out to the devastated tract, showed them what he wished done.

Late afternoon found the project complete, the last of the equipment installed and Magnus Ridolph engaged in testing the machinery.

A heavy concrete pill-box now rose on the border of the blighted acreage, a windowless building reinforced with steel and set on a heavy foundation. A hundred yards from the pill-box a ten-foot cylindrical block stood anchored deep into the ground. An endless herculoy cable ran from the pill-box, around a steel-collared groove in the block, back into the pill-box, where it passed around the drum of an electric winch, then out again to the block.

Magnus Ridolph glanced around the little room with satisfaction. There had been no time for attention to detail, but the winch ran smoothly, pulled the cable easily out, around the anchor block, back again. Inside the door rose a stack of resilian plates, each an inch thick, each trailing three feet of herculoy chain.

Magnus Ridolph took a last look about the pill-box, then strolled sedately to his copter, flew back to the cottage.

Chook was standing in the doorway.

"Chook," said Magnus Ridolph, "do you consider yourself brave, resourceful, resolute?"

Chook's bottle-green eyes moved in two different directions. "I am cook."

"*Mmph*," said Magnus Ridolph. "Of course. But tonight I wish to observe the Howling Bounders at close quarters, and desiring some assistance, I have selected you to accompany me."

Chook's eyes turned even farther out of focus. "Chook busy tonight."

"What is the nature of your task?" inquired Magnus Ridolph frostily.

"Chook write letter."

Magnus Ridolph turned away impatiently. During the course of the meal he once more suggested that Chook join him, but Chook remained obdurate. And so about an hour before sunset Magnus Ridolph shouldered a light knapsack and set out on foot for his pill-box.

The shadow of the foremost spur had engulfed the little concrete dome when he finally arrived. Without delay he ducked into the dark interior, dropped the knapsack to the floor.

He tested the door. It slid easily up and down, locked securely. He moved the rheostat controlling the winch. The drum turned, the cable slid out to the anchor block, around, returned. Magnus Ridolph now took one of his resilian plates, shackled the tail-chain to the cable, set it down directly before the doorway, lowered the door to all but a slit, seated himself, lit a cigarette, waited.

Shade crept across the dark purple field; the blue-green sky shaded through a series of deepening sub-marine colors. There was silence, an utter hush.

From the mountains came a yelp, far but very keen. It echoed down the rock-canyons. As if it were a signal, a series of other yells followed, a few louder and closer, but for the most part nearly lost out in the wasteland.

"*Ow-ow-ow-ow.*"

This time the cries were louder, mournful, close at hand, and Magnus Ridolph, peering through the peep-hole in the door, saw the tumble of figures come storming down the hill, black against the sky. He dipped a brush into a pan of liquid nearby, slid the door up a trifle, reached out, swabbed the resilian plate, slid the door shut. Rising, he put his eye to the peep-hole.

The howling sounded overhead now, to all sides, full of throbbing new overtones, and Magnus Ridolph caught the flicker of dark figures close at hand.

A thud on top of the pill-box, a yell from directly overhead, and Magnus Ridolph clenched his thin old hands.

Bumps sounded beside the pill-box; the cable twitched. The howling grew louder, higher in pitch, the roof resounded to a series of thuds. The cable gave a furious jerk, swung back and forth.

Magnus Ridolph smiled grimly to himself. Outside now he heard a hoarse yammering, then angry panting, the jingle of furiously shaken chain. And he glimpsed a form longer than a man, with long lank arms and legs, a narrow head, flinging itself savagely back and forth from the snare.

Magnus Ridolph started the winch, pulled the plate and its captive approximately ten feet out toward the anchor block, shackled another plate to the cable, daubed it with hesso-penthol, raised the door a trifle, shoved the plate outside. It was snatched from his hands. Magnus Ridolph slammed the door down, rose to the peep-hole. Another dark form danced, bounded back and forth across the cable, which, taking up the slack in the chain, threw the creature headlong to the ground with every bound.

The yells outside almost deafened Magnus Ridolph, and the pill-box appeared to be encircled. He prepared another plate, raised the door a slit, slid the plate under. Again it was snatched from his hands, but this time black fingers thrust into the slit, heaved with a bone-crushing strength.

But Magnus Ridolph had foreseen the contingency, had a steel bar locking down the door. The fingers strained again. Magnus Ridolph took his heat-pencil, turned it on the fingers. The steel changed color, glowed, the fingers gave off a nauseating stench, suddenly were snatched back. Magnus Ridolph shackled another plate to the cable.

Two hours passed. Every plate he shoved under the door was viciously yanked out of his hands. Sometimes fingers would seek the slit, to be repelled by the heat-pencil, until the room was dense with stifling organic smoke. Shackle the plate, daub it, slide it out, slam the door, run the cable further out on the winch, look through the peep-hole. The winch creaked, the pill-box vibrated to the frenzied tugging from without. He sent out his last plate, peered through the peep-hole. The cable was lined out to the anchor block and back with frantic tireless forms, and overhead others pelted the pill-box.

Magnus Ridolph composed himself against the concrete wall, found a flask in his knapsack and took a long drink.

A groaning from the winch disturbed him. He arose painfully, old joints stiff, peered through the peep-hole.

A form of concerted action was in progress: the cable was lined solidly on both sides with black shapes. They bent, rose, and the drum of the winch creaked, squawked. Magnus Ridolph released the winch brake, jerked the cable forward and back several times, and the line of black figures swayed

71

willy-nilly back and forth. Suddenly, like a flight of black ghosts, they left the cable, bounded toward the pill-box.

Clang! Against the steel door—the jar of a great weight. Clang! The door ground back against its socket. Magnus Ridolph rubbed his beard. The steel presumably would hold, and likewise the sill, bolted deep into the concrete. But, of course, no construction was invulnerable. Thud! Fine dust sprang away from the wall.

Magnus Ridolph jumped to the peep-hole, in time to glimpse a hurtling black shape, directed seemingly at his head. He ducked. THUD! Magnus Ridolph anxiously played a torch around the interior of the pill-box. Should there be a crack—

He returned to the peep-hole. Suppose the Bounders brought a length of steel beam, and used it for a battering-ram? Probably their powers of organization were unequal to the task. Once more he seated himself on the floor, addressed himself to his flask. Presently he fell into a doze.

He awoke to find the air hot, heavy, pungent. Red light flickered in through the peep-hole, an ominous crackling sound came to his ears. A moment he sat thoughtfully, while his lungs demanded oxygen from the vitiated atmosphere. He rose, looked forth into a red and white pyre of blazing ticholama. He sat down in the center of the room, clear of the already warm concrete.

"Is it my end, then, to be fired like a piece of crockery in a kiln?" he asked himself. "No," came the answer, "I shall undoubtedly suffocate first. But," he mused, "on second thought—"

He took his water bottle from the knapsack, brought forth the power pack, ran leads into the water. He dialed up the power, and bubbles of hydrogen and oxygen vibrated to the surface. He pressed his face to the bottle, breathed the synthetic atmosphere. . . .

Blantham's copter dropped to Magnus Ridolph's landing and Blantham stepped out, spruce in dark gray and red. Magnus Ridolph appeared in the doorway, nodded.

"Good morning, good morning." Blantham stepped forward jauntily. "I dropped by to tell you that the harvesters have nearly finished on my property and that they'll be ready for you at the first of the week."

"Excellent," said Magnus Ridolph.

"A pity those Bounders have done so much damage," sighed Blantham, looking off in the direction of the devastated area. "Something will have to be done to abate that nuisance."

Magnus Ridolph nodded in agreement.

Blantham inspected Magnus Ridolph. "You're looking rather tired. I hope the climate agrees with you?"

"Oh entirely. I've been keeping rather irregular hours."

"I see. What are those two domes out in the field? Did you have them built?"

Magnus Ridolph waved a modest hand. "Observation posts, I suppose you'd call them. The first was too limited, and rather vulnerable, in several respects, so I installed the second larger unit."

"I see," said Blantham. "Well, I'll be on my way. Those Bounders seem to have gotten pretty well into the plantation. Do you still have hope of a sixty-nine thousand munit profit on the property?"

Magnus Ridolph permitted a smile to form behind his crisp white beard. "A great deal more, I hope. My total profit on our transaction should come to well over two hundred thousand munits."

Blantham froze, his wide-set eyes blue, glassy. "Two hundred thousand munits? Are you— May I ask exactly how you arrive at that figure?"

"Of course," said Magnus Ridolph affably. "First of course is the sale of my harvest. Two thousand acres of good ti-cholama, which should yield forty-six thousand munits. Second, two hundred forty tons—estimated—of raw resilian, at a quarter munit a pound, or five hundred munits a ton. Subtract freight charges, and my profit here should be well over a hundred thousand munits—say one hundred and ten thousand—"

"But," stammered Blantham, his jowls red, "where did you get the resilian?"

Magnus Ridolph clasped his hands behind his body, looked across the field. "I trapped a number of the Bounders."

"But how? Why?"

"From their habits and activities, as well as their diet, I deduced that the Bounders were either resilian or some closely allied substance. A test proved them to be resilian. In the last two weeks, I've trapped twenty-four hundred, more or less."

"And how did you do that?"

"They are curious and aggressive creatures," said Magnus Ridolph, and explained the mechanism of his trap.

"How did you kill them? They're like iron."

73

"Not during the day time. They dislike the light, curl up in tight balls, and a sharp blow with a machete severs the prime chord of their nervous system."

Blantham bit his lips, chewed at his mustache. "That's still only a hundred fifty or sixty thousand. How do you get two hundred thousand out of that?"

"Well," said Magnus Ridolph, "I'll admit the rest is pure speculation, and for that reason I named a conservative figure. I'll collect a hundred thirty thousand munits from you, which will return my original investment, and I should be able to sell this excellent plantation for a hundred seventy or eighty thousand munits. My trapping expenses have been twelve thousand munits so far. You can see that I'll come out rather well."

Blantham angrily turned away. Magnus Ridolph held out a hand. "What's your hurry? Can you stay to lunch? I admit the fare is modest, only stew, but I'd enjoy your company."

Blantham stalked away. A moment later his copter was out of sight in the green-blue sky. Magnus Ridolph returned inside. Chook raised his head. "Eat lunch."

"As you wish." Magnus Ridolph seated himself. "What's this? Where's our stew?"

"Chook tired of stew," said his cook. "We eat chili con carne now."

THE KING OF THIEVES

IN ALL the many-colored worlds of the universe no single ethical code shows a universal force. The good citizen on Almanatz would be executed on Judith IV. Commonplace conduct of Medellin excites the wildest revulsion on Earth and on Moritaba a deft thief commands the highest respect. I am convinced that virtue is but a reflection of good intent.

—*Magnus Ridolph.*

"THERE's much wealth to be found here on Moritaba," said the purser wistfully. "There's wonderful leathers, there's rare

74

hardwoods—and have you seen the coral? It's purple-red and it glows with the fires of the damned! But"—he jerked his head toward the port—"it's too tough. Nobody cares for anything but telex—and that's what they never find. Old Kanditter, the King of Thieves, is too smart for 'em."

Magnus Ridolph was reading about Moritaba in *Guide to the Planets*:

The climate is damp and unhealthy, the terrain is best described as the Amazon Basin superimposed on the Lunar Alps . . .

He glanced down a list of native diseases, turned the page.

In the early days Moritaba served as a base and haven for Louie Joe, the freebooter. When at last the police ships closed in Louie Joe and his surviving followers fled into the jungles and there mingled with the natives, producing a hybrid race, the Men-men—this despite the protests of orthodox biologists that such a union is impossible.

In the course of years the Men-men have become a powerful tribe occupying the section of Moritaba known as Arcady Major, the rumored site of a large lode of telex crystals . . .

Magnus Ridolph yawned, tucked the book in his pocket. He rose to his feet, sauntered to the port, looked out across Moritaba.

Gollabolla, chief city of the planet, huddled between a mountain and a swamp. There were a Commonwealth Control office, a Uni-Culture Mission, a general store, a school, a number of dwellings, all built of corrugated metal on piles of native wood and connected by rickety catwalks.

Magnus Ridolph found the view picturesque in the abstract, oppressive in the immediate.

A voice at his elbow said, "Quarantine's lifted, sir. You may go ashore."

"Thank you," said Magnus Ridolph and turned toward the door. Ahead of him stood a short barrel-chested man of pugnacious aspect. He darted Magnus Ridolph a bright suspicious glance, then hunched a step closer to the door. The heavy jaw, the small fire-black eyes, the ruff of black hair were suggestive of the simian.

"If I were you, Mr. Mellish," said Magnus Ridolph affably,

"I would not take any luggage ashore until I found adequate thief-proof lodgings."

Ellis B. Mellish gave his briefcase a quick jerk. "No thief will get anything from me, I'll guarantee you."

Magnus Ridolph pursed his lips reflectively. "I suppose your familiarity with the tricks is an advantage."

Mellish turned his back. There was a coolness between the two, stemming from the fact that Magnus Ridolph had sold Mellish half of a telex lode on the planet Ophir, whereupon Mellish had mined not only his own property but Magnus Ridolph's as well.

A bitter scene had ensued in Mellish's office, with an exchange of threats and recriminations—the whole situation aggravated by the fact that the field was exhausted. Coincidentally both found themselves on the first packet for Moritaba, the only other known source of telex crystal.

Now the port opened and the pungent odor of Moritaba rolled into their faces—a smell of dank soil, exultant plant-life, organic decay. They descended the ladder, blinking in the hot yellow light of Pi Aquarii.

Four natives squatted on the ground nearby—slender wiry creatures, brownish-purple, more manlike than not. These were the Men-men—the hybrid race ruled by Kanditter, the King of Thieves. The ship's purser, standing at the foot of the gangplank, turned on them a sharp glance.

"Be careful of those boys," he told Magnus Ridolph and Mellish. "They'll take your eyeteeth if you open your mouth in front of them."

The four rose to their feet, came closer with long sliding steps.

"If I had my way," said the purser, "I'd run 'em off with a club. But—orders say 'treat 'em nice.'" He noticed Mellish's camera. "I wouldn't take that camera with me, sir. They'll make off with it sure as blazes."

Mellish thrust his chin forward. "If they get this camera, they'll deserve it."

"They'll get it," said the purser.

Mellish turned his head, gave the purser a challenging look. "If anyone or anything gets this camera away from me I'll give you another just like it."

The purser shrugged. A buzzing came from the sky. "Look," he said. "There's the copter from Challa."

It was the oddest contraption Magnus Ridolph had ever seen. An enormous hemisphere of wire mesh made a dome over the whole vehicle, an umbrella of close-mesh wire under which the supporting blades swung.

"That's just how fast these johnnies are," said the purser in grudging admiration. "That net is charged—high voltage—as soon as the copter lands. If it wasn't for that there wouldn't be a piece left of it an hour after it touched ground."

Mellish laughed shortly. "This is quite a place. I'd like to be in charge here for a couple of months." He glanced to where Magnus Ridolph stood, quietly watching the copter.

"How about you, Ridolph? Think you're going to leave with your shirt?" He laughed.

"I am usually able to adapt myself to circumstances," said Magnus Ridolph, observing Mellish with detached curiosity. "I hope your camera was not expensive?"

"What do you mean?" Mellish reached for the case. The lid hung loosely; the case was empty. He glanced at the purser, who had tactfully turned his back, then around the field. The four natives sat in a line about thirty feet distant, watching the three with alert amber eyes.

"Which one of them got it?" demanded Mellish, now suffused with a red flush.

"Easy, Mr. Mellish," said the purser, "if you hope to do business with the king."

Mellish whirled on Magnus Ridolph. "Did *you* see it? Which one—"

Magnus Ridolph permitted a faint smile to pull at his beard. He stepped forward, handed Mellish his camera. "I was merely testing your vigilance, Mr. Mellish. I'm afraid you are poorly equipped for conditions on Moritaba."

Mellish glared a moment, then grinned wolfishly. "Are you a gambling man, Ridolph?"

Magnus Ridolph shook his head. "I occasionally take calculated risks—but gamble? No, never."

Mellish said slowly, "I'll put you this proposition. Now—you are going to Challa?"

Magnus Ridolph nodded. "As you know. I have business with the king."

Mellish grinned his wide yellow-toothed smile. "Let us each take a number of small articles—watch, camera, micromac, pocket screen, energizer, shaver, cigarette case, cleanorator, a micro library. Then we shall see who is the more vigilant, the more alert." He raised his bushy black eyebrows.

"And the stakes?" inquired Magnus Ridolph coolly.

"Oh"—Mellish made an impatient gesture.

"You owe me a hundred thousand munits for the telex you

77

filched from my property," said Magnus Ridolph. "I'll take double or nothing."

Mellish blinked. "In effect," he said, "I'd be placing two hundred thousand munits against nothing—since I don't recognize the debt as collectable. But I'll bet you fifty thousand munits cash to cash. If you have that much."

Magnus Ridolph did not actually sneer but the angle of his fine white eyebrows, the tilt of his thin distinguished nose, conveyed an equivalent impression. "I believe I can meet the figure you mention."

"Write me a check," said Mellish. "I'll write you one. The purser will hold the stakes."

"As you wish," said Magnus Ridolph.

The copter took Mellish and Magnus Ridolph to Challa, the seat of Kanditter, the King of Thieves. First they crossed an arm of the old sea-bottom, an unimaginable tangle of orange, purple and green foliage, netted by stagnant pools and occasional pad-covered sloughs.

Then they rose over an army of white cliffs, flew low over a smooth plateau where herds of buffalo-like creatures on six splayed legs cropped mustard-colored shrubs. Down into a valley dark with jungle, toward a grove of tall trees looming above them like plumes of smoke. A clearing opened below, the copter sat down and they were in Challa.

Magnus Ridolph and Mellish stepped out of the copter, looked out through the cage of charged wire. A group of dark, big-eyed natives stood at a respectful distance, shuffling their feet in loose leather sandals with pointed toes.

On all sides houses sat off the ground on stilts, houses built of a blue white-veined wood, thatched with slabs of gray pith. At the end of a wide avenue stood a larger taller building with wings extending under the trees.

Three Earthmen stood watching the arrival of the copter with listless curiosity. One of these, a sallow thin man with a large beak of a nose and bulging brown eyes, suddenly stiffened in unbelief. He darted forward.

"Mr. Mellish! What on earth? I'm glad to see you!"

"I'm sure, Tomko, I'm sure," said Mellish. "How's everything going?"

Tomko glanced at Magnus Ridolph, then back to Mellish. "Well—nothing definite yet, sir. Old Kanditter—that's the king—won't make any concessions whatever."

"We'll see about that," said Mellish. He turned, raised his voice to the copter pilot. "Let us out of this cage."

The pilot said, "When I give you the word, sir, you can open that door—right there." He walked around the copter. "Now."

Mellish and Magnus Ridolph passed outside, each carrying a pair of magnesium cases.

"Can you tell me," inquired Magnus Ridolph, "where lodging may be found?"

Tomko said doubtfully, "There's usually a few empty houses around. We've been living in one of the wings of the king's palace. If you introduce yourself he'll probably invite you to do likewise."

"Thank you," said Magnus Ridolph. "I'll go pay my respects immediately."

A whistle came to his ears. Turning, he saw the copter pilot beckoning to him through the wire. He went as close to the charged mesh as he dared.

"I just want to warn you," said the pilot. "Watch out for the king. He's the worst of the lot. That's why he's king. Talk about stealing—*whoo!*" Solemnly shaking his head, he turned back to his copter.

"Thank you," said Magnus Ridolph. He felt a vibration through his wrist. He turned, said to the nearby native, "Your knife makes no impression in the alloy of the case, my friend. You would do better with a heat-needle."

The native slid quietly away. Magnus Ridolph set out for the king's palace. It was a pleasant scene, he thought, reminiscent of ancient Polynesia. The village seemed clean and orderly. Small shops appeared at intervals along the avenue—booths displaying yellow fruit, shiny green tubes, rows of dead shrimp-like insects, jars of rust-colored powder. The proprietors sat in front of the booths, not behind them.

A pavilion extended forward from the front of the palace, and here Magnus Ridolph found Kanditter, the King of Thieves, sitting sleepily in a low deep chair. He was to Magnus Ridolph's eye distinguishable from the other natives only by his headdress—a coronet-like affair woven of a shiny red-gold metal and set with telex crystals.

Unaware of the exact formalities expected of him, Magnus Ridolph merely approached the king, bowed his head.

"Greetings," said the king in a thick voice. "Your name and business?"

"I am Magnus Ridolph, resident of Tran, on Lake Sahara, Earth. I have come—to state the matter briefly—to—"

"To get telex?"

"I would be foolish to deny it."

79

"Ho!" The king rocked back and forth, pulled back his sharp dark features in a fish-like grin. "No luck. Telex crystal stay on Moritaba."

Magnus Ridolph nodded. He had expected refusal. "In the meantime may I trespass on the royal hospitality?"

The king's grin slowly faded. "Eh? Eh? What you say?"

"Where do you suggest that I stay?"

The king made a sweep of his arm toward the end of his palace. "Much room there. Go around, go in."

"Thank you," said Magnus Ridolph.

To the rear of the palace Magnus Ridolph found suitable quarters—one of a row of rooms facing out on the path like stalls in a stable. The resemblance was heightened by the stable-type door.

It was a pleasant lodging with the trees swaying far overhead, the carpet of red-gold leaves in front. The interior was comfortable though Spartan. Magnus Ridolph found a couch, a pottery ewer filled with cool water, a carved chest built into the wall, a table.

Humming softly to himself, Magnus Ridolph opened the chest, peered within. A soft smile disturbed his beard as he noted the back panel of the chest. It looked solid, felt solid, but Magnus Ridolph knew it could be opened from the outside.

The walls seemed sound—poles of the blue wood were caulked with a putty-like resin and there was no window.

Magnus Ridolph opened his suitcases, laid the goods out on the couch. From without he heard voices, and, looking forth, he saw Mellish rocking on his short legs down the center of the path, bulldog jaw thrust out, hands clenched, elbows swinging wide as he walked. Tomko came to the rear, carrying Mellish's luggage.

Magnus Ridolph nodded courteously, withdrew into his room. He saw Mellish grin broadly to Tomko, heard his comment: "They've got the old goat penned up for sure. Damned if he doesn't look natural with that beard hanging over the door."

Tomko snickered dutifully. Magnus Ridolph frowned. Old goat? He turned back to his couch—in time to catch a dark flicker, a glint of metal.

Magnus Ridolph compressed his lips. His micromac and power pack had disappeared. Peering under the couch, Magnus Ridolph saw a patch of slightly darker fiber in the matting. He straightened his back, just in time to see his pocket

80

screen swinging up through the air into a hole high in the wall.

Magnus Ridolph started to run outside and into the adjoining room, then thought better of it. No telling how many natives would be pillaging his room if he left for an instant. He piled everything back into his suitcases, locked them, placed them in the middle of the floor, sat on the couch, lit a cigarette.

Fifteen minutes he sat in reflection. A muffled bellow made him look up.

"Thieving little blackguards!" he heard Mellish cry. Magnus Ridolph grinned ruefully, rose to his feet and, taking his suitcases, he stepped out into the street.

He found the copter pilot reading a newspaper inside his thief-proof cage. Magnus Ridolph looked through the mesh.

"May I come in?"

The pilot arose, cast the switch. Magnus Ridolph entered, set his suitcases on the ground.

"I just been reading about you," said the pilot.

"Is that right?" asked Magnus Ridolph.

"Yeah—in one of these old newspapers. See—" he pointed out the article with a greasy forefinger. It read:

GHOST-ROBBER APPREHENDED

STARPORT BANK LAUDS
EARTH CRIME-DOCTOR

A million munits looted from the Starport Bank were recovered by Magnus Ridolph, noted savant and freelance troubleshooter, who this morning delivered the criminal, Arnold McGurk, 35, unemployed space-man, to Starport police. After baffling Starport authorities two weeks, Arnold McGurk refused to divulge how he robbed the supposedly thief-proof bank, other than to hint at the aid of 'ghosts.' Magnus Ridolph was similarly uncommunicative and the police admit ignorance of the criminal's *modus operandi* . . .

"Wouldn't ever have knowed you was a detective," said the pilot, eyeing Magnus Ridolph reverently. "You don't look the type."

"Thank you," said Magnus Ridolph. "I'm glad to hear it."

The pilot appraised him. "You look more like a professor or a dentist."

Magnus Ridolph winced.

"Just what was them 'ghosts' the article speaks of, Mr. Ridolph?" the pilot inquired.

"Nothing whatever," Magnus Ridolph assured him. "An optical illusion."

"Oh," said the pilot.

"There's something I'd like you to do for me," said Magnus Ridolph.

"Sure—glad to be of help."

Magnus Ridolph scribbled on a page in his notebook. "Take this to the ship right away before it leaves. Give it to the radio operator, ask him to send it ulrad special."

The pilot took the message. "That all?"

"No," said Magnus Ridolph. "There's another ship leaving Starport for Moritaba in—let's see—in four days. Six days passage makes ten days. I should have a parcel on that next ship.

"I want you to meet that ship, take that parcel aboard your copter, deliver it to me here immediately. When I get that parcel I'll pay you two hundred munits. Does that satisfy you?"

"Yes," said the pilot. "I'm off right now."

"Also," said Magnus Ridolph, "there is need for secrecy. Can you keep a close tongue in your head?"

"Haven't heard me say much yet, have you?" The pilot stretched his arms. "I'll see you in about ten days."

"Er—do you have any extra wire and a spare powerpack?" inquired Magnus Ridolph. "I think I'll need some sort of protection."

Magnus Ridolph returned to his room with his suitcases and what electrical equipment the pilot was able to spare. A half hour later he stood back. Now, he thought, next move to the Men-men.

A face appeared at the door—narrow, purple-brown, big-eyed, with a long thin nose, slit mouth, long sharp chin.

"King he want you come eat." The face peered cautiously around the room, brushed the wires Magnus Ridolph had strung up. *Crackle—spat.* The native yelped, bounded away.

"Ho, ho!" said Magnus Ridolph. "What's the trouble?"

The native uttered a volley of angry syllables, gesticulating, showing his pointed white teeth. Magnus Ridolph at last understood him to say, "Why you burn me, eh?"

"To teach you not to steal from me," Magnus Ridolph explained.

The native hissed scornfully. "I steal everything you got. I great thief. I steal from king. Sometimes I steal everything he got. Then I be king. I best stealer in Challa, you bet. I steal king's crown pretty soon."

Magnus Ridolph blinked his mild blue eyes. "And then?"

"And then—"

"Yes—and then?" came a third voice, harsh, angry. King Kanditter sprang close to the native, struck furiously with a length of cane. The native howled and leapt into the bushes. Magnus Ridolph hastily disconnected the powerpack lest the king receive a shock and inflict a like punishment on himself.

Kanditter threw the cane stalk to the ground, gestured to Magnus Ridolph. "Come, we eat."

"I'll be with you right away," said Magnus Ridolph. He picked up his suitcases, disconnected the powerpack, slung it under his arm and presented himself to the king. "Your invitation comes as a pleasant surprise, your Majesty. I find that carrying my possessions everywhere gives me quite an appetite."

"You careful, eh?" said Kanditter with a wide thin-lipped grin.

Magnus Ridolph nodded solemnly. "A careless man would find himself destitute in a matter of minutes." He looked sidewise at the king. "How do you guard your own property? You must own a great deal—micromacs, powerpacks and the like."

"Woman, she watch now. Woman, she very careful. She lose—*ugh!*" He flailed his long dark arms significantly.

"Women indeed are very useful," agreed Magnus Ridolph.

They marched in silence for a few yards.

"What you like telex for?" the king asked.

"The telex crystal," said Magnus Ridolph, "vibrates—shakes—very fast. Very, very, very, very fast. We use it to send voices to other stars. Voices go very far, very fast, when given shake with telex."

"Too much noise," was the king's observation.

"Where are your fields?" asked Magnus Ridolph ingenuously. "I've heard a great deal about them."

Kanditter merely turned him a side-glance, grinned his narrow grin.

Days passed, during which Magnus Ridolph sat quietly in his lodgings, reviewing recent progress in mathematics, developing some work of his own in the new field of contiguous-opposing programs.

He saw little of Mellish, who spent as much time as possible with the king—arguing, pleading, bluffly flattering, while Tomko was relegated to guarding the luggage.

Magnus Ridolph's barricade proved effective to the extent that his goods were safe so long as he sat within his room. When circumstances compelled him to walk abroad he packed everything into his suitcases, carried them with him. His behavior by no means set him apart or made him conspicuous.

Everywhere could be seen natives carrying their possessions in bags made from the thoraxes of large tree-dwelling insects. Mellish had fitted Tomko with a sack strapped to his chest and locked, in which reposed the objects named in the wager with Magnus Ridolph—or rather, those which still remained to him.

With disturbance Magnus Ridolph noted a growing ease and familiarity between Mellish and the King Kanditter. They talked by the hour, Mellish plying the king with cigars, the king in his turn supplying wine. Observing this camera-derie, Magnus Ridolph shook his head, muttered. If Kanditter signed away any rights now, before Magnus Ridolph was ready to apply persuasion—what a fiasco!

His worst fears were realized when Kanditter strolled up to where he sat in the shade before his room.

"Good day, your Majesty," said Magnus Ridolph with urbane courtesy. Kanditter flipped a long black hand. "You come tonight. Big eat, big drink—everybody come."

"A banquet?" inquired Magnus Ridolph, debating within himself how best to avoid participation.

"Tonight we make everybody know big new thing for Men-men. Mellish, he good man—fine man. He need telex, not hurt land. No noise, no bad man, lots of money."

Magnus Ridolph raised his eyebrows. "Have you decided then to award the franchise to Mellish?"

"Mellish good man," said the king, watching Magnus Ridolph interestedly.

"What will you derive personally from the agreement?" inquired Magnus Ridolph.

"How you say?"

"What will you get?"

"Oh—Mellish he make me machine that go round-round in circles. Sit in, music-noise come. Good for king. Name merry-go-round. Mellish he build five-dime store here in Challa. Mellish good man. Good for Men-men, good for king."

"I see," said Magnus Ridolph.

"You come tonight," said Kanditter, and before Magnus Ridolph could state his excuses he passed on.

The banquet commenced shortly after sundown on the pavilion before the palace. Torches, hanging high in the trees, provided a flaring red light, glanced on the purple-brown natives, glinted on King Kanditter's crown and Magnus Ridolph's suitcases, these latter gripped firmly between their owner's knees.

There was little ceremony connected with the eating. Women passed around the loose circle of men, carrying wooden trays full of fruit, young birds, the shrimp-like insects. Magnus Ridolph ate sparingly of the fruit, tasted the birds, dismissed the dish of insects.

A tray came by with cups of native wine. Magnus Ridolph sipped, watching Mellish, as he talked and made jocose gesticulations near the king. Now the king arose and passed out into the darkness and Mellish occupied himself with his wine.

A great flare like a meteor—down from the darkness hurtled a great cloud of flame, past Magnus Ridolph's head, smashing into the ground at his feet in a great crush of sparks.

Magnus Ridolph relaxed—only a torch had fallen. But how close to his head! Negligence, reprehensible negligence! Or—and he looked around for his suitcases—*was* it negligence? The suitcases were gone. Perhaps the element of chance was lacking from the episode.

Magnus Ridolph sat back. Gone not only were the articles of the wager but also all his fresh clothes, his papers, his careful work on the contiguous-opposed programs.

King Kanditter presently stepped forward into the light, vented a short shrill scream. The banqueters immediately became quiet.

Kanditter pointed to Mellish. "This man is friend. He give good things to Kanditter, to all Men-men. He give merry-go-round, he give five-dime store, he build big water that shoot into the air—right here in Challa. Mellish is good. Tomorrow Kanditter, king of Men-men, give telex to Mellish."

Kanditter sat down, and the normal chitter and clatter was resumed. Mellish sidled on his short legs around behind the stiffly formal Magnus Ridolph.

"You see, my friend," said Mellish hoarsely, "that's how I do things. I get what I go after."

"Remarkable, remarkable."

"By the way," and Mellish pretended to be searching

85

around Magnus Ridolph's feet. "Where are your suitcases? Don't tell me they're gone! Stolen? What a pity! But then—a mere fifty thousand munits—what's that, eh, Ridolph?"

Magnus Ridolph turned Mellish a deceptively mild glance. "You have a negligent attitude toward money."

Mellish swung his long arms vigorously, looked across the pavilion at Kanditter. "Money means very little to me, Ridolph. With the telex concession—or without it for that matter—I can arrange that things happen the way I want them to happen."

"Let us hope," said Magnus Ridolph, "that events continue to respond so facilely to your wishes. Excuse me, I think I hear the copter."

He hurried to the clearing. The pilot was climbing out of the cabin. He waved to Magnus Ridolph. "Got your package."

"Excellent." He reached in his pocket. "Ho! The black-guards have even picked my pocket!" He turned a rueful look to the pilot. "I'll pay you your fee in the morning—with a bonus. Now—would you assist me with this parcel to my room?"

"Sure thing." The pilot lifted one end of the long package, Magnus Ridolph the other, and they set off along the avenue.

Halfway they met King Kanditter, who eyed the bundle with a great deal of interest. "What that?"

"Ah," said Magnus Ridolph, "it's a wonderful new machine—very fine."

"Ch-ch-ch," said the king, gazing after them.

At his room Magnus Ridolph paused, mused a moment. "Now lastly," he said, "may I borrow your flash-lamp till tomorrow?"

The pilot handed him the article. "Just don't let those little devils snitch it."

Magnus Ridolph made a noncommittal remark, bade the pilot goodnight. Alone, he snapped loose the tapes, tore aside the fabric, pulled a can from out the case, then a large alumin box with a transparent window.

Magnus Ridolph peered within, chuckled. The box seemed full of moving flitting shapes—gauzy things only half visible. In a corner of the box lay a rough black pitted sphere, three inches in diameter.

Magnus Ridolph opened the can which had come with the parcel, poured a few drops of its contents over the flash-lamp, set the lamp on his bed. Then, carrying the box outside, he sat and waited. Five—ten minutes passed.

He looked inside, nodded in satisfaction. The flash-lamp had disappeared. He returned within, rubbed his beard. Best to make sure, he thought. Looking outside, he saw the pilot lounging in front of Mellish's room, talking to Tomko. Magnus Ridolph called him over.

"Would you be kind enough to watch my box till I get back? I'll be gone only a moment."

"Take your time," said the pilot. "No hurry."

"I won't be long," said Magnus Ridolph. He poured some of the oil from the can upon his handkerchief, while the pilot watched curiously, then set off back down the street to the king's quarters.

He found Kanditter in the pavilion, quaffing the last of the wine. Magnus Ridolph made him a courteous greeting.

"How is your machine?" inquired Kanditter.

"In good condition," said Magnus Ridolph. "Already it has produced a cloth which makes all metal shine like the sun. As a sign of my friendship, I want you to have it."

Kanditter took the handkerchief gingerly. "Make shine, you say."

"Like gold," said Magnus Ridolph. "Like telex crystal."

"Ah." Kanditter turned away.

"Good night," said Magnus Ridolph, and returned to his quarters. The pilot departed and Magnus Ridolph, with a brisk rub of his hands, opened the alumin box, reached within, took the pitted black ball out, laid it on his bed. Flipping, running, flowing out of the box came two—four—six—a dozen filmy creatures, walking, gliding, flitting on gossamer legs, merging into shadows, sometimes glimpsed, for the most part barely sensed.

"Be off with you," said Magnus Ridolph. "Be off and about, my nimble little friends. You have much work to do."

Twenty minutes later a ghostly flickering shape scuttled in through the door, up upon the bed, laid a powerpack tenderly beside the rough black sphere.

"Good," said Magnus Ridolph. "Now off again—be off!"

Ellis B. Mellish was wakened the next day by an unusual hubbub from the pavilion. He raised his head from the pillow, peered out through puffed red eyes.

"Shut off that racket," he grunted.

Tomko, who slept spread-eagled across Mellish's luggage, sat up with a jerk, rose to his feet, stumbled to the door, squinted up the street.

"There's a big crowd up by the pavilion. They're yelling something or other—can't make it out."

A slender purple-brown face looked in the door. "King say come now." He waited expectantly.

Mellish made a rasping noise in his throat, turned over in his bed. "Oh—all right. I'll come." The native left. "Officious barbarians," muttered Mellish.

He rose, dressed, rinsed his face in cold water. "Confounded glad to be leaving," he told Tomko. "Just as soon live back in the Middle Ages."

Tomko expressed his sympathy, handed Mellish a fresh towel.

At last Mellish stepped out in the street, ambled up toward the palace. The crowd in the pavilion had not dwindled. Rather it seemed thicker—rows of Men-men, squatting, rocking, chattering.

Mellish paused, looked across the narrow purple-brown back. His mouth dropped as if a weight had jerked his chin down.

"Good morning, Mellish," said Magnus Ridolph.

"What are you doing there?" barked Mellish. "Where's the king?"

Magnus Ridolph puffed at his cigarette, flicked the ashes, crossed his legs. "I'm the king now—the King of Thieves."

"Are you crazy?"

"In no respect," was the reply. "I wear the coronet—*ergo*, I am king." He nudged with his foot a native squatting beside him. "Tell him, Kanditter."

The ex-monarch turned his head. "Magnus now king. He steal crown—he king. That is law of the Men-men. Magnus he great thief."

"Ridiculous!" stormed Mellish, taking three steps forward. "Kanditter, what about our deal?"

"You'll have to dicker with me," came Magnus Ridolph's pleasant voice. "Kanditter has been removed from the situation."

"I'll do no such thing," declared Mellish, black eyes glittering. "I made a bargain with Kanditter—"

"It's no good,' said Magnus Ridolph. "The new king has annulled it. Also—before we get too far astray—in the matter of that fifty-thousand munit bet I find that I have all my own gear except my watch and, I believe, a large proportion of yours also. Stolen honestly, you understand—not confiscated by royal decree."

Mellish chewed his lip. He looked up suddenly. "Do you know where the telex lode is?"

"Exactly."

"Well," said Mellish bluffly, coming forward, "I'm a reasonable man."

Magnus Ridolph bent his head, became interested in the heatgun he had extricated from his pocket. "Another one of Kanditter's treasures—you were saying?"

"I'm a reasonable man," stuttered Mellish, halting.

"Then you will agree that five hundred thousand munits is a fair value to set on the telex concession. And I'd like a small royalty also—one percent of the gross yield is not exorbitant. Do you agree?"

Mellish swayed. He rubbed his hand across his face.

"In addition," said Magnus Ridolph, "you owe me a hundred thousand for looting my property on Ophir and fifty thousand on our wager."

"I won't let you get away with this!" cried Mellish.

"You have two minutes to make up your mind," said Magnus Ridolph. "After that time I will send an ulrad message filing the concession in my own name and ordering equipment."

Mellish sagged. "King of thieves—king of bloodsuckers—extortioners—that's a better name for you! Very well, I'll meet your terms."

"Write me a check," suggested Magnus Ridolph. "Also a contract stipulating the terms of the agreement. As soon as the check is deposited and a satisfactory entry made in my credit book the required information will be divulged."

Mellish began to protest against the unexpected harshness of Magnus Ridolph's tactics—but, meeting the mild blue eyes, he halted in mid-sentence. He looked over his shoulder.

"Tomko! Where are you, Tomko?"

"Right here, sir."

"My checkbook."

Tomko hesitated.

"Well?"

"It has been stolen, sir."

Magnus Ridolph held up a hand. "Hush, Mr. Mellish, if you please. Don't rail at your subaltern. If I'm not mistaken I believe I have that particular checkbook among my effects."

Night had fallen in Challa and the village was quiet. A few fires still smouldered and cast red flickers along the network of stilts supporting the huts.

A pair of shadows moved along the leaf-carpeted lane. The bulkiest of these stepped to the side, silently swung open a door.

Crackle! Snap! "Ouch!" brayed Mellish. *"Hoo!"*

His lunges and thrashing broke the circuit. The current died and Mellish stood gasping hoarsely.

"Yes?" came a mild voice. "What is it?"

Mellish took a quick step forward, turned his hand-lamp on the blinking Magnus Ridolph.

"Be so good as to turn the light elsewhere," protested the latter. "After all, I am King of Thieves, and entitled to some small courtesy."

"Sure," said Mellish, with sardonic emphasis. "Certainly, Your Majesty. Tomko—fix the light."

Tomko set the light on the table, diffused the beam so as to illuminate the entire room.

"This is a late hour for a visit," observed Magnus Ridolph. He reached under his pillow.

"No you don't," barked Mellish, producing a nuclear pistol. "You move and I'll plug you."

Magnus Ridolph shrugged. "What do you wish?"

Mellish settled himself confortably in a chair. "First I want that check and the contract. Second I want the location of that lode. Third I want that crown. Seems like the only way to get what you want around here is to be king. So I intend to be it." He jerked his head. *"Tomko!"*

"Yes, sir?"

"Take this gun. Shoot him if he moves."

Tomko gingerly took the gun.

Mellish leaned back, lit a cigar. "Just how did you get to be king, Ridolph? What's all this talk about ghosts?"

"I'd prefer to keep that information to myself."

"You *talk!*" said Mellish grimly. "I'd just as soon shoot you as not."

Magnus Ridolph eyed Tomko steadying the nuclear gun with both hands. "As you wish. Are you familiar with the planet Archaemandryx?"

"I've heard of it—somewhere in Argo."

"I have never visited Archaemandryx myself," said Magnus Ridolph. "However, a friend describes it as peculiar in many respects. It is a world of metals—mountain ranges of metallic silicon—"

"Cut the guff," snapped Mellish. "Get on with it!"

Magnus Ridolph sighed reproachfully. "Among the types of life native to this planet are the near-gaseous creatures which you call ghosts. They live in colonies, each centered on a nucleus. The nucleus serves as the energizer for the colony. The ghosts bring it fuel, it broadcasts energy on a convenient

90

wavelength. The fuel is uranium and any uranium compound is eagerly conveyed to the nucleus.

"My friend thought to see commercial possibilities in this property—namely the looting of the Starport Bank. He accordingly brought a colony to New Acquitain, where he daubed a number of hundred-Munit notes with an aromatic uranium compound, deposited them at the bank. Then he opened the box and merely waited till the ghosts returned with millions in uranium-permeated banknotes.

"I chanced to be nearby when he was apprehended. In fact"—and Magnus Ridolph smoothed the front of his blue and white nightshirt—"I played a small part in the event. However, when the authorities thought to ask how he had perpetrated the theft the entire colony had disappeared."

Mellish nodded appreciatively. "I see. You just got the king to daub everything he owned with uranium and then let the things loose."

"Correct."

Mellish blew out a plume of smoke. "Now I want directions to get to the lode."

Magnus Ridolph shook his head. "That information will be given to you only when I have deposited your check."

Mellish grinned wolfishly. "You'll tell me alive—or I'll find out from Kanditter tomorrow with you dead. You have ten seconds to make up your mind."

Magnus Ridolph raised his eyebrows. "Murder?" He glanced at Tomko, who stood with beaded forehead holding the nuclear pistol.

"Call it that," said Mellish. "Eight—nine—*ten!* Are you going to talk?"

"I can hardly see my way clear to—"

Mellish looked at Tomko. "Shoot him."

Tomko's teeth chattered; his hand shook like a twig in a strong wind.

"*Shoot* him!" barked Mellish.

Tomko squeezed shut his eyes, pulled the trigger. *Click!*

"Perhaps I should have mentioned," said Magnus Ridolph, "that among the first of the loot my ghosts brought me was the ammunition of your pistol which as you know is uranium." He produced his own heat-gun. "Now, goodnight, gentlemen. It is late and tomorrow will be more convenient for levying the fifty-thousand munit fine your offenses call for."

"What offenses?" blustered Mellish. "You can't prove a thing."

"Disturbing the rest of the King of Thieves is a serious crime," Magnus Ridolph assured him. "However, if you wish to escape, the trail overland back to Gollabolla begins at the end of this lane. You would not be pursued."

"You're crazy. Why, we'd die in the jungle."

"Suit yourself," was Magnus Ridolph's equable reply. "In any event, good night."

THE SPA OF THE STARS

JOE BLAINE sat, limp as a pillow, in his swivel chair, chewing morbidly at a dead cigar. The desk supported his feet. He stroked his pink jowl with a hand that was all flesh and no bone. His mood was one of gloom.

Many extremes had enlivened Joe Blaine's life: triumphs, failures, vicissitudes of many sorts. But never such an abysmal piece of cheese as the Spa of the Stars.

Outside, the white sun Eta Pisces shone with a tingling radiance on a landscape sparkling white, blue and green. ("Enjoy the zestful light of the Cluster's healthiest sun in surroundings of inexpressible beauty"—excerpt from the Spa's brochure.)

A lazy sea folded surf along a beach of pure sand behind which a wall of jungle rose four hundred feet, steep as a cliff. ("Vacation at the edge of unexplored jungle mysteries," read the brochure, and the illustration showed a lovely nude woman with apple-green skin standing under a tree blazing with red and black flowers.)

A big hotel, miles of beach, a hundred orange and green cabanas, an open-air dance pavilion, a theater, tennis courts, sail boats, an arcade of expensive shops, a race-track with grandstand and stables—this was the Spa of the Stars just as Joe Blaine had conceived it. Nothing was lacking but the nude green woman. If Joe Blaine had known where to get one, she'd have been there too.

There was another discrepancy. Joe had envisioned the lobby full of stylish women, the beach covered with bronze flesh. In his mind's-eye he had seen the grandstand black with sportsmen, all anxious to dispute the wisdom of the odds he had set. Each of the seven bars—as he had pictured them—were lined three deep, with the bartenders sweating and complaining of overwork. . . . Joe Blaine grunted and threw his cigar out the window.

The door split back and Mayla, his secretary, entered. Her hair was bright as the sands of the beach; she had eyes blue as the sea before it toppled to surf. She was slender, flexible, and her flesh had the compelling, clutchable look of a marshmallow. She was a creature of instinct, rather than intellect, and this suited Joe Blaine very well. Crossing the room, she patted the pink spot on his scalp.

"Cheer up, Joe, it can't be that bad."

The words catalyzed Joe's smouldering dejection to an angry bray.

"How could it be worse? You tell me. . . . Ten million munits sunk into the place and three paying guests!"

Mayla settled herself into a chair, thoughtfully puffed alight a cigarette.

"Just wait till the noise of those accidents dies down. . . . They'll be back like flies. After all, we got a lot of publicity—"

"Publicity! *Huh!* Nine bathers killed by sea-beetles the first day. The gorilla-things dragging those girls into the jungle: Not to mention the flying snakes and the dragons—Lord, the dragons! And you talk about publicity!"

Mayla pursed her lips. "Well—maybe you're right. I suppose it would look bad to somebody who didn't know the circumstances."

"What circumstances?"

"I mean about Kolama being a wild planet, and not explored or civilized."

"You think, then," said Blaine with great earnestness, "that people don't mind being chewed up by horrible creatures so long as it's out on a wild planet?"

She shook her head. "No, not that exactly—"

"Good," said Joe. "I'm relieved."

"—I just mean that maybe they'd make a few allowances."

Blaine threw up his hands and sank back in an attitude of defeat. He reached for a new cigar and lit it.

"Maybe," said Mayla after a short pause, "we could advertise it like a big game lodge, and people would come for excitement."

He reproached her with a glance. "You ought to know that nobody hunts big game—or any kind of game—if there's a

93

chance of *them* getting hurt. The odds are even out here; that'll keep away the jokers after cheap blood. . . ."

The telescreen buzzed. Joe turned impatiently. "Now what . . ." He snapped the switch. The screen glowed pink. "Long distance, looks like."

"Starport calling Joe Blaine," came the operator's voice.

"Speaking."

On the screen appeared a narrow face—all eyes, nose and teeth, a face that was crafty and calculating, and yet possessed of a quality that women thought attractive. This was Blaine's partner, Lucky Woolrich.

"Now what the devil do you want?" demanded Joe. "Do you know it costs eight munits a minute interplanet?"

Lucky said curtly, "Just wanted to find out if you've got it licked."

"Licked!" yelled Joe. "Are you crazy? I'm scared to set foot outside the hotel!"

"We've got to do something," Woolrich told him. "Ten million munits is an awful swipe of scratch!"

"We sure agree there."

"I don't get it," said Lucky. "The place got built without accidents. Nothing bothered us until we started to operate. Don't that seem fishy to you?"

"Fishy as all get out. I can't figure it. I've tried."

Lucky said, "Well, I called mainly to tell you I'm coming on out. Ought to be there in four days or so. I'm bringing a trouble-shooter—"

"We don't need a trouble-shooter," snapped Blaine. "We need a dragon-shooter and a water-beetle shooter and a flying-snake shooter. Lots of 'em."

Lucky ignored the comment. "I've got the man to help us out if anyone can. He's highly recommended. Magnus Ridolph. A well-known genius. Invented the musical-kaleidoscope."

"That's the ticket," said Blaine. "We'll dance 'em to death."

"Lay off the comics, Joe!" rasped Lucky. "Eight munits a minute is cheap when we're talking business; for jokes it's extravagant."

"I might as well have some fun for my money," said Blaine peevishly. "Ten million munits and every cent buying headaches."

"See you in four days," said Lucky coldly. The screen went dull.

Joe stood up, walked back and forth. Mayla watched with

proud possessiveness. She, who could have had forty-nine out of any fifty men, thought Joe was the cutest thing she'd ever seen.

A tall angular man in the red and blue uniform of the Spa came bounding into the office, knees raising as high as his chin with every step.

"Well, Wilbur?" snapped Blaine.

"Golly, Joe—you know that little old deaf lady? The cranky one?"

"Of course I know her. I know every one of our three guests. What about her?"

"One of them dragons just now came at her. Would have got her, too, if she hadn't ducked under a bench. Just swung down out of the sky, big as a house. Lordy, she's spittin' mad! Says she's gonna sue you, because the thing dove at her on hotel property."

Joe Blaine pulled at his scant hair, turned his cigar up between clenched teeth. "Give me strength, give me strength. . . ."

"How about a drink?" Mayla suggested.

Wilbur concurred. "Mix one for me too."

Seen in the flesh, Lucky was not as tall as he looked on the telescreen—hardly as tall as Joe, but thinner, neater.

"Joe," he said, "meet Mr. Ridolph. He's the expert I was telling you about." Lucky waved an arm at the slight man with the distinguished white beard who had wandered abstractedly into the lobby, looking here and there, in all directions, like a child on a circus midway.

Blaine took one look, eyed Lucky in disgust.

"Expert? That old goat? On what?" he muttered. Aloud, with effusive cordiality: "How do you do, Mr. Ridolph? So glad you could come to help. We sure need an expert out here to figure out our problems."

Magnus Ridolph shook hands fastidiously. "Yes," he said. "How do you do, Mr. Woolrich?"

"I'm Woolrich," said Lucky briskly. "This is Mr. Blaine."

"How do you do?" And Magnus Ridolph nodded, to assure them that he took the correction in good part. "You have a pleasant resort, very peaceful and quiet, just as I like it."

Blaine rolled his eyes upwards. "It's not peaceful and I don't like it quiet."

Lucky laughed, slapped Magnus Ridolph across his skinny shoulder blades. Magnus Ridolph turned, gave Lucky a cold stare.

"Don't let him throw you, Joe," said Lucky. "That's just an act he puts on for the customers. He's as shrewd as they come."

Joe eyed Magnus Ridolph like a housewife turning down a piece of meat at the butcher shop, then turned away and shook his head. He stiffened. A sudden grinding explosion of sound outside, a savage howling . . .

Lucky and Joe exchanged glances and ran for the door. High in the sky, almost overhead, two tremendous shapes flapped and tore at each other with fangs like hay-hooks. Drifting down came a roaring and fierce yelling. Blaine reached out, took Magnus Ridolph's elbow.

"There's thousands of 'em!" he yelled into Magnus Ridolph's ear. "Just waiting for somebody to set foot out on the beach. We got to get rid of them! Also the twenty-foot pincer-beetles that infest the ocean, and some half-ton gorillas that got a lot of human tendencies. Not to mention the flying snakes."

"They certainly seem a ferocious set of creatures," said Magnus Ridolph mildly.

The battle in the sky took a sudden lurch in their direction, and the three spectators jerked back involuntarily.

"Shoo!" yelled Joe. "Get outa here!"

A spatter of blood began to fall like rain. Talons ripped, yanked—brought a tooth-grinding screech. One of the forms toppled, started to fall with a tremendous slow majesty.

Lucky gave a strangling cry. Joe yelled, "No, no, no—"

End over end came the torn body, almost at their heads. It fell through the roof of the hotel, into the dining room. Glass sprayed a hundred feet in all directions. A convulsive flap of wings made further destruction. And now the victor swooped on vast leather pinions. It dropped hissing into the wreckage, began to tear at the flesh.

Joe cried in wordless anguish. Lucky turned, ran to the desk, returned with a grenade rifle.

"I'll show that overgrown lizard something." He sighted, pulled the trigger. Fragments of dragon and hotel spattered across the beach.

There was a sudden heavy silence. Then Blaine said in a crushed voice, "This is it. We're through."

Magnus Ridolph cleared his throat mildly. "Perhaps the situation is not as bad as you think."

"What's the use? We made a mistake. Kolama is just too tough. We might as well face it, take our loss."

96

"Now, Joe," said Lucky, "brace up. Maybe it's not so bad after all. Mr. Ridolph thinks we got a chance."

Joe snorted.

"Couldn't you post guards in copters, and kill any that came down?" suggested Magnus Ridolph.

Blaine shook his head. "They fly high, drop down like hawks. I've watched 'em. We couldn't keep 'em out. And one or two would be as bad for business as a hundred."

Lucky pulled at his lip. "What I want to know is how come we never had trouble while the place was going up."

Joe shook his head. "Beats me. Seems like when the Mollies were around, nothing ever bothered us. As soon as they took off our grief began."

Magnus Ridolph glanced inquiringly at Lucky. "Mollies? And what are they?"

"That's what Joe calls the natives," Lucky told him. "They helped us out while we were building."

"Did the excavating," said Joe.

"Possibly you could keep natives here and there around the property," suggested Magnus Ridolph.

Blaine shook his head. "Nobody could stand the stink. It must be the stink that keeps the beasts away. God knows I don't blame 'em."

Magnus Ridolph considered the theory. "Well, possibly, if the odor were extremely strong and pungent."

"It's not anything else."

Magnus Ridolph stroked his beard thoughtfully. "Just what sort of creatures are these—'Mollies'?"

"Well," said Joe, "think of a shrimp four feet tall, walking around on little stumpy legs. A sort of a fat gray shrimp with big stary eyes. That's a Molly for you."

"Are they intelligent? Do you have any contact with them?"

"Oh, I guess you'd call 'em intelligent. They live in big hives back in the jungle. Don't do any harm, and they helped us out quite a bit. We paid 'em in pots, pans, knives."

"How did you communicate with them?"

"They got a language of squeaks." Joe pursed up his lips. "*Squeak—squick, squick.*" He cleared his throat. "That means 'come here.'"

"Hm," said Magnus Ridolph. "And how do you say 'go away'?"

"*Squick—keek, keek,*"

"Hm."

"*Squeak, keek, keek, keek*—that means 'time to knock off for the day.' I learned that lingo pretty good."

"And you say the wild beasts never bothered them?"

"Nope. Only twice did anything even come near. Once a gorilla, once a dragon."

"And then?"

"They all stood still looking, as if asking themselves, now just what does this johnny think *he's* doing? And the gorilla and the dragon both turned 'round and took off." Joe shook his head. "Must have got a close whiff of them. Like skunk and sewage and half a dozen tannery vats. I had to wear a mask."

Woolrich said, "We've got movies of everything, if you think there's anything to it."

Magnus Ridolph nodded gravely, "They might be useful. I'd like to see them."

"This way," said Joe. He added glumly, "You can see them, but you can't smell them."

"Just as well," said Lucky.

The first scene showed virgin territory—the beach, the blue ocean, the sharp cliff of the jungle. On the beach sat the small prospect ship, and beside it stood Joe, self-consciously waving at the camera.

The second scene showed the Mollies excavating foundations. They worked in a crouched position with heads extended, and the sand exploded out of the trench ahead of them. They were rather more manlike than Joe had described them—gray whiskered creatures with soft segmented bodies. They had bulging pink blind-looking eyes, horny bowed legs, a concave area around their mouths.

Magnus Ridolph leaned forward. "They have a peculiar method of digging."

"Yeah," said Blaine. "It's fast, though. They blow it out."

Magnus Ridolph moved in his seat. "Run that again, please."

With a tired sigh and a helpless glance at Lucky, Joe complied. Once again they watched the crouched natives, saw the sand broken loose, thrown up and out of the ditch as if by a strong jet of air.

Magnus Ridolph sat back in his seat. "Interesting."

The scene changed. The concrete slab had been poured. A dozen natives were carrying a length of timber.

"Hear 'em talking? Listen. . . ." And Joe turned the volume control. They heard rising and falling eddies of shrill noise.

"Squeak—squeeeek!" came a peremptory sound.

"That's me," said Joe, "telling them to look up and pose for the pictures."

There was a general turning of the conical whiskered heads.

"Keek, keek, keek," said the speaker.

"That's 'back to work' " said Blaine. A few minutes later: "Here's where the dragon goes after them. . . . They saw it first. See? They're excited. . . . Then I saw it." The view swept up in the sky, showed the bottle-shaped body circling down on wings that seemed to reach across the horizon. The picture jerked, quivered, blurred, and suddenly showed the scene from a crazy angle, the view obscured by blades of grass.

"That's where I—put the camera down," said Joe. "Listen to those Mollies. . . ." And the speaker shrilled with the sound. It rose in pitch, high up through the scale, died.

"Now they're just looking at him—and now the dragon catches a whiff and man! he says, none of that for me, I'd rather chew bark off of the big trees, and he's away."

The view shifted from the odd angle, resumed its normal perspective. The dragon became a blurring dot in the sky.

"The next scene is where the gorilla comes at 'em. . . . There he is." The watchers saw a tall anthropoid with sparse brown fur, red eyes the size of saucers, a row of gland-like sacs dangling under his chin. He dropped out of a tree, came lurching toward the natives, roaring vastly. Again came the shrill squealing, gradually rising and dying, and the silent stare. The gorilla turned, flung his hands in an almost comical gesture of disgust and hurried away.

"Whatever it is," observed Lucky, "it's good."

Magnus Ridolph said reflectively, "Extremely disagreeable, those beasts."

"Humph," snorted Joe. "You haven't seen the sea-beetles yet."

Magnus Ridolph rose to his feet. "I think I've seen enough for tonight. If you'll excuse me, I think I'll try to get a little rest."

"Sure," said Lucky abstractedly. "Wilbur will show you your room."

"Thank you." Magnus Ridolph left the room.

"Well," said Blaine heavily, "there goes your great detective."

"Now Joe," said Mayla, looping an arm around his neck,

"don't be mean. I think he's sort of cute. So prim and tidy-like. And that little white beard, isn't it a scream?"

"Magnus Ridolph's got brains," said Lucky, without conviction.

"He looks like an old faker to me," said Joe. "Notice how he jumped when the gorilla dropped out of the tree? Cowardly old goat . . ."

"Excuse me," said Magnus Ridolph, "may I have that film? I'd like to study it under a viewer."

There was a pause.

"Ah—help yourself," said Woolrich.

Magnus Ridolph removed the cartridge. "Thank you very much. Good night."

Joe watched the door close. Then he turned and blurted, "Lucky, I always thought you had sense. When you said you were bringing out an expert, I had faith in you. Look at him. Senile. A pussy-footer. . . ."

"Now Joe," said Mayla, "don't be hasty now. Remember you thought I was dumb once too; remember? You told me so yourself."

"Ah-h-h-h-h," breathed Joe. "For two cents I'd—"

"Ten million munits," warned Lucky. "Lotsa scratch!"

Blaine pulled himself up in his chair. "You know what I'm gonna do?"

"What?"

"I'm going out to that Mollie hive. I'm going to find out what gives 'em that stink. Whatever it is, we can have it analyzed and maybe treated so that it won't be so vile."

Mayla said, "Honey, do you think it's safe?"

Lucky said, "Do you really think that's what does the trick?"

" 'Think'?" scoffed Joe. "I *know* it."

Joe's jungle suit was the best money could buy. The metallic fabric mirrored away the sun-glare. The plastic bubble surrounding his head was similarly silvered on top. The boots fitted his feet as comfortably as his own skin. By twisting a valve he could inflate vanes that would enable him to walk across swamp and ooze without sinking. A small pack on his back pumped cool clean air around him, supplied power for the sound pickup, the torch and power-knife at his belt. His pouch contained concentrated food for three days and an air mattress of material so tough and thin that when deflated it could be crumpled up inside his clenched fist. He carried a grenade rifle and a dozen extra clips of ammunition.

100

Early in the morning he set off, before Magnus Ridolph had arisen. Lucky watched him go with unconcern. The Lord protects fools and drunkards, thought Lucky; Joe was doubly secure. Mayla was not so impassive, and finally Lucky had to hold her until Joe was out of sight. Her cries followed him as he trudged across the sand toward the beetling rampart of vegetation. He found a trail and plunged into the green gloom.

As soon as the forest surrounded him, he halted to take stock. The flying snakes could knock him down and constrict, though the fabric of the suit would protect him from their teeth. He turned his eyes apprehensively into the air. Somehow the expedition seemed less urgent now than it had the previous evening. Magnus Ridolph—there was the man who should be investigating the natives. He was being paid for it! Joe chewed on his pink tongue. No, he couldn't very well go back now. Lucky would never let him forget it.

Once more he searched the fronds and foliage, golden-green where the light struck, dark rich green in the shadow. Moths flitted across the open spaces, in and out of the slanting beams of sunlight. Up, up, up—big green leaves, clots of red, yellow and black flowers, trailing chalk-blue vines. A snake could just about pick his time, thought Joe. A gorilla now, would make a noise crashing through the brush. Hm, Blaine thought, noise. He dialed up the power on his head phone until he could hear the hum of the insects. The crash of each of his footsteps was like a tree falling.

He continued, more at ease. The thrum of the snake's short wings should reach him long before the snake.

The trail wound without apparent direction here and there around the giant boles and up and down slopes. Joe became confused almost at once. Twice he heard the throb of wings and once a far thrashing, but he progressed a mile before he was molested. It was a gorilla.

Joe heard the snapping and the grunting as it climbed through the trees, then silence as it sighted him. There was a sliding sound, not too stealthy, as if the gorilla were confident. He glimpsed the mottled hide, aimed. He stopped in time. Golly! the amplifier!

He turned it down. The sound would have beat a hole in his head. He aimed again, pulled the trigger. A section of the jungle became a globe of empty space, with seared, bruised boundaries.

Joe turned the volume of the amplifier back up and continued. He walked three hours, killing five snakes with his torch and two more gorillas. At times he had to turn loose his power-knife, so thick was the tangle of shoots and vines. And after three hours the jungle looked no different from the jungle where he had set out.

Thud, thud, thud, sounded in his ear. Blaine stood still, waited. The Mollie appeared, halted, looked at him with blind-looking pink eyes. Blaine could see no expression or sign of surprise.

"Skeek," said Joe. "Hello."

"Keek, keek," returned the native. It stepped around Blaine, continued down the path. Joe shrugged, moved on.

A moment later he broke out into a clearing a hundred yards wide. In the center, a conical gray mound built of woven twigs and plastered with mud like a wasp's nest rose an amazing two hundred feet. It had been built around a living tree; from the apex the trunk extended and held an umbrella of foliage out into the sunlight.

Joe Blaine halted. The five hundred Mollies ambling around the clearing paid him no heed. And Joe had no interest in their simple occupations other than the source of the stench. Cautiously he opened the gate in his head-dome. He reeled, slammed it shut, eyes swimming. An odor so ripe, so putrid, so violently strong, it seemed impossible that the air could remain clear.

Where did it come from?

Across the clearing he glimpsed a depression, a wallow, where several dozen Mollies lay, moving languidly. Blaine approached, watched. A dozen Mollies appeared from the shadows of the forest, bearing crude baskets. About half held pulpy black balls; others, gray-green slugs six inches long; others, pink cylinders that looked as if they were cut from watermelon hearts.

The Mollies turned the baskets over into the wallow. Then they stood back, looked intently at the piles. And the black balls burst, the green slugs melted, the red cylinders spread out like oil. A moment later they were a mixture homogeneous with the rest of the wallow.

So, thought Joe, here it is. Food and chemical warfare from the same trough. He went to the depression, inspected it. The occupants gave him no heed. He dipped a quantity of the thick green-black ooze into a jar, sealed it. This would be enough for a test. Fast work, he thought. Now back to the hotel.

He looked across the clearing—stared. Through a gap in the trees gleamed a patch of brilliant white and, beyond, a bright blue. Could it be . . . He crossed the clearing, looked through the gap. It was the beach, the ocean. A half-mile to his right the hotel rose. Joe beat his head-dome with furious fists. Three hours of plodding through the jungle!

Blaine found Woolrich in the office. Lucky looked up in surprise.

"Hello. Didn't expect you back so soon." He wrinkled his nose. "You don't smell so good, Joe."

"I got it," Blaine said. "Here it is, the real magoo. If that don't keep them away, my name's not Joe Blaine."

"Get it out of here," said Lucky in a stifled voice. "I can smell it through the bottle."

"Must have got some on the outside," said Blaine. And he told Lucky his adventures.

Lucky's thin face still looked skeptical. "And now?"

"Now we test the stuff. One of us paints himself with it, wanders around the beach. The other stands guard with a grenade-rifle just in case. If the dragons come down, and shy off, we'll know for sure."

Lucky tapped his fingers on the desk. "Sounds good. Well," he said carelessly, "since you already got some of the stuff on you, you might as well be the decoy."

Joe stared unbelievingly. "Are you crazy, Lucky? I got to run the camera. You know that. It's got to be you."

After a half-hour's debate, they finally selected Magnus Ridolph to serve as the guinea pig.

"He won't like it," said Woolrich doubtfully.

"He's got to like it. What are we paying him for? He hasn't turned a hand so far. He ought to be glad we've solved the problem for him."

"He might not see it that way."

Joe opened a drawer in the desk, pulled out a metal can.

"See this? It's a somnol spray, to be used on drunks and roughnecks. We'll give him a dose, and he won't even know what's happening. Where is he now?"

"In the engine room. He's been puttering around all morning, working on the lathe."

Blaine sneered. "Now, isn't that the limit? He's supposed to be the brains, the trouble-shooter, and he leaves it to us. Well, we'll fix that. He'll earn his money, whether he wants to or not."

Lucky reluctantly rose to his feet. "Maybe if we asked him—"

"Better this way," said Joe. "It's not as if there's any danger. We know the stuff works. Don't the Mollies run around scot-free? And besides, we'll be standing right there with guns."

They found Magnus Ridolph in the workshop. polishing a metal blue tube with a piece of crocus cloth. As they entered he looked up, nodded, and fitted the tube through a hole in a metal cup. He coupled a hose to the tube, set the apparatus in a jig, turned a valve. There came a hiss of air, a thin blowing sound.

Magnus Ridolph gazed at the pattern on an oscillograph. "Hm," he muttered. "That's about right, I should say."

"What are you doing, Mr. Ridolph?" asked Blaine jocularly, one hand close behind his back.

Magnus Ridolph gave him a cool glance, then returned to his apparatus and detached it from the jig.

"I'm refining a certain musical principle . . ."

S-s-s-s, went the somnol bomb. A fine mist surrounded Magnus Ridolph's distinguished head. He gasped, stiffened, slumped.

"Did you hear him, Lucky?" Joe kicked at the metal tube Magnus Ridolph still clutched in his hand. "Fooling around with music, when we're in a jam."

Lucky said, "I guess that musical kaleidoscope sort of went to his head. He used to be a good man, so I've heard."

"You must have heard wrong," said Joe. "Well, let's take him out on the beach. Here's a wheelbarrow. That should do the trick."

They trundled the supine body out into the white blaze of the sun, two hundred yards down the beach.

"This is far enough," said Blaine. "Let's douse him and get back under the trees. It makes me nervous, being in the open like this. Those dragons are like flies this time of day."

They lifted Magnus Ridolph from the wheelbarrow, stretched him on the sand, and Joe poured the black liquid liberally across his chest.

"Gad!" coughed Lucky. "It even comes upwind!"

"She's rich," said Joe complacently. "When I go after something, I get it. Now come on, let's get out of the way. Hurry up, there's a dragon out there now."

They ran up to the edge of the jungle and waited. The speck low on the horizon expanded, became a flapping monster. Joe held his rifle ready.

"Just in case," he told Lucky.

The dragon bulked large in the sky. It saw Magnus Ridolph's prone figure, circled.

Lucky said, "Golly, I just thought of something!"

"What?" snapped Joe.

"If that stuff doesn't work, we won't know until the dragon's pretty close. And then—"

"Rats!" said Joe bluffly. "It'll work. It's got to."

The dragon made a sudden swoop to the beach, waddled forward.

Twenty yards— "It don't faze him!" cried Lucky.

Ten yards. Blaine raised the gun, lowered it again.

"Shoot, Joe—for Pete's sake, shoot!"

"I can't!" cried Blaine. "I'll blow Ridolph to pieces!"

Lucky Woolrich ran out on the beach, yelled, jumped up and down. The dragon paid no heed.

Five yards. Magnus Ridolph stirred. Perhaps the odor of the black liquid had aroused him, perhaps some sensation of danger. He shook his head, propped himself on his elbow.

It was a rude awakening for Magnus Ridolph. Eye to eye he stared at the dragon.

The dragon opened its maw, darted its head forward, snapped. Magnus Ridolph rolled over, escaped by an inch.

Blaine shook his head. "That stuff doesn't work at all!"

The dragon made a quick hop, darted its head forward again. Magnus Ridolph again stumbled back, and the fangs clanged past his ribs. He still clutched his metal tube. He frantically put it to his lips, puffed out his cheeks, blew, blew, blew.

The dragon pulled its head back like a turtle. It jerked its legs, its wings. Magnus Ridolph blew. The dragon gave a great belching roar, in almost comical haste lumbered away. The tremendous leather pinions flapped; it sluggishly took to the air, departed across the ocean.

Magnus Ridolph sat down on the sand. For a long moment he sat limply. Then he looked down at his tunic, once crisp and white, now befouled with a black viscosity. As the wind changed, Joe and Lucky felt the odor. Joe coughed, and Magnus Ridolph slowly looked in their direction.

And slowly Magnus Ridolph got to his feet, threw aside his tunic, and slowly marched back to the hotel.

Magnus Ridolph appeared at dinnertime scrubbed, polished, in clean clothes. His white beard was brushed till it shone like angelical floss, and his manner was unusually affable.

Lucky and Joe were relieved to find him in such good humor. They had expected angry accusations, threats and demands. Magnus Ridolph's genial attitude came as a glad surprise, and they vied with each other in cordiality. Mayla, in bed with a headache, was not present.

Blaine explained the circumstances which had led to the experiment, and Magnus Ridolph seemed genuinely interested.

Lucky went so far as to be jocular. "—and Lord, Magnus, when you looked up at that dragon, I swear your beard stuck out from your face like it was electrified!"

"Of course we had you covered all the time," said Joe. "We had a bead on that dragon every instant. One false move and he'd have been a goner."

"Just what was that tube, Magnus?" asked Lucky. "It sure did the trick. Marvelous." He nudged Blaine. "I told you he had brains."

Magnus Ridolph held up a deprecatory hand. "Simple application of what I learned from the movies you showed me."

"How's that?" asked Joe, lighting a cigar.

"Have you noticed the voice-box on the Mollies? It's a paraboloid surface, and the vibrator is at the focus. It gives them exquisite control over sound. By moving the vibrator they can concentrate a node at any given point; I wouldn't doubt but what they see the pressure patterns in some peculiar manner. In other words, they can use their voices as men use an air-hammer, especially in the supersonic ranges. I suspected as much when I saw them excavating those foundations. They were not blowing the sand out with air, they were blasting it out with appropriately applied pressure waves."

"Why, of course!" said Joe, disgustedly spitting a bit of tobacco to the side. "That's how they mixed up the mess in that terrible wallow. Just dumped it in, looked at it, and it all seemed to melt and stir in by itself."

Lucky reproached Joe with a look; best to keep Magnus Ridolph's mind away from wallows and vile black ooze.

Magnus Ridolph lit a cigarette and puffed a thoughtful gust into the air.

"Now when one of the native beasts attacked them, they projected a supersonic beam in a frequency to which the creatures were most sensitive. Probably aimed for a tender spot—the eye, for instance. A study of the sound track proved my theory. I found a clear record of strong inaudible sounds. I calculated the rate of what seemed the most effective frequency, and this morning built a suitable projector."

Joe and Lucky shook their heads in admiration. "Don't see how he does it." "Beats everything I've ever heard of."

Magnus Ridolph smiled. "Now for the hotel, I recommend several large oscillators, mounted permanently, and arranged to project a curtain of the most effective frequency around the property. Any competent sonic engineer can set up such a dome for you."

"Good, good," said Lucky.

"I'll get a man out here right away," said Blaine. "Sure lucky we got you."

Magnus Ridolph made a courteous acknowledgment. "Thank you; perhaps the association will prove of equal value for me."

Blaine stared curiously into Magnus Ridolph's calm countenance.

Lucky said hurriedly, "Now Joe, as to Magnus' fee, I originally mentioned the figure of five thousand munits—"

"Make it ten," said Joe heartily, reaching for his pen. "I think we owe Mr. Ridolph a bonus."

"Gentlemen, gentlemen," murmured Magnus Ridolph. "You make me uncomfortable with your generosity. I'm well content with my stipulated fee."

"Well, now, look here—" stammered Joe, making feeble gestures with his pen.

"Surely you can't believe that I'd accept five thousand munits for the—hm, inconsequential events of this afternoon?"

"Well," said Joe, "you never know how a person takes things. Sometimes they'll sue you, ha, ha, for a hair in the soup. Of course, in your case—well," he finished lamely, "we hadn't really thought about it."

Ridolph frowned thoughtfully. "Ah, if I had an exaggerated sense of dignity, a sop of five thousand munits might only further offend me. But since I am what I am, I'm sure we can let events adjust themselves naturally."

"Sure," said Lucky enthusiastically. "Gentlemen to gentlemen."

Joe Blaine twirled the cigar in his mouth, looked into space trying to trace the implications of the words.

"Well, suits me," he said reluctantly. He wrote. "Here's your fee, then."

"Thank you." Magnus Ridolph pocketed the check. He looked out the window. "I believe your franchise ends about a half-mile up the beach?"

Blaine nodded. "Just about where I came out of the jungle this morning. Maybe a little this way."

Magnus Ridolph said abstractedly, "The closer to the Mollie village, the better."

"Eh? How's that?"

Magnus Ridolph looked up in surprise. "Haven't I described my plans for the bottling and processing plant? No? Today I applied via space-wave for a use permit of the beach."

Joe and Lucky had turned their heads simultaneously, staring. Their faces wore the expressions seen on small animals, who, tripping a baited trigger, snap their own flash-light photographs.

"Processing plant?"

"For what?"

Magnus Ridolph said in a pedantic tone. "I've tentatively decided on the name Mephitoline—which to some extent describes the product."

"But—"

"But—"

"It has been my experience," continued Magnus Ridolph, "that the more noxious a salve, an unguent, or a beauty aid, the more eagerly it is purchased, and the greater its therapeutic or psychological value. In this respect, that unspeakably vile liquid which you used this afternoon in your experiment can hardly be improved upon. Mephitoline, suitably bottled and attractively packaged, will be a valuable specific against psychosomatic disorders."

"But—"

"Possibly Mephitoline may be used as a fixative in the perfume industry, as being more positive than either ambergris, musk, or any of the synthetics. I also anticipate a large and steady sale to college fraternities, lodges, and secret organizations, where it might become an important adjunct to their rituals."

Magnus Ridolph turned a grave glance upon Joe and Lucky.

"I have you two to thank for putting this opportunity in my way. But then, the Spa of the Stars will doubtless share in any prosperity which might come to the Mephitoline Bottling Works. Plant workers will no doubt spend part of their pay at your bars, only three minutes walk away. . . ."

"Look here," said Blaine, in a voice like an old-fashioned wagon crossing a graveled road, "you know darn well that a plant bottling that black stuff a few hundred yards upwind from the hotel would chase every guest back on the same packet that brought him!"

108

"Not at all," argued Magnus Ridolph. "The Mephitoline planet would add a great deal of color and atmosphere. I believe that the plant and the Spa would complement each other very well. I'm sure you must have thought of it yourself: 'Spa of the Stars, Health Center of the Cluster. If You've Got It, Mephitoline Will Cure It'—something of the sort. But, as you see"—and Magnus Ridolph smiled apologetically—"I'm a dreamer. I have no head for business. You two are really better suited to managing a modern medical laboratory. I suppose it would be better for us all if I sold out to you for—say, twenty-five thousand munits. Cheap at the price."

Joe Blaine spat in a wordless futility of anger and disgust.

"Pah!" snorted Lucky. "You're selling us a gold brick. You haven't got a plant, you don't even know whether the stuff is any good."

Magnus Ridolph seemed impressed with Lucky's reasoning. He rubbed his beard thoughtfully.

"That's a very good point. After all, how can we be sure of Mephitoline's efficacy? The sensible solution is to test it. Hm—I see that you have a rather severe case of acne. And—yes—Mr. Blaine appears to be suffering from—is it heat-rash? or some sort of itch?"

"Heat-rash!" snapped Joe.

"We'll put Mephitoline to a test. Each of you can rub Mephitoline over your lesions—or better yet, submerge yourselves in a Mephitoline bath. Give it a fair chance. Then if your conditions are not alleviated, we'll know that Mephitoline is useful only in a psychological sense, and my price will drop to fifteen thousand munits. If your ailments are cured, and Mephitoline has a specific value, the price remains at twenty-five thousand munits. Of course, if you and Mr. Woolrich do not avail yourselves of this opportunity, I personally can't afford to give it up."

There was a short silence.

"Well, Joe," said Lucky wearily, "he's got us over a barrel."

"Not at all," protested Magnus Ridolph. "By no means! I am offering you a valuable property at a ridiculously—"

Blaine interrupted him. "Ten thousand munits is our top price. Take it or leave it."

"Very well," said Magnus Ridolph readily. "Ten thousand—if the Mephitoline does not cure your itch. But unless the test is made, I'll have to hold out for twenty-five thousand."

In a tight-lipped atmosphere the Mephitoline was gingerly swabbed over the afflicted parts. Magnus Ridolph, however, insisted on a liberal application.

"If the job is scamped, we will never be sure in our minds."

But when the Mephitoline was finally scraped off with sticks, the itch and the acne were found still to be in evidence.

"Now are you satisfied?" asked Joe, glaring from behind the application like a tiger made-up with grease-paint. "It don't work. I itch like fury. It's even worse than before."

"The substance is evidently no cure-all," said Magnus Ridolph regretfully.

Lucky had been scrubbing himself with alcohol. "How do you get this stuff off? Soap and water I guess would be better. . . ."

But thorough scouring still did not entirely erase the Mephitoline; a strong odor still clung to the persons of Joe Blaine and Lucky Woolrich.

"Cripes," muttered Joe, "how long does this stuff last?" He looked suspiciously at Magnus Ridolph. "How did you get it off you?"

Magnus Ridolph, standing carefully aloof, said, "That's a rather valuable bit of information, I'm sorry to say. I arrived at the formula after considerable—"

"All right," said Joe brutally. "How much?"

Magnus Ridolph drew his fine white eyebrows up into an injured line. "Oh, negligible. I'll make only a token charge of a thousand munits. If you perform—ah, further experiments with Mephitoline, you'll need the solution time and time again."

There were several bitter statements, but finally Joe wrote Magnus Ridolph a check, eleven thousand munits in all.

"Now, how do we get rid of this horrible stench?"

"Apply a ten percent solution of hydrogen peroxide," said Magnus Ridolph.

Joe started to bellow; Lucky stifled him, and went off to the hotel dispensary. He returned with an empty gallon jug.

"I can't find any!" he said querulously. "The bottle's empty!"

"There is no more," said Magnus Ridolph frankly. "I used it all myself. Of course, if you wish to retain me as a consultant, I can outline a simple chemical process . . ."

COUP DE GRACE

I

THE HUB, a cluster of bubbles in a web of metal, hung in empty space, in that region known to Earthmen as Hither Sagittarius. The owner was Pan Pascoglu, a man short, dark and energetic, almost bald, with restless brown eyes and a thick mustache. A man of ambition, Pascoglu hoped to develop the Hub into a fashionable resort, a glamor-island among the stars—something more than a mere stopover depot and junction point. Working to this end, he added two dozen bright new bubbles—"cottages," as he called them—around the outer meshes of the Hub, which already resembled the model of an extremely complex molecule.

The cottages were quiet and comfortable; the dining salon offered an adequate cuisine; a remarkable diversity of company met in the public rooms. Magnus Ridolph found the Hub at once soothing and stimulating. Sitting in the dim dining salon, the naked stars serving as chandeliers, he contemplated his fellow-guests. At a table to his left, partially obscured by a planting of dendrons, sat four figures. Magnus Ridolph frowned. They ate in utter silence and three of them, at least, hulked over their plates in an uncouth fashion.

"Barbarians," said Magnus Ridolph, and turned his shoulder. In spite of the mannerless display he was not particularly offended; at the Hub one must expect to mingle with a variety of peoples. Tonight they seemed to range the whole spectrum of evolution, from the boors to his left, across a score of more or less noble civilizations, culminating with—Magnus Ridolph patted his neat white beard with a napkin—himself.

From the corner of his eye he noticed one of the four shapes arise, approach his own table.

"Forgive my intrusion, but I understand that you are Magnus Ridolph."

Magnus Ridolph acknowledged his identity and the other, without invitation, sat heavily down. Magnus Ridolph wa-

111

vered between curtness and civility. In the starlight he saw his visitor to be an anthropologist, one Lester Bonfils, who had been pointed out to him earlier. Magnus Ridolph, pleased with his own perspicacity, became civil. The three figures at Bonfils' table were savages in all reality: paleolithic inhabitants of S-Cha-6, temporary wards of Bonfils. Their faces were dour, sullen, wary; they seemed disenchanted with such of civilization as they had experienced. They wore metal wristlets and rather heavy metal belts: magnetic pinions. At necessity, Bonfils could instantly immobilize the arms of his charges.

Bonfils himself was a large fair man with thick blond hair, heavy and vaguely flabby. His complexion should have been florid; it was pale. He should have exhaled easy good-fellowship, but he was withdrawn and diffident. His mouth sagged, his nose was pinched; there was no energy to his movements, only a nervous febrility. He leaned forward. "I'm sure you are bored with other people's troubles, but I need help."

"At the moment I do not care to accept employment," said Magnus Ridolph in a definite voice.

Bonfils sat back, looked away, finding not even the strength to protest. The stars glinted on the whites of his eyes; his skin shone the color of cheese. He muttered, "I should have expected no more."

His expression held such dullness and despair that Magnus Ridolph felt a pang of sympathy. "Out of curiosity—and without commiting myself—what is the nature of your difficulty?"

Bonfils laughed briefly—a mournful empty sound. "Basically—my destiny."

"In that case, I can be of little assistance," said Magnus Ridolph.

Bonfils laughed again, as hollowly as before. "I use the word 'destiny' in the largest sense, to include"—he made a vague gesture—"I don't know what. I seem predisposed to failure and defeat. I consider myself a man of good-will—yet there is no one with more enemies. I attract them as if I were the most vicious creature alive."

Magnus Ridolph surveyed Bonfils with a trace of interest. "These enemies, then, have banded together against you?"

"No . . . at least, I think not. I am harassed by a woman. She is busily engaged in killing me."

"I can give you some rather general advice," said Magnus Ridolph. "It is this: Have nothing more to do with this woman."

Bonfils spoke in a desperate rush, with a glance over his shoulder toward the paleolithics. "I had nothing to do with her in the first place! That's the difficulty! Agreed that I'm a fool; an anthropologist should be careful of such things, but I was absorbed in my work. This took place at the southern tip of Kharesm, on Journey's End; do you know the place?"

"I have never visited Journey's End."

"Some people stopped me on the street—'We hear you have engaged in intimate relations with our kinswoman!'

"I protested: 'No, no, that's not true!'—because naturally, as an anthropologist, I must avoid such things like the plague."

Magnus Ridolph raised his brows in surprise. "Your profession seems to demand more than monastic detachment."

Bonfils made his vague gesture; his mind was elsewhere. He turned to inspect his charges; only one remained at the table. Bonfils groaned from the depths of his soul, leapt to his feet—nearly overturning Magnus Ridolph's table—and plunged away in pursuit.

Magnus Ridolph sighed, and after a moment or two, departed the dining salon. He sauntered the length of the main lobby, but Bonfils was nowhere to be seen. Magnus Ridolph seated himself, ordered a brandy.

The lobby was full. Magnus Ridolph contemplated the other occupants of the room. Where did these various men and women, near-men and near-women, originate? What were their purposes, what had brought them to the Hub? That rotund moon-faced bonze in the stiff red robe, for instance. He was a native of the planet Padme, far across the galaxy. Why had he ventured so far from home? And the tall angular man whose narrow shaved skull carried a fantastic set of tantalum ornaments: a Lord of the Dacca. Exiled? In pursuit of an enemy? On some mad crusade? And the anthrope from the planet Hecate sitting by himself: a walking argument to support the theory of parallel evolution. His outward semblance caricatured humanity; internally he was as far removed as a gastropod. His head was bleached bone and black shadow, his mouth a lipless slit. He was a Meth of Maetho, and Magnus Ridolph knew his race to be gentle and diffident, with so little mental contact with human beings as to seem ambiguous and secretive. . . . Magnus Ridolph focused his gaze on a woman, and was taken aback by her miraculous beauty. She was dark and slight, with a complexion the color of clean desert sand; she carried herself with a self-awareness that was immensely provoking. . . .

Into the chair beside Magnus Ridolph dropped a short nearly-bald man with a thick black mustache: Pan Pascoglu, proprietor of the Hub. "Good evening, Mr. Ridolph; how goes it with you tonight?"

"Very well, thank you. . . . That woman: who is she?"

Pascoglu followed Magnus Ridolph's gaze. "Ah. A fairy-princess. From Journey's End. Her name—" Pascoglu clicked his tongue. "I can't remember. Some outlandish thing."

"Surely she doesn't travel alone?"

Pascoglu shrugged. "She says she's married to Bonfils, the chap with the three cave-men. But they've got different cottages, and I never see them together."

"Astonishing," murmured Magnus Ridolph.

"An understatement," said Pascoglu. "The cave-men must have hidden charms."

The next morning the Hub vibrated with talk, because Lester Bonfils lay dead in his cottage, with the three paleolithics stamping restlessly in their cages. The guests surveyed each other nervously. One among them was a murderer!

II

PAN PASCOGLU came to Magnus Ridolph in an extremity of emotion. "Mr. Ridolph, I know you're here on vacation, but you've got to help me out. Someone killed poor Bonfils dead as a mackerel, but who it was—" He held out his hands. "I can't stand for such things here, naturally."

Magnus Ridolph pulled at his little white beard. "Surely there is to be some sort of official inquiry?"

"That's what I'm seeing you about!" Pascoglu threw himself into a chair. "The Hub's outside all jurisdiction. I'm my own law—within certain limits, of course. That is to say, if I were harboring criminals, or running vice, someone would interfere. But there's nothing like that here. A drunk, a fight, a swindle—we take care of such things quietly. We've never had a killing. It's got to be cleaned up!"

Magnus Ridolph reflected a moment or two. "I take it you have no criminological equipment?"

"You mean those truth machines, and breath-detectors and cell-matchers? Nothing like that. Not even a fingerprint pad."

"I thought as much," sighed Magnus Ridolph. "Well, I can hardly refuse your request. May I ask what you intend to do with the criminal after I apprehend her—or him?"

Pascoglu jumped to his feet. Clearly the idea had not oc-

114

curred to him. He held out his clenched hands. "What should I do? I'm not equipped to set up a law court. I don't want to just shoot somebody."

Magnus Ridolph spoke judiciously. "The question may resolve itself. Justice, after all, has no absolute values."

Pascoglu nodded passionately. "Right! Let's find out who did it. Then we'll decide the next step."

"Where is the body?" asked Magnus Ridolph.

"Still in the cottage, just where the maid found it."

"It has not been touched?"

"The doctor looked him over. I came directly to you."

"Good. Let us go to Bonfils' cottage."

Bonfils' "cottage" was a globe far out on the uttermost web, perhaps five hundred yards by tube from the main lobby.

The body lay on the floor beside a white chaise-longue—lumpy, pathetic, grotesque. In the center of the forehead was a burn; no other marks were visible. The three paleolithics were confined in an ingenious cage of flexible splines, evidently collapsible. The cage of itself could not have restrained the muscular savages; the splines apparently were charged with electricity.

Beside the cage stood a thin young man, either inspecting or teasing the paleolithics. He turned hastily when Pascoglu and Magnus Ridolph stepped into the cottage.

Pascoglu performed the introductions. "Dr. Scanton, Magnus Ridolph."

Magnus Ridolph nodded courteously. "I take it, doctor, that you have made at least a superficial examination?"

"Sufficiently to certify death."

"Could you ascertain the time of death?"

"Approximately midnight."

Magnus gingerly crossed the room, looked down at the body. He turned abruptly, rejoined Pascoglu and the doctor, who waited by the door.

"Well?" asked Pascoglu anxiously.

"I have not yet identified the criminal," said Magnus Ridolph. "However, I am almost grateful to poor Bonfils. He has provided what appears to be a case of classic purity."

Pascoglu chewed at his mustache. "Perhaps I am dense—"

"A series of apparent truisms may order our thinking," said Magnus Ridolph. "First, the author of this act is currently at the Hub."

115

"Naturally," said Pascoglu. "No ships have arrived or departed.

"The motives to the act lie in the more or less immediate past."

Pascoglu made an impatient movement. Magnus Ridolph held up his hand, and Pascoglu irritably resumed the attack on his mustache.

"The criminal in all likelihood had had some sort of association with Bonfils."

Pascoglu said, "Don't you think we should be back in the lobby? Maybe someone will confess, or—"

"All in good time," said Magnus Ridolph. "To sum up, it appears that our primary roster of suspects will be Bonfils' shipmates en route to the Hub."

"He came on the *Maulerer Princeps;* I can get the debarkation list at once." And Pascoglu hurriedly departed the cottage.

Magnus Ridolph stood in the doorway studying the room. He turned to Dr. Scanton. "Official procedure would call for a set of detailed photographs; I wonder if you could make these arrangements?"

"Certainly. I'll do them myself."

"Good. And then—there would seem no reason not to move the body."

III

MAGNUS RIDOLPH returned along the tube to the main lobby, where he found Pascoglu at the desk.

Pascoglu thrust forth a paper. "This is what you asked for."

Magnus Ridolph inspected the paper with interest. Thirteen identities were listed:

1. Lester Bonfils, with
   a. Abu
   b. Toko
   c. Homup
2. Viamestris Diasporus
3. Thorn 199
4. Fodor Impliega
5. Fodor Banzoso
6. Scriagl
7. Hercules Starguard
8. Fiamella of Thousand Candles

9. Clan Kestrel, 14th Ward,
   6th Family, 3rd Son
10. (No name)

"Ah," said Magnus Ridolph. "Excellent. But there is a lack. I am particularly interested in the planet of origin of these persons."

"Planet of origin?" Pascoglu complained. "What is the benefit of this?"

Magnus Ridolph inspected Pascoglu with mild blue eyes. "I take it that you wish me to investigate this crime?"

"Yes, of course, but—"

"You will then cooperate with me, to the fullest extent, with no further protest or impatient ejaculations." And Magnus Ridolph accompanied the words with so cold and clear a glance that Pascoglu wilted and threw up his hands. "Have it your own way. But I still don't understand—"

"As I remarked, Bonfils has been good enough to provide us a case of definitive clarity."

"It's not clear to me," Pascoglu grumbled. He looked at the list. "You think the murderer is one of these?"

"Possibly, but not necessarily. It might be me, or it might be you. Both of us have had recent contact with Bonfils."

Pascoglu grinned sourly. "If it were you, please confess now and save me the expense of your fee."

"I fear it is not quite so simple. But the problem is susceptible to attack. The suspects—the persons on this list and any other Bonfils had dealt with recently—are from different worlds. Each is steeped in the traditions of his unique culture. Police routine might solve the case through the use of analyzers and detection machines. I hope to achieve the same end through cultural analysis."

Pascoglu's expression was that of a castaway on a desert island watching a yacht recede over the horizon. "As long as the case gets solved," he said in a hollow voice, "and there's no notoriety."

"Come, then," said Magnus Ridolph briskly. "The worlds of origin."

The additions were made; Magnus Ridolph scrutinized the list again. He pursed his lips, pulled at his white beard. "I must have two hours for research. Then—we interview our suspects."

Two hours passed, and Pan Pascoglu could wait no longer. He marched furiously into the library, to find Magnus Ridolph gazing into space, tapping the table with a pencil. Pascoglu opened his mouth to speak, but Magnus Ridolph turned his head, and the mild blue gaze seemed to operate some sort of relay within Pascoglu's head. He composed himself, and made a relatively calm inquiry as to the state of Magnus Ridolph's investigations.

"Well enough," said Magnus Ridolph. "And what have you learned?"

"Well—you can cross Scriagl and the Clan Kestrel chap off the list. They were gambling in the game-room and have foolproof alibis."

Magnus Ridolph said thoughtfully, "It is of course possible that Bonfils met an old enemy here at the Hub."

Pascoglu cleared his throat. "While you were here studying, I made a few inquiries. My staff is fairly observant; nothing much escapes them. They say that Bonfils spoke at length only to three people. They are myself, you and that moon-faced bonze in the red robes."

Magnus Ridolph nodded. "I spoke to Bonfils, certainly. He appeared in great trouble. He insisted that a woman—evidently Fiamella of Thousand Candles—was killing him."

"What?" cried Pascoglu. "You knew all this time?"

"Calm yourself, my dear fellow. He claimed that she was engaged in the process of killing him—vastly different from the decisive act whose effect we witnessed. I beg of you, restrain your exclamations; they startle me. To continue, I spoke to Bonfils, but I feel secure in eliminating myself. You have requested my assistance and you know my reputation: hence with equal assurance I eliminate you."

Pascoglu made a guttural sound, and walked across the room.

Magnus Ridolph spoke on. "The bonze—I know something of his cult. They subscribe to a belief in reincarnation, and make an absolute fetish of virtue, kindness and charity. A bonze of Padme would hardly dare such an act as murder; he would expect to spend several of his next manifestations as a jackal or a sea-urchin."

The door opened, and into the library, as if brought by some telepathic urge, came the bonze himself. Noticing the attitudes of Magnus Ridolph and Pascoglu, their sober appraisal of himself, he hesitated. "Do I intrude upon a private conversation?"

"The conversation is private," said Magnus Ridolph, "but inasmuch as the topic is yourself, we would profit by having you join us."

"I am at your service." The bonze advanced into the room. "How far has the discussion advanced?"

"You perhaps are aware that Lester Bonfils, the anthropologist, was murdered last night."

"I have heard the talk."

"We understand that last evening he conversed with you."

"That is correct." The bonze drew a deep breath. "Bonfils was in serious trouble. Never had I seen a man so despondent. The bonzes of Padme—especially we of the Isavest Ordainment—are sworn to altruism. We render constructive service to any living thing, and under certain circumstances to inorganic objects as well. We feel that the principle of life transcends protoplasm; and in fact has its inception with simple—or perhaps not so simple—motion. A molecule brushing past another—is this not one aspect of vitality? Why can we not conjecture consciousness in each individual molecule? Think what a ferment of thought surrounds us; imagine the resentment which conceivably arises when we tread on a clod! For this reason we bonzes move as gently as possible, and take care where we set our feet."

"Aha, hum," said Pascoglu. "What did Bonfils want?"

The bonze considered. "I find it difficult to explain. He was a victim of many anguishes. I believe that he tried to live an honorable life, but his precepts were contradictory. As a result he was beset by the passions of suspicion, eroticism, shame, bewilderment, dread, anger, resentment, disappointment and confusion. Secondly, I believe that he was beginning to fear for his professional reputation—"

Pascoglu interrupted. "What, specifically, did he require of you?"

"Nothing specific. Reassurance and encouragement, perhaps."

"And you gave it to him?"

The bonze smiled faintly. "My friend, I am dedicated to serious programs of thought. We have been trained to divide our brains left lobe from right, so that we may think with two separate minds."

Pascoglu was about to bark an impatient question, but Magnus Ridolph interceded. "The bonze is telling you that only a fool could resolve Lester Bonfils' troubles with a word."

"That expresses something of my meaning," said the bonze.

Pascoglu stared from one to the other in puzzlement, then threw up his hands in disgust. "I merely want to find who burnt the hole in Bonfils' head. Can you help me, yes or no?"

The bonze smiled faintly. "My friend, I am dedicated to wonder if you have considered the source of your impulses? Are you not motivated by an archaic quirk?"

Magnus Ridolph interpreted smoothly. "The bonze refers to the Mosaic Law. He warns against the doctrine of extracting an eye for an eye, a tooth for a tooth."

"Again," declared the bonze, "you have captured the essence of my meaning."

Pascoglu threw up his hands, stamped to the end of the room and back. "Enough of this foolery!" he roared. "Bonze, get out of here!"

Magnus Ridolph once more took it upon himself to interpret. "Pan Pascoglu conveys his compliments, and begs that you excuse him until he can find leisure to study your views more carefully."

The bonze bowed and withdrew. Pascoglu said bitterly, "When this is over, you and the bonze can chop logic to your heart's content. I'm sick of talk; I want to see some action." He pushed a button. "Ask that Journey's End woman—Miss Thousand Candles, whatever her name is—to come into the library."

Magnus Ridolph raised his eyebrows. "What do you intend?"

Pascoglu refused to meet Magnus Ridolph's gaze. "I'm going to talk to these people and find out what they know."

"I fear that you waste time."

"Nevertheless," said Pascoglu doggedly. "I've got to make a start somewhere. Nobody ever learned anything lying low in the library."

"I take it, then, that you no longer require my services?"

Pascoglu chewed irritably at his mustache. "Frankly, Mr. Ridolph, you move a little too slow to suit me. This is a serious affair. I've got to get action fast."

Magnus Ridolph bowed in acquiescence. "I hope you have no objection to my witnessing the interviews?"

"Not at all."

A moment passed, then the door opened and Fiamella of Thousand Candles stood looking in.

Pan Pascoglu and Magnus Ridolph stared in silence. Fiamella wore a simple beige frock, soft leather sandals. Her arms and legs were bare, her skin only slightly paler than the frock. In her hair she wore a small orange flower.

Pascoglu somberly gestured her forward; Magnus Ridolph retired to a seat across the room.

"Yes, what is it?" asked Fiamella in a soft, sweet voice.

"You no doubt have learned of Mr. Bonfils' death?" asked Pascoglu.

"Oh yes!"

"And you are not disturbed?"

"I am very happy, of course."

"Indeed." Pascoglu cleared his throat. "I understand that you have referred to yourself as Mrs. Bonfils."

Fiamella nodded. "That is how you say it. On Journey's End we say he is Mr. Fiamella. I pick him out. But he ran away, which is a great harm. So I came after him, I tell him I kill him if he will not come back to Journey's End."

Pascoglu jumped forward like a terrier, stabbed the air with a stubby forefinger. "Ah! then you admit you killed him!"

"No, no," she cried indignantly. "With a fire gun? You insult me! You are as bad as Bonfils. Better be careful, I kill you."

Pascoglu stood back, startled. He turned to Magnus Ridolph. "You heard her, Ridolph?"

"Indeed, indeed."

Fiamella nodded vigorously. "You laugh at a woman's beauty; what else does she have? So she kills you, and no more insult."

"Just how do you kill, Miss Fiamella?" asked Magnus Ridolph politely.

"I kill by love, naturally. I come like this—" She stepped forward, stopped, stood rigid before Pascoglu, looking into his eyes. "I raise my hands—" She slowly lifted her arms, held her palms toward Pascoglu's face. "I turn around, I walk away." She did so, glancing over her shoulder. "I come back." She came running back. "And soon you say, 'Fiamella, let me touch you, let me feel your skin.' And I say, 'No!' And I walk around behind you, and blow on your neck—"

"Stop it!" said Pascoglu uneasily.

"—and pretty soon you go pale and your hands shake and you cry, 'Fiamella, Fiamella of Thousand Candles, I love you, I die for love!' Then I come in when it is almost dark

121

and I wear only flowers, and you cry out, 'Fiamella!' Next I—"

"I think the picture is clear," said Magnus Ridolph suavely. "When Mr. Pascoglu recovers his breath, he surely will apologize for insulting you. As for myself, I can conceive of no more pleasant form of extinction, and I am half-tempted to—"

She gave his beard a playful tweak. "You are too old."

Magnus Ridolph agreed mournfully. "I fear that you are right. For a moment I had deceived myself. . . . You may go, Miss Fiamella of Thousand Candles. Please return to Journey's End. Your estranged husband is dead; no one will ever dare insult you again."

Fiamella smiled in a kind of sad gratification, and with soft lithe steps went to the door, where she halted, turned. "You want to find out who burned poor Lester?"

"Yes, of course," said Pascoglu eagerly.

"You know the priests of Cambyses?"

"Fodor Impliega, Fodor Banzoso?"

Fiamella nodded. "They hated Lester. They said, 'Give us one of your savage slaves. Too long a time has gone past; we must send a soul to our god.' Lester said, 'No!' They were very angry, and talked together about Lester."

Pascoglu nodded thoughtfully. "I see. I'll certainly make inquiries of these priests. Thank you for your information."

Fiamella departed. Pascoglu went to the wall mesh. "Send Fodor Impliega and Fodor Banzoso here, please."

There was a pause, then the voice of the clerk responded: "They are busy, Mr. Pascoglu—some sort of rite or other. They said they'll only be a few minutes."

"Mmph. . . . Well, send in Viamestris Diasporus."

"Yes, sir."

"For your information," said Magnus Ridolph, "Viamestris Diasporus comes from a world where gladiatorial sports are highly popular, where successful gladiators are the princes of society, especially the amateur gladiator, who may be a high-ranking nobleman, fighting merely for public acclamation and prestige."

Pascoglu turned around. "If Diasporus is an amateur gladiator, I would think he'd be pretty callous. He wouldn't care who he killed!"

"I merely present such facts as I have gleaned through the morning's research. You must draw your own conclusions."

Pascoglu grunted.

In the doorway appeared Viamestris Diasporus, the tall

man with the ferocious aquiline head whom Magnus Ridolph had noticed in the lobby. He inspected the interior of the library carefully.

"Enter, if you please," said Pascoglu. "I am conducting an inquiry into the death of Lester Bonfils. It is possible that you help us."

Diasporus' narrow face elongated in surprise. "The killer has not announced himself?"

"Unfortunately, no."

Diasporus made a swift gesture, a nod of the head, as if suddenly all were clear. "Bonfils was evidently of the lowest power, and the killer is ashamed of his feat, rather than proud."

Pascoglu rubbed the back of his head. "To ask a hypothetical question, Mr. Diasporus, suppose you had killed Bonfils, what reason—"

Diasporus cut the air with his hand. "Ridiculous! I would only mar my record with a victory so small."

"But, assuming that you had reason to kill him—"

"What reason could there be? He belonged to no recognized gens, he had issued no challenges, he was of stature insufficient to drag the sand of the arena."

Pascoglu spoke querulously: "But if he had done you an injury—"

Magnus Ridolph interjected a suggestion: "For the sake of argument, let us assume that Mr. Bonfils had flung white paint on the front of your house."

In two great strides Diasporus was beside Magnus Ridolph, the feral bony face peering down. "What is this, what has he done?"

"He has done nothing. He is dead. I ask the question merely for the enlightenment of Mr. Pascoglu."

"Ah! I understand. I would have such a cur poisoned. Evidently Bonfils had committed no such solecism, for I understand that he died decently, through a weapon of prestige."

Pascoglu turned his eyes to the ceiling, held out his hands. "Thank you, Mr. Diasporus, thank you for your help."

Diasporus departed; Pascoglu went to the wall-mesh. "Please send Mr. Thorn 199 to the library."

They waited in silence. Presently Thorn 199 appeared, a wiry little man with a rather large round head, evidently of a much mutated race. His skin was a waxy yellow; he wore gay garments of blue and orange, with a red collar and rococo red slippers.

Pascoglu had recovered his poise. "Thank you for coming, Mr. Thorn. I am trying to establish—"

Magnus Ridolph said in a thoughtful voice, "Excuse me. May I make a suggestion?"

"Well?" snapped Pascoglu.

"I fear Mr. Thorn is not wearing the clothes he would prefer for so important an inquiry as this. For his own sake he will be the first to wish to change into black and white, with, of course, a black hat."

Thorn 199 darted Magnus Ridolph a glance of enormous hatred.

Pascoglu was puzzled. He glanced from Magnus Ridolph to Thorn 199 and back.

"These garments are adequate," rasped Thorn 199. "After all, we discuss nothing of consequence."

"Ah, but we do! We inquire into the death of Lester Bonfils."

"Of which I know nothing!"

"Then surely you will have no objection to black and white."

Thorn 199 swung on his heel and left the library.

"What's all this talk about black and white?" demanded Pascoglu.

Magnus Ridolph indicated a strip of film still in the viewer. "This morning I had occasion to review the folkways of the Kolar Peninsula on Duax. The symbology of clothes is especially fascinating. For instance, the blue and orange in which Thorn 199 just now appeared induces a frivolous attitude, a light-hearted disregard for what we Earthmen would speak of as 'fact'. Black and white, however, are the vestments of responsibility and sobriety. When these colors are supplemented by a black hat, the Kolarians are constrained to truth."

Pascoglu nodded in a subdued fashion. "Well, in the meantime, I'll talk to the two priests of Cambyses." He glanced rather apologetically at Magnus Ridolph. "I hear that they practice human sacrifice on Cambyses; is that right?"

"Perfectly correct," said Magnus Ridolph.

The two priests, Fodor Impliega and Fodor Banzoso, presently appeared, both corpulent and unpleasant-looking, with red flushed faces, full lips, eyes half-submerged in the swelling folds of their cheeks.

Pascoglu assumed his official manner. "I am inquiring into the death of Lester Bonfils. You two were fellow passengers

124

with him aboard the *Maulerer Princeps;* perhaps you noticed something which might shed some light on his death."

The priests pouted, blinked, shook their heads. "We are not interested in such men as Bonfils."

"You yourselves had no dealings with him?"

The priests stared at Pascoglu, eyes like four knobs of stone.

Pascoglu prompted them. "I understand you wanted to sacrifice one of Bonfils' paleolithics. Is this true?"

"You do not understand our religion," said Fodor Impliega in a flat plangent voice. "The great god Camb exists in each one of us, we are all parts of the whole, the whole of the parts."

Fodor Banzoso amplified the statement. "You used the word 'sacrifice'. This is incorrect. You should say, 'go to join Camb'. It is like going to the fire for warmth, and the fire becomes warmer the more souls that come to join it."

"I see, I see," said Pascoglu. "Bonfils refused to give you one of his paleolithics for a sacrifice—"

"Not 'sacrifice'!"

"—so you became angry, and last night you sacrificed Bonfils himself!"

"May I interrupt?" asked Magnus Ridolph. "I think I may save time for everyone. As you know, Mr. Pascoglu, I spent a certain period this morning in research. I chanced on a description of the Camgian sacrificial rites. In order for the rite to be valid, the victim must kneel, bow his head forward. Two skewers are driven into his ears, and the victim is left in this position, kneeling, face down, in a state of ritual composure. Bonfils was sprawled without regard for any sort of decency. I suggest that Fodor Impliega and Fodor Banzoso are guiltless, at least of this particular crime."

"True, true," said Fodor Impliega. "Never would we leave a corpse in such disorder."

Pascogul blew out his cheeks. "Temporarily, that's all."

At this moment Thorn 199 returned, wearing skin-tight black pantaloons, white blouse, a black jacket, a black tricorn hat. He sidled into the library, past the departing priests.

"You need ask but a single question," said Magnus Ridolph. "What clothes was he wearing at midnight last night?"

"Well?" asked Pascoglu. "What clothes were you wearing?"

"I wore blue and purple."

"Did you kill Lester Bonfils?"

125

"No."

"Undoubtedly Mr. Thorn 199 is telling the truth," said Magnus Ridolph. "The Kolarians will perform violent deeds only when wearing gray pantaloons or the combination of green jacket and red hat. I think you may safely eliminate Mr. Thorn 199."

"Very well," said Pascoglu. "I guess that's all, Mr. Thorn."

Thorn 199 departed, as Pascoglu examined his list with a dispirited attitude. He spoke into the mesh. "Ask Mr. Hercules Starguard to step in."

Hercules Starguard was a young man of great physical charm. His hair was a thick crop of flaxen curls; his eyes were blue as sapphires. He wore mustard-colored breeches, a flaring black jacket, swaggering black short-boots. Pascoglu rose from the chair into which he had sunk. "Mr. Starguard, we are trying to learn something about the tragic death of Mr. Bonfils."

"Not guilty," said Hercules Starguard. "I didn't kill the swine."

Pascoglu raised his eyebrows. "You had reason to dislike Mr. Bonfils?"

"Yes, I would say I disliked Mr. Bonfils."

"And what was the cause of this dislike?"

Hercules Starguard looked contemptuously down his nose at Pascoglu. "Really, Mr. Pascoglu, I can't see how my emotions affect your inquiry."

"Only," said Pascoglu, "if you were the person who killed Mr. Bonfils."

Starguard shrugged. "I'm not."

"Can you demonstrate this to my satisfaction?"

"Probably not."

Magnus Ridolph leaned forward. "Perhaps I can help Mr. Starguard."

Pascoglu glared at him. "Please, Mr. Ridolph, I don't think Mr. Starguard needs help."

"I only wish to clarify the situation," said Magnus Ridolph.

"So you clarify me out of all my suspects," snapped Pascoglu. "Very well, what is it this time?"

"Mr. Starguard is an Earthman, and is subject to the influence of our basic Earth culture. Unlike many men and near-men of the outer worlds, he has been inculcated with the idea that human life is valuable, that he who kills will be punished."

"That doesn't stop murderers," grunted Pascoglu.

"But it restrains an Earthman from killing in the presence of witnesses."

"Witnesses? The paleolithics? What good are they as witnesses?"

"Possibly none whatever, in a legal sense. But they are important indicators, since the presence of human onlookers would deter an Earthman from murder. For this reason, I believe we may eliminate Mr. Starguard from serious consideration as a suspect."

Pascoglu's jaw dropped. "But—who is left?" He looked at the list. "The Hecatean." He spoke into the mesh. "Send in Mr. . . ." He frowned. "Send in the Hecatean."

The Hecatean was the sole non-human of the group, although outwardly he showed great organic similarity to true man. He was tall and stick-legged, with dark brooding eyes in a hard chitin-sheathed white face. His hands were elastic fingerless flaps: here was his most obvious differentiation from humanity. He paused in the doorway, surveying the interior of the room.

"Come in, Mr.—" Pascoglu paused in irritation. "I don't know your name; you have refused to confide it, and I cannot address you properly. Nevertheless, if you will be good enough to enter . . ."

The Hecatean stepped forward. "You men are amusing beasts. Each of you has his private name. I know who I am—why must I label myself? It is a racial idiosyncrasy, the need to fix a sound to each reality."

"We like to know what we're talking about," said Pascoglu. "That's how we fix objects in our minds, with names."

"And thereby you miss the great intuitions," said the Hecatean. His voice was solemn and hollow. "But you have called me here to question me about the man labeled Bonfils. He is dead."

"Exactly," said Pascoglu. "Do you know who killed him?"

"Certainly," said the Hecatean. "Does not everyone know?"

"No," said Pascoglu. "Who is it?"

The Hecatean looked around the room, and when he returned to Pascoglu, his eyes were blank as holes in a crypt.

"Evidently I was mistaken. If I knew, the person involved wishes his deed to pass unnoticed, and why should I disoblige him? If I did know, I don't know."

Pascoglu began to splutter, but Magnus Ridolph interceded in a grave voice. "A reasonable attitude."

Pascoglu's cup of wrath boiled over. "I think his attitude is

127

disgraceful! A murder has been committed, this creature claims he knows, and will not tell. . . . I have a good mind to confine him to his quarters until the patrol ship passes."

"If you do so," said the Hecatean, "I will discharge the contents of my spore sac into the air. You will presently find your Hub inhabited by a hundred thousand animalcules, and if you injure a single one of them, you will be guilty of the same crime that you are now investigating."

Pascoglu went to the door, flung it aside. "Go! Leave! Take the next ship out of here! I'll never allow you back!"

The Hecatean departed without comment. Magnus Ridolph rose to his feet and prepared to follow. Pascoglu held up his hand. "Just a minute, Mr. Ridolph. I need advice. I was hasty; I lost my head."

Magnus Ridolph considered. "Exactly what do you require of me?"

"Find the murderer! Get me out of this mess!"

"These requirements might be contradictory."

Pascoglu sank into a chair, passed a hand over his eyes. "Don't make me out puzzles, Mr. Ridolph."

"Actually, Mr. Pascoglu, you have no need of my services. You have interviewed the suspects, you have at least a cursory acquaintance with the civilizations which have shaped them."

"Yes, yes," muttered Pascoglu. He brought out the list, stared at it, then looked sidewise at Magnus Ridolph. "Which one? Diasporus? Did he do it?"

Magnus Ridolph pursed his lips doubtfully. "He is a knight of the Dacca, an amateur gladiator evidently of some reputation. A murder of this sort would shatter his self-respect, his confidence. I put the probability at one percent."

"Hmph. What about Fiamella of Thousand Candles? She admits she set out to kill him."

Magnus Ridolph frowned. "I wonder. Death by means of amorous attrition is of course not impossible—but are not Fiamella's motives ambiguous? From what I gather, her reputation was injured by Bonfils' disinclination, and she thereupon set out to repair her reputation. If she could harass poor Bonfils to his doom by her charm and seductions, she would gain great face. She had everything to lose if he died in any other fashion. Probability: one percent."

Pascoglu made a mark on the list. "What of Thorn 199?"

Magnus Ridolph held out his hands. "He was not dressed in his killing clothes. It is as simple as that. Probability: one percent."

128

"Well," cried Pascoglu, "what of the priests, Banzoso and Impliega? They needed a sacrifice to their god."

Magnus Ridolph shook his head. "The job was a botch. A sacrifice so slipshod would earn them ten thousand years of perdition."

Pascoglu made a half-hearted suggestion. "Suppose they didn't really believe that?"

"Then why trouble at all?" asked Magnus Ridolph. "Probability: one percent."

"Well, there's Starguard," mused Pascoglu, "But you insist he wouldn't commit murder in front of witnesses . . ."

"It seems highly unlikely," said Magnus Ridolph. "Of course, we could speculate that Bonfils was a charlatan, that the paleolithics were impostors, that Starguard was somehow involved in the deception . . ."

"Yes," said Pascoglu eagerly. "I was thinking something like that myself."

"The only drawback to the theory is that it cannot possibly be correct. Bonfils is an anthropologist of wide reputation. I observed the paleolithics, and I believe them to be authentic primitives. They are shy and confused. Civilized men attempting to mimic barbarity unconsciously exaggerate the brutishness of their subject. The barbarian, adapting to the ways of civilization, comports himself to the model set by his preceptor—in this case Bonfils. Observing them at dinner, I was amused by their careful aping of Bonfils' manners. Then, when we were inspecting the corpse, they were clearly bewildered, subdued, frightened. I could discern no trace of the crafty calculation by which a civilized man would hope to extricate himself from an uncomfortable situation. I think we may assume that Bonfils and his paleolithics were exactly as they represented themselves."

Pascoglu jumped to his feet, paced back and forth. "Then the paleolithics could not have killed Bonfils."

"Probability minuscule. And if we concede their genuineness, we must abandon the idea that Starguard was their accomplice, and we rule him out on the basis of the cultural qualm I mentioned before."

"Well—the Hecatean, then. What of him?"

"He is a more unlikely murderer than all the others," said Magnus Ridolph. "For three reasons: First, he is non-human, and has no experience with rage and revenge. On Hecate violence is unknown. Secondly, as a non-human, he would have no points of engagement with Bonfils. A leopard does not at-

129

tack a tree; they are different orders of beings. So with the Hecatean. Thirdly, it would be, physically as well as psychologically, impossible for the Hecatean to kill Bonfils. His hands have no fingers; they are flaps of sinew. They could not manipulate a trigger inside a trigger-guard. I think you may dispense with the Hecatean."

"But who is there left?" cried Pascoglu in desperation.

"Well, there is you, there is me and there is—"

The door slid back; the bonze in the red cloak looked into the room.

V

"COME IN, COME IN," said Magnus Ridolph with cordiality. "Our business is just now complete. We have established that of all the persons here at the Hub, only you would have killed Lester Bonfils, and so now we have no further need for the library."

"What?" cried Pascoglu, staring at the bonze, who made a deprecatory gesture.

"I had hoped," said the bonze, "that my part in the affair would escape notice."

"You are too modest," said Magnus Ridolph. "It is only fitting that a man should be known for his good works."

The bonze bowed. "I want no encomiums. I merely do my duty. And if you are truly finished in here, I have a certain amount of study before me."

"By all means. Come, Mr. Pascoglu; we are inconsiderate, keeping the worthy bonze from his meditations." And Magnus Ridolph drew the stupefied Pan Pascoglu into the corridor.

"Is he—is he the murderer?" asked Pascoglu feebly.

"He killed Lester Bonfils," said Magnus Ridolph. "That is clear enough."

"But why?"

"Out of the kindness of his heart. Bonfils spoke to me for a moment. He clearly was suffering considerable psychic damage."

"But—he could be cured!" exclaimed Pascoglu indignantly. "It wasn't necessary to kill him to soothe his feelings."

"Not according to our viewpoint," said Magnus Ridolph. "But you must recall that the bonze is a devout believer in— well, let us call it 'reincarnation'. He conceived himself performing a happy release for poor tormented Bonfils, who came to him for help. He killed him for his own good."

They entered Pascoglu's office; Pascoglu went to stare out the window. "But what am I to do?" he muttered.

"That," said Magnus Ridolph, "is where I cannot advise you."

"It doesn't seem right to penalize the poor bonze. . . . It's ridiculous. How could I possibly go about it?"

"The dilemma is real," agreed Magnus Ridolph.

There was a moment of silence, during which Pascoglu morosely tugged at his mustache. Then Magnus Ridolph said, "Essentially, you wish to protect your clientele from further application of misplaced philanthropy."

"That's the main thing!" cried Pascoglu. "I could pass off Bonfils' death—explain that it was accidental. I could ship the paleolithics back to their planet . . ."

"I would likewise separate the bonze from persons showing even the mildest melancholy. For if he is energetic and dedicated, he might well seek to extend the range of his beneficence."

Pascoglu suddenly put his hand to his cheek. He turned wide eyes to Magnus Ridolph. "This morning I felt pretty low. I was talking to the bonze . . . I told him all my troubles. I complained about expense—"

The door slid quietly aside; the bonze peered in, a half-smile on his benign face. "Do I intrude?" he asked as he spied Magnus Ridolph. "I had hoped to find you alone, Mr. Pascoglu."

"I was just going," said Magnus Ridolph politely. "If you'll excuse me . . ."

"No, no!" cried Pascoglu. "Don't go, Mr. Ridolph!"

"Another time will do as well," said the bonze politely. The door closed behind him.

"Now I feel worse than ever," Pascoglu moaned.

"Best to conceal it from the bonze," said Magnus Ridolph.

THE SUB-STANDARD SARDINES

Banish Evil from the world? Nonsense! Encourage it, foster it, sponsor it. The world owes Evil a debt beyond imagination. Think! Without greed ambition falters. Without vanity art becomes idle musing. Without cruelty benevolence lapses to passivity. Superstition has shamed man into self-reliance and, without stupidity, where would be the savor of superior understanding?

—MAGNUS RIDOLPH

MAGNUS RIDOLPH lay on a deck-chair, a green and orange umbrella bearing the brunt of the African sunlight. The table beside him supported a smouldering cigar, Shemmlers *News Discussions* turned face downward, a glass containing ice and a squeezed half-lime. In short, a picture of relaxation, idyllic peace . . . The transgraf clanged from within.

After a restless interval Magnus Ridolph arose, entered the apartment, took the message from the rack. It read:

> Dear Magnus,
> My chef's report on tomorrow's dinner—broiled grouse with truffles and compote of Marchisand cherries, Queen Persis salad, Sirius Fifth artichokes. A subsidiary report of my own—wines from three planets, including an incredible Fragence claret, a final course of canned sardines.
> If you are free, I'd like your verdict on the menu—especially the sardines, which are unusual.
>
> Joel Karamor.

Magnus Ridolph returned to the deck-chair, re-read the invitation, folded it, laid it on the table beside him. He rubbed his short white beard, then, leaning back in his deckchair, half-closed his eyes, apparently intent on a small sailboat, white as the walls of Marrakech, plying the dark blue face of Lake Sahara.

He rose abruptly, crossed into his study, seated himself at his Mnemiphot, keyed the combination for *Sardines*.

For several minutes information played across the screen. Very little seemed significant and he found no notes of his own on the topic. The *sardina pilchardis*, according to the Mnemiphot, belonged to the herring family, swam in large shoals and fed on minute pelagic animals. There were further details of scale pattern, breeding, habits, natural enemies, discussion of variant species.

Magnus Ridolph wrote an acceptance to the invitation, ticked off Joel Karamor's address code, dropped the message into the transgraph slot.

Karamor was a large healthy man with a big nose, a big chin, a brush of brindle-gray hair. He was an honest man and conducted his life on a basis of candor, simplicity and goodwill. Magnus Ridolph, accustomed to extremes of deception and self-interest, found him a refreshing variant.

The dinner was served in a high room paneled in Congo hardwoods, decorated with primitive masks hung high in the shadows. One glass wall opened up on a magnificent expanse of clear blue twilight and, twenty miles south, the loom of the Tibesti foothills.

The two sat at a table of burnished lignum vitæ, between them a centerpiece of carved malachite which Magnus Ridolph recognized for a Three-Generation Work from the Golwana Coast of the planet Mugh—a product of father, son and son's son, toiled over a hundred years to the minute.*

The dinner surpassed Karamor's usual standard. The grouse was cooked to a turn, the salad beyond exception. The wines were smooth and brilliant, rich but not cloying. Dessert was a fruit ice, followed by coarse crackers and cheese.

"Now," said Karamor, watching Magnus Ridolph slyly, "for our sardines and coffee."

Magnus Ridolph obliged with the wry face he knew to be expected of him. "The coffee, at least, I shall enjoy. The sardines will have to be of spectacular quality to tempt me."

Karamor nodded significantly. "They're unusual." He

---

* The catalogue of Pomukka-Dhen, last of the Golwana emperors, listed seven thousand Century pieces, 136 Millennium pieces, and fourteen Ten-Thousand-Year pieces. A rumor had reached Magnus Ridolph of a Hundred-Thousand-Year work nearing completion in the Backlands, a gigantic carved tourmaline.

arose, slid back the panel of a wall-cabinet, returned to the table with a flat can, embossed in red, blue and yellow.

"It's yours," and Karamor, seating himself, watched his guest expectantly.

The label read: *Premier Quality. Select Sardines in oil. Packed by Chandaria Canneries, Chandaria.*

Magnus Ridolph's fine white eyebrows rose. "Imported from Chandaria? A long way to bring fish."

"The sardines are top-grade," said Karamor. "Better than anything on earth—delicacies of prime quality and they bring a premium price."

"I still should not, at first thought, imagine it profitable," was Magnus Ridolph's doubtful comment.

"That's where you're wrong," declared Karamor. "Of course you must understand the cannery expenses are very low, and compensate for the shipping costs. And then space-freight is not especially expensive. Actually we're doing very well."

Magnus Ridolph looked up from the can. "We?"

"George Donnels, my partner in the canning business, and myself. I financed the proposition, and I look after the sales. He runs the cannery and fishing operations."

"I see," said Magnus Ridolph vaguely.

"A few months ago," continued Karamor, frowning, "he offered to buy me out. I told him I'd consider it. And then—" Karamor gestured toward the can. "Open it."

Magnus Ridolph bent over the can, raising a tab, pressing the lid-release button. . . . Bang! The lid flew high in the air, the contents of the can sprayed in all directions.

Magnus Ridolph sat back, raising eyebrows mutely at Karamor. He felt his beard, combing out the fragments of fish which had become entangled in the hairs.

"Spectacular indeed," said Magnus Ridolph. "I agree. What were the other tests you wished me to make?"

Karamor rose to his feet, circled the table. "Believe me, Magnus, that surprised me as much as it did you. I expected nothing like that . . ."

"What did you expect?" inquired Magnus Ridolph drily? "A flight of birds?"

"No, no, please believe me, Magnus. You must know I wouldn't indulge in a stupid joke of that sort?"

Magnus Ridolph wiped his face with a napkin. "What is the explanation for the—" he licked his lips—"the occurrence?"

Karamor returned to his seat. "I don't know. I'm worried. I want to find out. I've opened a dozen cans of sardines in

134

the last week. About half were in good condition. The rest—all tampered with, one way or another.

"In one can the fish were threaded with fine wires. In another the flesh tasted of petroleum. Another gave off a vile odor. I can't understand it. Someone or something wants to ruin Chandaria Cannery's reputation."

"How widespread is this tampering?"

"Only the last shipment, so far as I know. We've had nothing but compliments on the product up to now."

"Whom do you suspect?"

Karamor spread out his big hands. "I don't know. Donnels couldn't benefit, that's certain—unless he figured he could scare me into selling and I think he knows me better than that. I thought you might investigate—act for me."

Magnus Ridolph considered a moment. "Well—at the moment, so it happens, I'm free."

Karamor relaxed, smiled. "The import seals were all intact," he told his guest.

"And they are applied at the cannery?"

"Right."

"Then," said Magnus Ridolph, "it is evident that the mischief occurs on Chandaria."

Magnus Ridolph rode the passenger packet to City of the Thousand Red Candles, on Rhodope, Fomalhaut's fourth planet, where he took a room at the Ernst Delabri Inn.

He enjoyed a quiet dinner in the outdoor dining room, then hired a barge and let the boatman paddle him along the canals till long after dark.

Next morning Magnus Ridolph assumed a new character. Ignoring his white and blue tunic, he buttoned himself into a worn brown work-suit, pulled a gray cloth cap over his ruff of white hair. Then, crossing the King's Canal and the Panalaza, he threaded the dingy street of the Old Town to the Central Employment Pool.

Here he found little activity. A few men, a few nervous tom-tickers, a knot of Capellan anthropoids, one Yellowbird, a few native Rhodopians listlessly watched the call-screen. Prominent on the wall was a sign reading:

CANNERY WORKERS!

WANTED ON CHANDARIA!

—a notice which excited little attention.

135

Magnus Ridolph strolled to the assignment window. The velvet-skinned Rhodopian clerk bobbed his head courteously, lisped, "Yes, sir?"

"I'd like to try the cannery on Chandaria," said Magnus Ridolph.

The Rhodopian flicked him a seal-brown glance. "In what capacity?"

"What positions are open?"

The Rhodopian glanced at a list. "Electrician—three hundred munits; integrator-feed mechanic—three hundred twenty munits; welder—two hundred ninety munits; labor—two hundred munits."

"Hm," said Magnus Ridolph. "No clerical work?"

"At the present, no."

"I'll try the electrician job."

"Yes sir," said the Rhodopian. "May I see your Union Journeyman Certificate?"

"My word," said Magnus Ridolph. "I neglected to pack it."

The Rhodopian showed blunt pink teeth. "I can send you out as a laborer. The steward will sign you up on the job."

"Very well," sighed Mangus Ridolph.

A cargo freighter conveyed the cannery recruits to Chandaria—a thick wobbly shell permeated through and through with the reek of hot oil, sweat and ammonia. Magnus Ridolph and a dozen others were quartered in an empty hold. They ate in the crew's mess and were allowed two quarts of water a day for washing. Smoking was forbidden.

Little need be said of the voyage. Magnus Ridolph for years afterward labored to expunge the memory from his brain. When at last the passengers filed, blinking, out on Chandaria, Magnus Ridolph looked his part. His beard was unkempt and dirty, his hair hung around his ears and he blended completely with his fellows.

His first impression of the planet was dismal watery distance, drifting patches of fog, wan maroon illumination. Chandaria was the ancient planet of an ancient red sun and the land lay on a level with the ocean—prone, a gloomy peneplain haunted with slow-shifting mists.

In spite of its age Chandaria supported no native life more advanced than reeds and a few fern trees. Protozoa swarmed the seas and, with no natural enemies, the twenty thousand sardines originally loosed into the waters throve remarkably well.

As the passengers alighted from the hold of the freighter a

young man with a long horse-like yellow face, very broad shoulders, very narrow hips, stepped forward.

"This way, men," he said. "Bring your luggage."

The newcomers obediently trooped at his heels, across ground that quaked underfoot. The path led into fog and, for a quarter-mile, the only features of the landscape were a few rotten trees thrusting forlorn branches through the mist, a few pools of stagnant water.

The mist presently thinned, revealing a huddle of long buildings and, beyond, an expanse of reeds and the glint of water.

"This is the bunkhouse for those of you who sleep," and the young man jerked his finger at the men and the anthropoids. "You go in and sign with the house-captain, You, Yellowbird, you, Portmar, and you, Rhodope, this way."

Magnus Ridolph ruefully shook his head as he mounted the soggy steps into the bunkhouse. This was probably the low point in his career. Two hundred munits a month, grubbing among the intimate parts of fish. He made a wry grimace, entered the bunkhouse.

He found an empty cubicle, threw his duffel-bag on the cot, strolled into the recreation room, which smelled of fish. Unpainted plyboard covered the walls, which were spanned by bare aluminum rafters. A cheap telescreen at the end of the room displayed a buxom young woman, singing and contorting her body with approximately equal vehemence.

Magnus Ridolph sighed once more, inquired for the house-captain.

He was assigned to the No. 4 Eviscerator. His duties were simple. At intervals of about three minutes he pulled a lever which raised a gate. From a pond outside came a rush of water, and thousands of sardines swam serenely into the machine, where fingers, slots and air jets sorted them for size, guided them against flashing knives, finally flung them through a spray and out on a series of belts, where, still flapping feebly, they were tucked into cans by a line of packers.

These packers were mostly Banshoos from nearby Thaddeus XII—bulbous gray torsos with twenty three-fingered tentacles, an eye and a sub-brain at the tip of each tentacle.

From the packers the cans were fitted with lids, conducted through a bank of electronic cookers and finally stacked into crates, sealed and ready for export.

Magnus Ridolph considered the process with a thoughtful eye. An efficient and well-organized sequence of operations,

137

he decided. The Banshoo packers were the only non-mechanical stage in the process and, watching the swift play of tentacles over the belt, Magnus Ridolph thought that no machine could work as quickly and flexibly.

Somewhere along this line, he reflected, the sardines had been, and possibly were being, adulterated. Where? At the moment no answer presented itself.

He ate his lunch in an adjoining cafeteria. The food was passable—precooked on Earth, served in sealed trays. Returning toward his post at Eviscerator No. 4 he noted a doorway leading out on a plank walk.

Magnus Ridolph paused, stepped outside. The walk, supported on piles driven into the morass, ran the length of the plant. Magnus Ridolph turned toward the ocean, hoping to catch a glimpse of the cannery's fishing fleet.

The mist had lifted somewhat, revealing endless miles of reed-covered mud-flats and a stagnant sea. The land proper was distinguishable from the mud-flats only by an occasional cycad which showed a dull frond to the gread somber sun. It was a landscape bleak and inexpressibly dreary, a world without hope or joy.

Magnus Ridolph rounded the corner of the plant, came upon the concentration pond from which the fish were channeled to the eviscerators. He looked right and left but—except for a neat aluminum dinghy—not a boat of any sort was visible. How then was the cannery supplied with fish?

He turned his attention to the concentration pond, a shallow concrete basin, fifty feet by twenty, with a break in the wall facing the sea three feet square. Magnus Ridolph, stepping closer, saw that a set of long transparent bristles pointed through the opening, permitting fish to swim in, but preventing their escape.

And as he watched, the dull surface of the ocean rippled. He caught the sheen of a thousand small fins, and into the basin darted first one fish, then a hundred, then a thousand and further thousands until the basin seethed and spattered with concentrated life.

Magnus Ridolph felt eyes on him. Lifting his head he saw standing across the pond the broad-shouldered young man with the long yellow face. He wore puttees, high field boots of nulastic, a tan jacket, and now he came striding around the pond toward Magnus Ridolph.

"You supposed to be out here? Or at work?"

"I am employed, yes," said Magnus Ridolph mildly. "I su-

138

pervise a"—he coughed—"an eviscerator. But now, I have only just finished my lunch."

The young man's mouth curled. "The whistle blew half an hour ago. Get in motion, Pop, because we didn't bring you three light-years out here to see the sights."

"If, as you say, the whistle has blown, I shall certainly return to my duties. Er—whom have I the pleasure of addressing?"

"My name's Donnels. I sign your check."

"Ah, yes. I see," said Magnus Ridolph, nodding. He thoughtfully returned to the eviscerator.

His duties were light but monotonous. Open the gate, shut it; open the gate, shut it—occasionally break up a jam of frantic silvery bodies in front of the segregators. Magnus Ridolph found ample time for reflection.

An explanation for the mysterious adulterations seemed as far away as ever. The man who could accomplish the mischief most easily was George Donnels but so far as Magnus Ridolph could see, the plant seemed completely efficient. True, Donnels wanted to buy out Karamor's interest but why should he endanger the reputation of his own product?

Especially when he had such admirable raw material—for the fish, so Magnus Ridolph noted, were larger and more plump than the specimens displayed by his Mnemiphot. Evidently conditions on Chandaria agreed with them or possibly Donnels had stocked the world with only the most select fish.

Open the gate, close it. And he noted that the surge of fish down the chute formed a recurring pattern. First one fish—rather larger, this one, perhaps the leader of the shoal—then the thousands, dashing helter-skelter after him into the knives. There was never any hesitation. The instant the gate opened, in surged the shoal-leader, followed by the eager thousands.

The races most numerously represented at the cannery were the Banshoos, Capellan anthropoids, men and Cordovan toricles, in that order. Each had its separate bunkhouse and mess-hall—though bunkhouse was perhaps a misnomer for the tanks of warm broth in which the Banshoos wallowed, or the airtight barracks of the Capellans.

After a shower and his evening meal, Magnus Ridolph wandered into the recreation room. The telescreen was for the moment lifeless and a pair of card games were in progress. Magnus Ridolph took a seat beside a stocky bald man with plump cheeks and little blue pig-eyes, who was reading the afternoon news-facsimile.

139

After a moment he laid the sheet to the side, stretched pudgy arms, belched. Magnus Ridolph with grave courtesy offered him a cigarette.

"Thanks, don't mind if I do," said the stocky man cheerfully.

"Rather dull isn't it?" said Magnus Ridolph.

"Sure is," and his new friend blew a plume of smoke into the already hazy atmosphere. "Think I'll take outa this jungle next ship."

"You'd think the company would provide better recreation facilities," said Magnus Ridolph.

"Oh, they don't care for anything but making money. These are the worst conditions I've ever worked in. Bare union minimum, no extras at all, whatever."

"A matter has been puzzling me—" began Magnus Ridolph.

"Lots of stuff puzzling me," sniffed his friend.

"How are the fish supplied to the cannery?"

"Oh," the man exhaled a wise cloud of smoke, "they're supposed to have bait in that pond. There's so many fish and they're so hungry they bite for anything. Donnels sure saves that way—gets the fish free, so to speak. Don't cost him a cent, far's I can see."

"And where does Donnels live?" inquired Magnus Ridolph.

"He's got him a nice little cabin over behind the laboratory."

"Oh—the laboratory," mused the white-bearded sage. "And where is the laboratory? I hadn't noticed it."

"She's off along the trail a little ways, down the shore."

"I see."

Magnus Ridolph presently rose to his feet and wandered around the room a moment or so. Then he slipped out into the night.

Chandaria had no moons and a heavy mist shrouded the face of the planet from the stars. Ten steps took Magnus Ridolph into utter darkness. He switched on his pocket flash, picked his way gingerly over the soggy ground, at last came upon the trail to the laboratory—a graveled path, dry and solid.

Once fairly on the path he doused the flash, halted, strained his ears for sound. He heard a far waver of voices from the direction of the cannery, a phonograph faintly squeaking Capellan music.

He continued along the path, guiding himself by the feel of the gravel, stopping often to listen. He walked an interminable time, through blackness so dense that it seemed to stream back from his face as he walked. Suddenly a row of lighted windows glowed through the fog. Magnus Ridolph moved as close as feasible to one of these windows, stood on his tiptoes, stared.

He was looking into a room equipped as a biological laboratory. Donnels and a slight dark man in a white smock stood talking beside a coffin-shaped crate.

As he watched Donnels took a pair of cutters, snapped the bands of metal tape binding the crate. The fiber sides fell away, wadding was torn aside, and now a factory-new diving-suit stood revealed—a semi-rigid shell with a transparent dome, oxygen generator and propulsion unit.

Donnels kicked aside the rubbish, stood viewing the gear with evident satisfaction. Magnus Ridolph strained to catch a word of the conversation. Impossible—the window was insulglass. He trotted to the door, inched it open.

"—ought to be a good outfit, four hundred and fifty munits worth," came Donnels' flat voice.

"The question is—is it what we need?"

"Sure." Donnels sounded confident, cocksure. "There's no current to speak of. In five minutes I can circle the colony, and before they know what's going on, the stessonite will kill 'em off like flies."

"Ha, hmph," the technician coughed. "They'll see you coming—ha, hmph—just as when you tried to blast them."

"Curse it, Naile," crowed Donnels, "you're a pessimist! I'll come in along the bottom. They won't see the suit like they did the boat. The suit can hit as fast as they can swim; no chance of word getting on ahead. Well, we'll try anyway. No harm trying. How're your pupils coming along?"

"Good, very good indeed. Two in D tank are ready for the fifth chart and in H tank—that big fellow—he's into the eighth chart."

Magnus Ridolph straightened slightly, then bent closer. "The Barnett Method?" He heard Donnels' voice. "And how about that fellow—in the tank by himself?"

"Ah," said Naile, "that's the wise one! Sometimes I think he knows more than I do."

"That's the boy that'll make millionaires out of both of us," said Donnels, a singing lilt in his voice. "Provided I can buy out Karamor."

There was a silence. Then Magnus Ridolph heard a faint movement of feet. He ducked back to the window, in time to see Donnels' broad-shouldered figure leaving the laboratory.

Naile came obliquely toward him, bent forward with mouth loosely open, staring at an object out of Magnus Ridolph's vision. Magnus Ridolph chewed his lip, fingered his beard. Hypotheses formed in his mind, only to be defeated by their eventual implications. Naile left the room through a door at the rear. Evidently he had his quarters in an annex to the laboratory.

Magnus Ridolph stirred himself. Further information must be collected. He marched to the door and, almost insolently casual, entered the laboratory.

Standard equipment—permobeam projector and viewer, radio-activator, microscopes—visual and quantumnal—balances, automatic dissectors, gene calibrators, mutation cradles. These he dismissed with a glance. At his shoulder stood the diving-suit. First things first, thought Magnus Ridolph. He inspected the suit with appreciation.

"Excellent apparatus," he said to himself. "Admirable design, conscientious workmanship. A shame to defeat the purpose of so much effort." He shrugged, reached inside, and detached the head of the seam-sealer—a small precisely-machined bit of metal, without which the suit could not be made water-tight.

Movement flickered across the room. *Naile!* Magnus Ridolph quietly stepped toward the door. The motion caught the technician's eye.

"Hey!" he cried. "What are you up to?" He bounded forward. "Come back here!" But Magnus Ridolph was away into the Chandaria night.

A beam of light tore a milky rent through the fog, rested a moment on Magnus Ridolph.

"You!" roared Naile. For so slight a man, thought Magnus Ridolph, his voice was remarkably powerful. He heard the thud of Naile's feet. The man also appeared to be agile, swift.

Magnus Ridolph groaned once, then—as the thud of feet grew louder—he jumped off the path into the swamp.

He sank to his knees in cool slime, crouched, threw himself prone. The beam of Naile's flash passed over his head, the steps pounded past. Darkness returned.

Magnus Ridolph struggled through the muck back to the path, proceeded cautiously.

The mist wandered away, vague as a sleepwalker. Magnus Ridolph saw the lights of his bunkhouse, a hundred yards distant. But as he watched they were obscured by something prowling the road in front. Naile?

Magnus Ridolph turned, trotted as fast as his old legs

142

would carry him, skirted far around to the left. Then he closed in to the rear of the bunkhouse. He made directly for the washroom, showered, rinsed out his clothes.

Returning to the recreation hall he found the stocky bald man sitting exactly where he had left him an hour previously.

Magnus Ridolph took a seat. "I understand," he said, "that Donnels was blasting out in the ocean."

The plump man guffawed. "Yes, sir, he surely was. What in the Lord's name for, I'm sure I can't tell you. Sometimes I think he's—well, he flies off the handle, like. A little excitable."

"Possibly he wished to kill some fish?" suggested Magnus Ridolph.

His friend shrugged, pushed plump lips out around his pipe-stem. "With hundreds of tons of fish swarming of their own free will into his cannery he wants to go out and kill more? I hardly think so. Unless he's crazier'n I think."

"Just where was he blasting?"

His friend darted him a glance from little blue pig-eyes. "Well, I'll tell you—though I don't see what difference it makes. He was right off the point of land that sticks into the ocean—the one with the three tall trees on it. About a mile down the shore."

"Strange," mused Magnus Ridolph. He pulled the small metal part from his pocket, fingering it thoughtfully. "Strange. Sardines flinging themselves headlong into cans—Donnels and Naile applying the Barnett Method to something in a tank—Donnels blasting, poisoning something in the ocean—and, too, the adulteration of the canned sardines. . . .

He reported to work at the eviscerator with a theory looming vague at the portals of his mind, like one of the fern trees through the Chandaria mist. He bent over the chute, eyes under the frosty eyebrows sparking with as much excitement as he ever permitted himself.

Open the gate—the surge of fish. Close the gate. Open the gate—the chute running thick with glinting silver crescents. Close the gate. Open the gate—the fish, first one, then the ranks behind. Close the gate.

Magnus Ridolph noted that always a lone sardine led the way down the chute, a swarm of followers close on his tail. And peering after them into the bowels of the eviscerator Magnus Ridolph noticed an inconspicuous side-channel into which the first fish ducked while his fellows poured on to their deaths.

143

Magnus Ridolph thoughtfully found a rag, reached far down, wadded shut the side-channel. Open the gate. The lead fish plunged down the chute—after him came the blind finny horde. He reached the side-channel, butted the rag frantically. The thrust of the others caught him. With desperate flapping of tail, he vanished into the knives. Close the gate. Open the gate. And the lead fish, thwarted in his escape by the wadded rag, was carried to death by his fellows.

Six times the sequence was repeated. Then, when Magnus Ridolph opened the gate, there was no rush of fish. He reached down, removed the rag, sat peering with an innocent eye up the chute.

A foreman presently bustled forward. "What's the trouble? What's wrong up here?"

"The fish evidently have learned the danger of the chute," said Magnus Ridolph. The foreman gave him a scornful glance. "Keep working the gate." He turned away.

Ten minutes later, when Magnus Ridolph opened the gate, fish poured down the chute as before. The foreman came to watch a moment, assured himself that the fish were running as usual, then departed. Mangus Ridolph replaced the rag in the side-passage. Six operations later the opened gate again drew blank. Magnus Ridolph immediately pulled out the rag.

The foreman came on the run. Magnus Ridolph shook his head ruefully, framed an apologetic smile behind his beard.

"We can't have this—we can't *have* this!" bawled the foreman. "What's going on here?"

He ran off, came back with a rock-eyed Donnels.

Donnels peered down the chute, felt into the side escape. He drew back, straightened, glanced sharply at Magnus Ridolph, who blandly returned the gaze.

"Throw another unit into the tank," said Donnels to the foreman. "Keep an eye on 'em. See what's happening."

"Yes, sir." The foreman hurried off.

Donnels turned to Magnus Ridolph, his long yellow face set hard, his mouth pulled far down at the corners.

"You come out on the last ship?"

"Why, yes," said Magnus Ridolph. "A dismal voyage. The quarters were cramped, the food was miserable."

The thin mouth quivered. "Where did you sign up?"

"On Rhodope. I remember it perfectly, it was—"

"Fine, fine," said Donnels. After a short pause. "You look like a pretty smart man."

"Ahr, ahem," said Magnus Ridolph. "Are you suggesting a

144

promotion? I'd be delighted to have a more responsible position, something clerical perhaps."

"If you're smart," said Donnels in an edged even tone, "you'll keep your mind on your work—and *nothing* else."

"Just as you say," said Magnus Ridolph with dignity.

The foreman returned. Donnels signaled Magnus Ridolph to raise the gate and fish once more flushed the chute.

Donnels stood close at hand for twenty minutes and the foreman remained ten minutes after Donnels had stalked away.

The rest of the shift Magnus Ridolph performed his duties well and skillfully—though by way of diversion he found it amusing to reach down and cuff the Judas fish as it passed, until at last the fish learned to keep to the far side of the chute. Magnus Ridolph could pursue his sport only with inconvenient exertion and so desisted.

Magnus Ridolph sat on the clammy bench before the bunkhouse, looking out over the landscape. There was little to see. Low in the sky hung the giant red sun, fitfully obscured by the shifting vapors. Ahead stretched the mud-flats and the leaden ocean, to his left rose the cannery and the warehouse. To his right the laboratory was visible, two hundred yards down the gravel path.

Magnus Ridolph reached for a cigar, then remembered that he had packed none in his meager luggage—and the brand sold at the commissary offended rather than soothed his palate.

Movement at the laboratory. Magnus Ridolph sat straighter on the bench. Donnels and Naile emerged, followed by two Capellan laborers, carrying the diving-suit.

Magnus Ridolph pursed his lips. Evidently the absence of the seam-sealer had not been discovered.

He watched impassively as the party turned toward the cannery wharf—Donnels darted him a long level stare as he strode by.

As soon as the group had passed Magnus Ridolph rose, jauntily set off down the path toward the laboratory. He found the door unlocked and, entering, turned directly to the wall which had been out of his vision when he stood at the window.

Tanks lined the wall, tanks full of fish—sardines. Some swam placidly to and fro, others hung close to the glass, staring out with intent eyes. Magnus Ridolph became aware of differences.

Some had monstrous tails, lizard-like heads. Others resembled tadpoles, with rudimentary fins and tail barely moving hyper-developed crania. Eyes bulged at Magnus Ridolph—eyes like bubbles, eyes flame red, eyes coal-pit black. One fish trailed a bridal-train of fins, another wore an antler-like head-growth.

Magnus Ridolph surveyed the array without emotion. He had seen like sights in other biological laboratories, freak distortions of every description. In the infamous clinic on the planet Pandora— Magnus Ridolph returned to the case at hand, sought a fish in a tank by himself—"the wise one."

There he was, at the far end—a fish normal except for a slightly enlarged head.

"Well, well," said Magnus Ridolph. "Well, well." He bent forward, peered into the tank and the sardine, eyes unwinking, expressionless, stared back. Magnus Ridolph turned, sought around the room. There—the twenty charts comprising the Barnett Method for Establishing Communication with Alien Intelligences.

Magnus Ridolph fanned out the master chart before the tank, and the fish pressed closer to the glass.

"Opening communication," Magnus Ridolph signaled and waited. The fish plunged to the bottom of the tank, returned with a bit of metal in its mouth. It tapped on the glass— once, twice, once.

Magnus Ridolph had no need to refer to the chart. "Proceed," was the message.

He bent over the chart, selected the symbols with care, pausing frequently to assure himself that the fish was following him.

"Instructor-man . . . of you . . . desire . . . utilize . . . you . . . purpose . . . injury . . . class of you. I . . . know (negative) . . . method."

The fish tapped on the glass: 5—3—5, 4—3—2. 5—6—1, 2—6—3—4.

Magnus Ridolph followed the code on the chart. "Class of me . . . exists . . . place (indefinite, interrogative)?"

Magnus Ridolph signaled back. "Large (emphatic) . . . extension . . . water . . . exists . . . exterior. Plurality (emphatic) . . . class of you . exists Class of instructor-man . . . kill . . . class of you . . . eat . . . class of you."

"Purpose (interrogative) . . . of you?" was the fish's pointed signal.

"Complex mixture," signaled Magnus Ridolph. "Construc-

146

tive. You . . . desire (interrogative . . . depart . . . tank . . . converge . . . plurality . . . class of you?"

The fish rattled his bit of metal indecisively. "Food?"

"Plurality," returned Magnus Ridolph. "Swim . . . extension (emphatic . . . barriers (negative) ."

The fish twitched his fins, retired to a dark corner. Presently, as Magnus Ridolph was becoming restive, the fish swam out in front once more, tapped twice on the glass.

Magnus Ridolph sought around the laboratory, found a bucket. He dipped it into the tank, but the fish nervously skittered out of reach. Magnus Ridolph scooped him out willy-nilly and, stuffing the Barnett charts into his pocket, he left the laboratory.

Briskly he traversed the path, turned toward the wharf. Now he spied Donnels and Naile coming toward him, lines dividing Donnels' yellow face into hard segments. Magnus Ridolph prudently set the bucket beside the bunkhouse, and was placidly seated on the bench when Donnels and Naile passed.

"—slider was there and working late night, I'm sure," Magnus Ridolph heard Naile say. Donnels shook his head curtly.

As soon as they had passed Magnus Ridolph took the bucket, continued toward the wharf.

The diving-suit stood at the edge of the pier, ready for use—except for the missing seam-sealer. The Capellan laborers stood dully nearby, watching without interest.

Magnus Ridolph rubbed his chin. Suit—seam-sealer—why not? He changed his mind about throwing the fish into the ocean; instead he approached the suit, looked it over carefully. Two dials on the breastplate; one controlled the drive-unit, the other the air generator. Simplicity itself.

He fitted the seam-sealer into place and, with a side-glance at the two Capellans, stepped into the suit, slid the seam-sealer home. The Capellans shifted uneasily, brains roiling at a sight which they knew to be unnatural—and yet which they had no orders to prevent. As an afterthought Magnus Ridolph unsealed the suit, transferred the Barnett charts to the exterior pouch, sealed himself into the suit once more.

At his belt hung a knife, an axe, a flash-lamp. Another lamp was set at the top of the transparent head dome. He reached to the breastplate, assured himself that the dials moved easily, set the air-generator in operation.

He looked over his shoulder. Motion near the laboratory.

He floated the bucket on the sluggish water, lurched off the dock. A last glimpse of the rear showed him George Donnels running in his direction, face twisted in a contortion of rage. Behind him scampered Naile, white smock flapping.

Magnus Ridolph tapped the side of the bucket, unsure of the code, hoping for the best. "Swim . . . proximity . . . me." Then he overturned the bucket. The fish darted out, away. Magnus Ridolph himself sank under the surface.

He twisted the propulsion dial. Water was sucked into the unit, spewed astern. Magnus Ridolph drove headlong through the water. And something tore hissing past the head-dome, made a vague clap in his ears.

Magnus Ridolph wrenched at the dial, and the water buffeted his suit.

Two or three minutes later he slowed, rose to the surface. The wharf was a quarter-mile to the rear and he could see Donnels' taut frame searching across the water. Magnus Ridolph chuckled.

The point of land with the three tall trees sloped into the ocean at his left. Turning on his head-lamp, fixing the direction by a compass set in the rim of the dome, he submerged, drove forward.

The water was emerald-green, clearer than it seemed from the surface. He swam into a gigantic underwater forest—sea-trees with delicate silver fronds pinned to the bottom by the slenderest of stalks, sea-vines rising straight as pencils of light from the depths, with shining globes spaced along the stalks.

These might not be true plants, thought Magnus Ridolph, but possibly groups of polyps like the anemones of Earth. And, recalling the sting of the Portuguese man-of-war, he gave the sea-vines a wide berth.

Everywhere swam sardines, shoal upon shoal, sardines by the millions, and the light in the dead-dome glinted on the flitting silver sides like moonlight along a wind-ruffled lake.

Magnus Ridolph looked about to see if possibly the fish he had liberated were near. If so he was indistinguishable among his fellows.

On he drove, suspended between the mirroring under-surface and the gloom of the depths, past shoulders of quiet mud, across sudden deeps, threading the groves of the sea-trees.

He rose once more to the surface, adjusted his course. The cannery was a ramshackle huddle far back along the gray shore. He submerged, continued.

148

A white wall glimmered ahead. He veered, slowed and saw the barrier to be a submarine dyke, a rampart of felsite or quartzite, striding mightily across the ocean floor. He drifted close to the wall, rose to the top face—a flat course of rock fifteen feet below the surface.

Magnus Ridolph floated quietly, considering. This was approximately where Donnels had blasted, possibly a little further out to sea. He turned, swam slowly through the lime-green water, just above the flat white rock-face. He halted, floated motionless.

Below him several-score bubbles clung to the stone, large globes arrayed in ordered rows. They seemed flexible, swayed slightly to random currents. Within, Magnus Ridolph glimpsed small intricate objects and a lurid flickering light came from several.

Magnus Ridolph suddenly became aware of the press of fish, thicker than anything he had seen to date. They were pushing slowly in upon him and now, noting the hyper-developed crania, the bulging eyes, the careful purposive movements, Magnus Ridolph felt that he knew a great deal about the Chandaria cannery.

He also experienced a sense of uneasiness. Why were several of the fish nudging a weighted bubble in his direction?

He whipped out the Barnett charts, found number one, gesticulated to the sequence which conveyed the notion of friendly intent.

Several of the fish darted close, followed his motions carefully. One of them—no different, so far as Magnus Ridolph could tell, from the multitude—came close, tapped on his headdome.

1—2—1— "opening communication."

Manus Ridolph sighed, relaxed in the diving suit, indicated symbols on the charts.

"I . . . come . . . purpose . . . help . . . class of you."

"Doubt. Class of you . . . destructive (interrogative)?"

"Class of me . . . in building . . . friends (negative) of me. I . . . constructive. Friend . . . class of you."

"Class of you . . . purpose . . . kill . . . class of us."

Magnus Ridolph struggled with the elemental concepts. Valuable as the charts were, conveying an exact sense was like repairing a watch with a pipe-wrench.

"Complex . . . thought. Class of me . . . carry . . . you . . . this place. Construct . . . thinking . . . of you . . . stronger."

A sudden small movement flurried through the throng, silver sides twinkled. Magnus Ridolph listened—the hum of a propeller. He rose to the surface. Not a hundred yards distant was the rowboat, propelled by an outboard motor. The man in the boat sighted Magnus Ridolph, swerved. In one hand he carried a long tube with a shoulder stock. Magnus Ridolph submerged quickly.

The propeller droned louder, closer. The black underbody of the little boat plunged directly at him.

Magnus Ridolph threw the propulsion dial hard to its stop. Water blasted back from the jet, scattering the fish, and Magnus Ridolph dove off at an angle.

The boat turned with him, following swiftly. The propeller halted, the boat slowed. Under the surface came the tube, pointing at Magnus Ridolph. It twitched, ejected a little projectile which bubbled fast toward him.

Magnus Ridolph doubled fast to the side and the spew of his drive caught the missile, diverted it slightly. From behind came a tremendous explosion—jarring Magnus Ridolph like a hammer blow. And the boat was once more after him.

Magnus Ridolph blinked, shook his head. He twisted, dove up at a slant for the boat. Up under the light boat he came, the head-dome under one side of the hull. Full power on the thrust-unit—up and over went the boat. Sprawling into the water toppled an awkward dark shape and the rocket-tube plunged steeply into the darkness below. The boat filled with water, settled into the gloom.

Magnus Ridolph surfaced, placidly watched Naile, the laboratory technician, paddling for land. He was a clumsy swimmer and the shore was a mile distant. If he reached the shore, there would still be several miles of morass to traverse back to the cannery. After a moment Magnus Ridolph sunk below the surface, returned to the great white underwater rampart.

Joel Karamor strode back and forth, hands behind his back, forehead furrowed. Magnus Ridolph, at his ease in an old-fashioned leather armchair, sipped a glass of sherry. This was Joel Karamor's business office, high in the French Pavilion Tower—one of the landmarks of Tran, the miracle-city on the shores of Lake Sahara.

"Yes," muttered Karamor, "but where was Donnels all this time? Where is he now?"

Magnus Ridolph coughed slightly, touched his white beard, this once more crisp, well-cropped.

"Ah, Donnels," he mused. "Did you value him as a partner?"

Karamor froze stock-still, stared at his visitor. "What do you mean? Where is Donnels?"

Magnus Ridolph touched the tips of his fingers together. "I'll continue my report. I returned to the dock and as it was somewhat after sunset, very dull and gloomy, I fancy I was not observed. A large number of the intelligent fish, I may add, accompanied me for reasons of their own, into which I did not inquire.

"I assumed that Donnels would be standing on the wharf, probably armed and emotionally keyed to shoot without permitting me to present my authority from you. I believe I have mentioned that the wharf provided the only access from the cannery to the ocean—the shore being an impassable swamp.

"If Donnels were standing on the wharf, he would completely dominate the ground. My problem then was to find a means to reach solid ground without being perceived by Donnels."

Karamor resumed his pacing. "Yes," he muttered. "Go on."

Magnus Ridolph sipped his sherry. "A suitable expedient had occurred to me. Understand now, Joel, I could not, at the risk of my life, climb boldly up on the wharf."

"I understand perfectly. What did you do?"

"I swam through the trap into the concentration pond. But I still would be exposed if I tried to emerge from the water, so . . ."

"So?"

"So I swam to the gate into the cannery, waited till it opened and propelled myself into the chute toward the eviscerator."

"Hah!" snorted Joel Karamor. "Just the grace of God I'm not opening a can of sardines and finding you. Canned Magnus Ridolph!"

"No," said the white-bearded sage. "There was little danger of the eviscerator. The chute is set at a gentle slope . . . As you may imagine, the operator of the machine was startled when I appeared before him. Fortunately for me he was a Capellan, excellent at routine tasks, short on initiative, and he raised no special outcry when I rose from the chute.

"I removed the diving suit, explained to the Capellan that I was testing the slope of the channel—which seemed to satisfy him—and then I strolled out on the wharf.

"As I expected, Donnels was standing there, watching across the water. He did not hear me—I walk rather quietly. It now occurred to me that inasmuch as Donnels was young

151

and athletic, of choleric disposition and furthermore carried a hand-weapon, my bargaining position was rather poor. Accordingly I pushed him into the water."

"You did! Then what?"

Magnus Ridolph put on a doleful countenance.

"Then what, confound it?" bawled Karamor.

"A tragic occurrence," said Magnus Ridolph. He shook his head. "I might have foreseen it had I thought. You remember, I mentioned the fish following me back from the dike."

Karamor stared. "You mean?"

"Donnels drowned," said Magnus Ridolph. "The fish drowned him. Feeble individually, in the mass they drove him away from the wharf, pulled him under. A distressing sight. I was very upset."

Karamor paced once, twice, across the room, flung himself into a chair opposite Magnus Ridolph.

"An accident, hey? Poor unfortunate Donnels, hey? Is that the story? The trouble is, Magnus, I know you too well. The whole thing sounds too precise. These—ah, intelligent sardines"—he made a sardonic mouth—"had no idea Donnels would be pushed into the water?"

"Well," said Magnus Ridolph thoughtfully. "I *did* mention that he would probably be waiting on the wharf. And the Barnett charts, though very useful of course, are not infallible. I suppose it's not impossible that the fish assumed—"

"Never mind, never mind," said Karamor wearily.

"Look at it this way," suggested Magnus Ridolph easily. "If Donnels had not attempted to blast and poison the fish they would not have drowned him. If Donnels had not sent Naile to blast me out of the water and had not been waiting on the dock for the honor of shooting me personally I would not have pushed him in."

"Yes," said Karamor, "and if you hadn't stolen his suit he probably wouldn't have been waiting for you."

Magnus Ridolph pursed his lips. "If we pursue the matter of ultimate responsibility to the limit we might arrive at you, who, as Donnels partner, is legally responsible for his actions."

Karamor sighed. "How did the whole thing start?"

"A natural evolution," said Magnus Ridolph. "Donnels and Naile, in stocking Chandaria with sardines, naturally selected the best sardines possible. Then in the laboratory, while waiting for the fish to multiply, they encouraged mutations to improve the stock even further.

"One of these mutations proved highly intelligent, and I fancy this gave Donnels his big idea. Why not breed a strain of intelligent fish which could be trained to work for him, like sheep-dogs or better, like the Judas-goat which leads the sheep into the abbatoir?

"They set to work breeding, cross-breeding, and indeed a very intelligent sardine resulted. Those which would cooperate with Donnels rendered very valuable service, enabling him to can fish without going to the trouble of catching them himself.

"A few of the fish, the most intelligent, preferred freedom and founded a colony near the dike. Donnels soon learned of this colony because all but the most servile of his Judas fish swam off and joined their brothers.

"Taming these fish, teaching them, was a laborious task and Donnels decided to exterminate the colony. He also feared that the intelligent fish might outnumber the normal ones and refuse to be led blindly into his concentration pond. He tried blasting and poison from the surface but was unsuccessful, as the fish could see him coming. So he ordered a diving-suit from Rhodope.

"Meanwhile the fish had launched a counter-offensive. They had no weapons—they could not attack Donnels directly. But they knew the purpose of the cannery, that it packed sardines for human consumption.

"They developed the skill to build the bubbles on the dike—a secretion, I believe—and prepare a series of offensive substances. Then a great number of ordinary sardines were captured, packed with these substances, sent into the cannery to be canned and exported."

Joel Karamor rose abruptly to his feet, once more paced the glossy floor. "And what happened to Naile?"

"He showed up a day later. A mere tool."

Karamor shook his head. "I suppose the plant is a total loss. Did you make arrangements to evacuate the help?"

Magnus Ridolph widened his eyes in surprise. "None whatever. Was I supposed to do so?"

"I gave you full powers," snapped Karamor. "You should have seen to it."

A buzzer sounded. Karamor pushed the button. A soft voice spoke. Karamor's brindle-gray hair rose in a startled ruff.

"Cargo of canned sardines? Hold on." He turned to Magnus Ridolph. "Who dispatched the sardines? What's going on here—and there?"

Magnus Ridolph shrugged. "The cannery is functioning as

153

before—under new management. Using my powers I made the necessary arrangements. Your share of the profits shall be as before."

Karamor halted in mid-stride. "So? And who is my partner? Naile?"

"By no means," said Magnus Ridolph. "He has nothing to offer."

"Who then?" bellowed Karamor.

"Naturally, the colony of intelligent sardines I told you about."

"What!"

"Yes, said Magnus Ridolph. "You are now associated commercially with a shoal of sardines. The Sardine-Karamor Company."

"My word," husked Karamor. *"My word!"*

"The advantages to all concerned are obvious," said Magnus Ridolph. "You are assured of efficient management with high-grade raw material guaranteed. The sardines receive whatever civilized amenities they desire."

Karamor was silent for some minutes. He turned a narrow eye on the bland Magnus Ridolph.

"I detect the Ridolph touch in this scheme. The characteristic lack of principle, the calculated outing of orthodox practise . . ."

"Tut, tut," said Magnus Ridolph. "Not at all, not at all."

Karamor snorted. "Do you deny that the whole program was your idea?"

"Well," said Magnus Ridolph carefully, "I admit that I pointed out to the fishes the advantages of the arrangement."

TO B OR NOT TO C OR TO D

WALKING on Caffron Beach in the planet Azul's watery blue-green twilight Magnus Ridolph was confronted by a scowling man of formidable appearance—very tall, very broad, with thundercloud eyebrows, a mouth and jaw like an ore-crusher.

"Are you Magnus Ridolph?" The tone was direct with overtones of bellicosity.

Magnus Ridolph wondered which of his creditors had been so importunate as to pursue him out here on the quiet blue sand beside Veridical Sea. Unfortunate—impossible to avoid him now.

Magnus Ridolph said frankly, "I am he."

The carbuncle eyes of the scowling man bored into Magnus Ridolph's pale blue ones. "I understand you're a detective."

Magnus Ridolph pursed his lips thoughtfully, touched his neat white beard. "Why, I suppose that term might be used. Generally I refer to myself as—"

The scowling man looked off across the ink-black water. "I don't care what you call yourself. John Southern recommended you."

"Ah, yes," Magnus Ridolph nodded. "I remember him. The statues in the King of Maherleon's harem."

The big man's scowl deepened. "You're not what I expected."

"Intelligence, facility, resourcefulness are not like neckties, to be displayed as ornaments," Magnus Ridolph pointed out.

"Maybe you can angle and argue but can you produce when the going's tough? That's what I want to know.

Confident that the man, no matter how unpleasant, was no bill collector Magnus Ridolph said affably, "That depends upon the circumstances."

The big man's expression became slightly contemptuous.

Magnus Ridolph said easily, "The circumstances include a feeling of sympathy with my client. So far you have aroused no such sensation."

The big man grinned. "I arouse what sympathy I need by writing my name to a check. My name is Howard Thifer. I'm in the heavy metals business."

Magnus Ridolph nodded. "I have heard your name mentioned."

"Probably as a high-flying free-wheeling financial hell-raiser."

"I believe the term 'unscrupulous blackguard' was used," said Ridolph.

Thifer made an impatient gesture with a forearm the size of a rolled-up welcome mat. "Never mind about that. The squealing of scalded shoats! I'm up against something fantastic. Something I can't fight. It's costing me money and I've got to lick it."

"Suppose you describe your problem."

Thifer turned the full gaze of his red-brown eyes on Mag-

155

nus Ridolph. "This is confidential, understand? If anything leaked out there'd be trouble for both of us. Get me?"

Magnus Ridolph shrugged, started to move away, across the pale blue beach. "I find that your proposition does not interest me."

A hand like a bear paw descended on his shoulder. In outrage Magnus Ridolph swung around. "Hands off, sir!"

Thifer said with a heavy leer, "At the Green Lion Hostel two process servers are waiting for you. They've got a multiple notice of judgment."

Magnus Ridolph chewed at his lip. "That confounded zoo," he muttered. Aloud, "Mr. Thifer, what is the nature of your problem, and how much are you able to pay?"

"First of all," said Thifer, "I'll warn you that if you take on this job there's a good chance you'll be killed. In fact you'll certainly be killed unless you do better than the last twenty men. You see, I'm being frank with you. Are you still interested?"

Magnus Ridolph remarked that if his death were a necessary adjunct to the solving of the mystery he feared that his fee would have to be disproportionately large.

Thifer said, "Well, here's the set-up. I own a planet."

"A planet *in toto?*"

"Yes," said Thifer roughly. "I own Jexjeka. I'm—quite wealthy."

Magnus Ridolph sighed. "I am not. My zoo is unsuccessful. It has cost me a great deal."

"Hm. So that howling menagerie of monsters is your doing?"

"No longer. I've sold the whole affair for two hundred munits."

Howard Thifer snorted, a sound that would have fractured the larynx of an ordinary man. "Here's the situation—or better, come aboard my ship, where I can show you on the chart."

"Jexjeka is rock, all rock," said Thifer. "There are what I call oases—four springs of good water. Only water on the planet. Two in each hemisphere, as you see. My headquarters is here"—he pointed—"at A, closest to the mines."

"Heavy metals?"

"I'm mining a crystal of pure tungsten the size of a house. I've got an open-pit of selenium oxide and I'm working a

156

three-foot vein of centaurium trioxide, with uranium. But that's neither here nor there," he said impatiently. "About two years ago I decided to make Jexjeka self-sustaining."

Magnus Ridolph frowned. "A planet all rock?"

Thifer said, "It's airless, lifeless—not even spores. But I'm using Thalurian labor—anaerobes from Thaluri Second. They eat like wolves and it costs me real money keeping them in supplies.

"I figured to plant some of the native vegetation at the oases, have them grow some of their own food. So I freighted in soil, planted an orchard of Thalurian trees, the fiber things with the glass leaves. Now, see here at oasis B, the closest to A—this is where I set out the first orchard, also a meadow for the Thalurian cows." He sat back, glowered at the chart.

"And?" Magnus Ridolph prompted.

"It's what I can't understand. It puzzles me. Everything went beautifully. The trees give bigger crops than they do on Thaluri Second. The cows—I call 'em that, they're big barrels with long legs for hanging on to the rocks—they multiplied like rabbits, really prospered."

Magnus Ridolph scanned the chart, glanced up into Thifer's big flat face. "Clearly I am dense. You have spoken at length and I still fail to understand your problem." He smoothed the front of his neat white and blue tunic.

Thifer scowled. "Let's understand each other, Ridolph. I'm not paying you for sarcasm. I don't like to be the butt of your jokes, anybody's jokes."

Magnus Ridolph inspected him coolly. "Calm yourself, Mr. Thifer. Your display of temper embarrasses me."

Thifer's face swelled with dark blood. He clenched his hands, then in a low thick voice he said, "About a year ago I decided to expand my orchard to oasis C. On the night of June thirteen, Earth-time, every man at the oasis disappeared. They vanished off the face of the planet as if they'd never been there. There were two Earthmen, a Rhodopian clerk, four Thalurians."

"Any ships missing?"

"No, nothing like that. We were mystified, naturally. An investigation told us nothing. But I still went ahead, expanded the farm to oasis D. Eighty-four days after the first disappearance the same thing happened.

"Every man vanished without trace from both C and D. No sign of violence, no struggle, no hint of any kind as to what happened. Naturally camp routine was disrupted. The Thalurians, as you may know, are a very superstitious

157

bunch—easily frightened. The second disappearance set them off into a serious demonstration. I finally got them quiet and imported a crew of men I could trust from another working.

"I sent this crew out to C and D. Eighty-four days after the previous disappearance they disappeared, the whole bunch—lock, stock and barrel. Gone into thin air—expect there's no air on Jexjeka. And at each disappearance went all the Thalurians I was able to persuade out to C and D to tend the orchard and the cows—and likewise all the cows."

Magnus Ridolph asked, "Have you appealed to the TCI?"

Thifer sounded his gargantuan snort. "That gang of scroungers? You know what they told me? They told me I had no business on Jexjeka in the first place. That, since it lay outside the legal bounds of the Commonwealth, they had no legal right to investigate. And mind you, every eighty-four days citizens of the Commonwealth were disappearing into nowhere. They wouldn't even turn their heads to spit in my direction."

Magnus Ridolph rubbed his beard. "You're sure there is not some simple explanation? The men are not working with a gang of hijackers or black-birders?"

Thifer said, "Nonsense!" and glowered indignantly at Magnus Ridolph.

Magnus Ridolph said, "I agree that you have given me an interesting story. I suppose your idea is that I take up residence at either C or D, risking my own disappearance?"

"That's right."

Magnus Ridolph said slowly, "Actually I have outlived my usefulness. If I am to be killed on Jexjeka my only concern is for my creditors. I would not care to have the stigma of debt soil my memory.

"Hm—you say that there are two process-servers waiting at the hostel? Well, I will be modest. Give me a check for ten thousand munits and satisfy the process-servers and I will undertake your problem for you."

Thifer growled, "Just what do you owe these process-servers?"

"I'm not sure," said Magnus Ridolph, looking blandly at the chart. "The bill was merely provisions for the creatures in my zoo."

"Provisions for how long?"

"Four months—no longer."

Thifer considered. "That shouldn't be too much. Very well, I'll do it."

"I'll write out a quick agreement," suggested Magnus Ridolph. He did so and Howard Thifer, after grumbling about the delay, put his signature to it.

Together they left the cruiser, returned to the Green Lion Hostel in the Vale of Tempe at the head of Caffron Beach.

Two young men, sitting in the lobby, jumped to their feet at the sight of Magnus Ridolph, advanced upon him like terriers.

"Gentlemen, gentlemen!" said Magnus Ridolph, holding his hands up in mock dismay. "There is no need for your unpleasant documents. Are you empowered to accept a settlement?"

"We'll settle for the exact sum of the judgment, not one cent less."

"Mr. Thifer here will pay you. Please submit him your bill."

Thifer pulled out a checkbook. "How much is it?" he rumbled.

"One hundred and twenty-two thousand, six hundred and twenty munits. Make it payable to Vanguard Organic Supply of Starport."

Thifer turned to Magnus Ridolph with a terrible slow fury. "You lying swindling old goat!"

"'Goat,'" said Magnus Ridolph, "is an epithet I dislike. Others have regretted its use. My beard is an affectation, I agree. Aside from this beard I have no hircine characteristics."

Thifer's eyes were level pools of hot fire. "You told me this bill was for animal food. You tricked me into—"

"No such thing!" protested Magnus Ridolph. "You need merely read the statement these gentlemen will hand you."

Thifer reached across, snatched a sheet of paper from the process-server, who protested feebly. The sheet read:

"To Magnus Ridolph, statement of indebtedness, as per invoice below, covering deliveries during last quarter.

100 kg. candied ceegee eggs @ M80/kg.	M 8,000
200 liters sap (from Yellow-Bounding Tree of Lennox IV) @ M45/liter	9,000
One ton live chancodilla grubs @ M4,235/ton	4,235
Two tons slime from bed of Lanklark Sinkhole @ 380/ton	760
50 lbs. California raisins, first quality @ M1/lb.	50
100 cases ripe ticholama buds from Naos VI @ M42/case	4,200
20 frozen mandrakes @ M600	12,000
400 cartons—"	

Thifer flung back the statement. He said briefly to Magnus Ridolph, "I won't pay it."

Magnus Ridolph asid, "I have no choice but to sue for breach of contract. And in addition you will be denied the pleasure of my disappearance from your oases C and D."

"True," said Thifer. "It's worth many times the money to assist, even in a small way, at your disappearance. I warn you, Ridolph, I'm not a forgiving man." He turned to the process-server. "How much was that again?"

"One hundred twenty-two thousand six hundred and twenty munits."

"Here's your check." He jerked his head to Magnus Ridolph. "Have your luggage sent out to my cruiser. We're leaving for Jexjeka at once."

"As you wish," said Magnus Ridolph.

During the eight-day voyage from Azul in Sagittarius to Jexjeka in Cancer 3/2, Magnus Ridolph spoke to Howard Thifer exactly twice. They lunched together the first day out and agreed to discuss the mystery in the observation dome over coffee.

The discussion began amiably—"a feast of reason, a flow of soul." Before long Magnus Ridolph expressed surprise at the fact that while Thifer had prospected the planet for minerals and organic life he had ignored the possible presence of the inorganic, sometimes supersensory, creatures found on certain planets, even on Earth, where they were known as ghosts.

Here Thifer vented his most devastating snort to date. "John Southern told me you were a detective, not an incense-swinging hoochy-macooch witch-doctor."

Magnus Ridolph nodded philosophically, remarking that his attitude was not unusual. He cited the animal world. Swine, bears, seals among others also took their sensory impressions to be an accurate picture of the world, said Magnus Ridolph.

Thifer's eyes began to glisten. Before long epithets were exchanged and the word 'goat' was used, whereupon Magnus Ridolph rose to his feet, bowed in icy politeness and left the dome.

The lunch and the discussion comprised the two occasions on which Howard Thifer and Magnus Ridolph spoke during the cruise. Only when the ship sank into a glass-smooth basin of what evidently had been a tremendous blister in the basalt

160

did the two once more exchange words. And now Thifer, on his home territory, was inclined to be affable.

"Rock, rock, rock," he said. "Damn impressive planet and not a bad place to live if it had an atmosphere. Not too hot, not too cold. Maybe one of these days I'll set up an air plant, build up some atmosphere. Should make a good tourist planet, wouldn't you say, Ridolph?"

"Very spectacular," agreed Magnus Ridolph. A year or so previously he had seen published in the Augustan Review a list of the settled planets arranged by Arthur Idry, the explorer, in order of their increasingly unearthly and bizarre quality.

Earth was naturally norm, with Fan, Naos VI, Exigencia, Omicron Ceti III, Mallard 42, Rhodope, New Sudan, high on the list. At the bottom were ranged such strange worlds as Formaferra, Julian Wolters IV, Alpheratz IX, Gengillee. Looking now across Jexjeka Magnus Ridolph decided that Idry had missed a good bet for last place on the list.

Jexjeka was the sole satellite of three suns—Rouge, a nearby red giant, Blanche, a white Sol-sized star at a greater distance, and Noir, Blanche's dark companion. Jexjeka revolved around Rouge so that for half of each sidereal year two suns shone during the day. For the other half Rouge shone during the day, Blanche during the so-called night.

Rouge filled half the black sky, a monster ball of molten red whose globular shape was manifest. Indeed its equatorial region seemed to bulge out into the observer's face. The dazzling white disk of Blanche hung slightly to the side. Noir was nowhere visible.

The ship had berthed at the center of a vast shallow basin. The black glass of the floor rose in a gradual catenary to a mile-high rampart of gray rock, at the base of which were a huddle of shiny domes and a tailings pile. Thifer's living quarters were in another dome slighty removed from the mine buildings, beside oasis A, a pool of clear water.

Formed by chemical action in the warm interior of Jexjeka it was conveyed to the surface in the form of vapor, to condense and trickle into a pool, where it gradually evaporated into interstellar space, which here began at the planet's surface. Magnus Ridolph was forced to admit that the planet had a certain mad beauty to it.

Distance on this airless world of gigantic proportions was hard to estimate. The perspectives had a peculiar distorted slant. Magnus Ridolph judged Thifer's dwelling to be a mile distant and he was surprised when the surface car, which

161

trundled along the glass-smooth bed of the blister, required ten minutes to make the trip.

The car entered an airlock. Thifer swung open the door. "We're here."

It was evident that Thifer had devoted neither time nor money to sybaritic niceties. Magnus Ridolph frowned at the unrelieved concrete floor, the blank walls, the rigid furniture.

"Your quarters are this way," said Thifer and led Magnus Ridolph down a hall walled with corrugated aluminum to a room overlooking the pool.

The room was furnished with a narrow bed, a chest of drawers painted gray-green, a straight-back chair painted white.

"You are very wise," Magnus Ridolph observed sagely. "Very sensitive."

"How so?" inquired Thifer.

"You have accurately grasped the personality of the planet and have carried the feeling in its most subtle nuances into the furnishings of your house. Quite correctly you decided that starkness and rigor was the only answer to the blank simplicity of the landscape."

"Mmmph," said Thifer, grinning sourly. "Glad you like it. Most people don't. Damned if I'll spend any money on padding fat buttocks. I made it the hard way—hard work and hard living—and blast it if I'll change my style now."

"Sensible," agreed Magnus Ridolph. "Ah—your food is as unaffected as your accommodations?"

"We eat," said Thifer. "Nothing fancy but we eat."

Magnus Ridolph nodded. "Well, I think I'll bathe and change clothes. Perhaps you'll have my luggage brought in?"

"Sure," said Thifer. "Bathroom's past that panel. Nice brisk shower does wonders for a man. Piped direct from the pool. Lunch in about an hour."

Reflecting that the sooner he resolved the mystery of Oases C and D the sooner he could return to civilization, at lunchtime Magnus Ridolph announced his intention of immediate investigation.

"Good, good," said Thifer. "You'll need an air-suit and something to get around in. You'll have to go by yourself—I've got a stack of work to attend to. You won't be bothered—there's nobody at either C or D. Getting close to the eighty-fourth day."

Magnus Ridolph nodded in polite acquiescence.

After lunch Thifer fitted him with an air-suit, took him behind the dome to an area cluttered with all types of boats, in varying degrees of repair.

Magnus Ridolph chose a small homemade hopper—two light I-beams welded to form an X and fitted with a plywood platform. The hopper was lifted by jets at the tips of the X, propelled and steered by a jet under the platform. Simple, useful, foolproof.

Armed with a small hand-gun—despite Thifer's assurance that no living creature roamed the planet—Magnus Ridolph climbed on the platform, settled himself in an orderly fashion, tested the power-pack, inspected the fuel cartridge, flicked the switch, jiggled the controls, slowly turned the wing-nut which served as a lift control.

The hopper rose like an elevator. Magnus Ridolph nodded coolly to Thifer, who stood watching him with a poorly concealed grin of amusement, and sent the hopper skidding up on a slant over the great gray pegmatite rampart.

Wilderness, thought Magnus Ridolph—wilderness in the most implacable magnitude. Incomprehensible chaos of black and gray, stained vermilion in the light of Rouge and Blanche. Tables, spires, crevasses the human eye had never been designed to see, the human brain to grasp.

Massiveness in terms of cubic miles, cubic tens of miles. Pillars of crystal threaded with crimson light. Fields of silver-shining gneiss, rippled in accurate sinusoidal waves. Canyons shadowed in the imperturable black of airless shade. Blisters with polished floors, craters, blowholes. . . .

As Magnus Ridolph flew he asked himself, if there were life on Jexjeka with a volition that permitted settlement at A and B but barred it at C and D, where and how would this life manifest itself? The repetition of the eighty-four-day period indicated cyclical activity, seasonal fluctuation, obedience to some sort of law.

Religious sacrifices? Disease with an eighty-four-day incubation period? Magnus Ridolph pursed his lips skeptically. He halted the hopper, scanned the face of Jexjeka below him, saw a vast obsidian mirror, tilted at ten or fifteen degrees. Ten miles it extended to its edge, where the surface was marred by striated conchoidal ripples.

Magnus Ridolph dropped to twenty feet above the glistening surface. The light from the two suns penetrated the clear glass, flittered and shone from tiny aventurine flakes. Magnus Ridolph landed, alighted, stooped, looked closely at the surface. Clean polished glass, not one puff of dust.

Magnus Ridolph climbed back on the hopper, raised it

three feet, let it skid down slope to where the obsidian surface curled up into a lip. Beyond was a precipice. Magnus Ridolph floated over the edge, peered into the darkness. Sight was swallowed in the blackness.

He let the hopper settle—down, down, down, out of the sunlight. He flicked on the lights stapled to the sides of the platform. Down, down, down—at last the bottom of the canyon loomed gray below, rose to meet him.

The hopper came gently to rest like a piece of water-logged wood settling to the dark bed of an ocean. The canyon floor was an unidentifiable black rock with large fibrous gray crystals. Magnus Ridolph looked up, down the stony waste to the edge of his private pool of light. No dust, no evidence that living foot had rested on this secret floor.

Raising the hopper a few feet over the rock floor he cruised slowly up the canyon. Nothing—bare rock bed, cold, dismal, forlorn. Magnus Ridolph suddenly felt a trace of uneasiness, a clamped-in feeling. He raised the hopper—up, up, up, into the pale red light of Rouge and Blanche, clear of the obsidian plain. He took his bearings and proceeded toward B.

He was impressed by the extent of Howard Thifer's development work. Thirty or forty acres surrounding the pool had been covered with light black loam from Thaluri II and the fiber-trunked trees with the square glass leaves ranged in row after row. On most of these trees orange-brown fruit swelled from the trunks the size of melons, ready for harvest.

On an area set aside for pasture a dozen Thalurian cows crawled, cropping at silver spiny grass. And from the orchard a dozen shiny-skinned Thalurian natives peered at Magnus Ridolph, ducking back behind the glass foliage when he turned to look at them.

They bore a strange resemblance to the cows, Magnus Ridolph noticed, though they stood upright and the cows half-crawled, half-wallowed. Their eyes rose on thick stalks above the headless shoulders, with the food-mouth between the eyes.

Magnus Ridolph alighted from the hopper. The Thalurians bent their eye-stalks through the foliage, danced nervously as he approached.

Magnus Ridolph nodded politely, glanced here, there, looked at the pool of water. Nothing of interest—he found it to be merely a pool of water, boiling slightly into the vacuum though the temperature was close to freezing. He returned to

164

the hopper, rose high, headed for C on the other side of the planet.

C appeared identical to B except for the absence of the Thalurians and the Thalurian cows. Peculiar, that resemblance thought Magnus Ridolph—evolutionary kinship. No doubt a similar organic relationship existed among Earth fauna in the eyes of the Thalurians.

He examined the trees. The ripe fruit had burst, releasing hordes of tiny pulsing corpuscles, round and red as pomegranate seeds. They jerked, quivered, urged themselves away from the parent tree.

Magnus Ridolph looked long and carefully through the orchard. He examined it intently, minutely. Nothing—as Thifer had told him, no sign of struggles, no damage, no clues. Magnus Ridolph strolled back and forth seeking tracks, bent grass, broken twigs.

Broken twigs? No—but several of the twigs which might have borne big glass leaves ended in bare nubbins of fiber. There was no sign of the missing leaves at the base of the tree. Magnus Ridolph whistled through his teeth. A few missing leaves might mean much or nothing. Perhaps it was normal for trees to carry leafless twigs. Magnus Ridolph tucked the idea to the back of his mind. He would question Thifer when opportunity offered.

Up in his hopper, away to D. Identical to B and C except that it lay at the foot of a tremendous spike of red granite, which shone like bronze where the dull light of Rouge—a sliver of Rouge bulging over the horizon—struck. D was as deserted as C. A few leaves were missing from some of the trees.

The sliver of Rouge disappeared. Darkness poured down as if the sky were a chute. Magnus Ridolph shivered in spite of the warmed air in his suit. Desolation, solitude, existed only by contrast with a mental picture of what might be.

Such concepts never occurred to a brain in mid-space. Space was tremendous, empty—the ultimate grandeur—but neither dismal nor desolate. The loneliness of the dark orchard at D preyed on the brain only because other orchards, warm, fragrant, hospitable, existed.

He flung the hopper high, returned to B, where it was still day. He alighted, examined the trees while the Thalurians hid and watched him with eye-stalks pushed through the glass foliage. Every twig ended in a square brittle leaf.

Back on his hopper, up into airless space. Very little power

165

gave the hopper great speed in the absence of friction. And Magnus Ridolph arrived back at Station A in time for dinner.

Thifer greeted him with initial curiosity then ignored him, conversing in a belligerent grumbling tone to Smitz, the mine foreman, a thin sad-eyed man with hair like salt-grass. Magnus Ridolph, at the far end of the table, ate sparingly of cucumbers and a poorly-seasoned pot-pie.

At last Thifer turned to Magnus Ridolph with an amused sardonic expression as if, now that important business had been dealt with, other matters could be considered.

"Well," said Thifer, "did you locate your ghosts?"

Magnus Ridolph raised his fine white eyebrows. "Ghosts? I don't understand you."

"You said once that you thought ghosts might be responsible for the disappearances."

"I fear you misinterpreted my words. I spoke on a level of abstraction you plainly did not comprehend. In reply to your question I saw no ghosts."

"See anything at all?"

"I noticed that leaves were missing from some of the trees at C and D. Do you know why this should be?"

Thifer, with a sly wink at Smitz, the foreman, who sat watching Magnus Ridolph with an open smile, said, "Nope. Maybe when the boys disappeared they took the leaves with 'em for souvenirs."

"You may have hit on the correct answer," said Magnus Ridolph evenly. "Some sort of explanation exists. Hm—there are no other planets in the system?"

"Nope. Not a one. Three stars, one planet."

"You're certain? After all, this system, lying outside the Commonwealth, has probably not been surveyed."

"I'm certain. There's just the three stars and Jexjeka."

Magnus Ridolph considered a moment. Then, "Jexjeka revolves around Rouge and the dark star Noir revolves around Blanche. Am I right?"

"Right as a trivet. And Rouge and Blanche revolve around each other. Regular merry-go-round."

"Ha-ha-ha," laughed Smitz.

"Have you checked the periods of these revolutions?"

"No. What difference does it make? It's about as foolish as your idea about ghosts."

Magnus Ridolph frowned. "Allow me to be the judge of that. After all you have paid a hundred and thirty-two thousand munits for my services."

Thifer laughed. "I've got that all figured out. Don't worry a minute. You'll earn it. If not by detecting you'll do it digging. We pay our men fifteen munits a day, board and room."

Magnus Ridolph's voice was mild. "Do I understand you correctly? That if I am unable to explain the disappearances I refund you your fee through manual labor?"

Thifer's laugh boomed out again and Smitz' drier chuckle joined his merriment.

"You got three choices," said Thifer. "Detect, disappear or dig. D'you think I'm such a patsy as to let you pull what you pulled on me at Azul and get away with it?"

"Ah," said Magnus Ridolph, "you think I dealt with you unfairly. And you brought me to Jexjeka to put me to work in your mines."

"You got it right, mister. I'm a hard man to deal with when I'm crowded."

Magnus Ridolph returned to the cucumbers. "Your unpleasant threats are supererogatory."

"Are *what?*"

"Unnecessary. I intend to solve the mystery of the disappearances."

Thifer's big mouth twisted in the aftermath of his laugh. "I'd say you were sensible."

"One more question," said Magnus Ridolph. "The interval between the disappearance is what?"

"Eighty-four days. A little over a year—a Jexjeka year, that is. The year is eighty-two days of twenty-six Earth hours each."

"According to this interval, when would the next critical night be due?"

"In—let's see—four days."

"Thank you," said Ridolph and addressed himself to his cucumbers.

"Got any ideas?" Thifer asked.

"A large number. It is the basis of my method. I examine every conceivable hypothesis. I make an outline, expanding the sub-headings as fully as possible. If I am sufficiently thorough among these hypotheses will be actuality.

"So far my theories range from crevasses gaping to engulf the men through ghosts to your murdering these men yourself for some purpose of your own. Possibly insurance."

Smitz' chin dropped, dangled, wobbled. He darted a startled glance at Thifer, drew slightly away.

Thifer's face was a blank blotch of tough leathery flesh. "Anything's possible," he said.

Magnus Ridolph made a pedantic gesture with his fork. "Many things are not possible. Your concept of ghosts—pseudo-religious bogies—is impossible. Mine is not. I'll grant that if your kind of ghosts were possible they would enjoy haunting Jexjeka. It is the bleakest most chilling world I have ever seen."

"You'll get used to it," said Thifer grimly. "A hundred and thirty-two thousand munits, at fifteen munits a day, is—eighty-seven hundred days. You're lucky I throw in board, room, work-clothes."

Magnus Ridolph rose. "I find your humor difficult to enjoy. Excuse me, please." He bowed and left them. As the door slid back into place he heard Thifer's booming laugh and Smitz' ready cackle. And Magnus Ridolph smiled quietly.

Four days to the critical night. Magnus Ridolph commandeered the hopper, flew high, flew low across the planet. He landed at the poles—to the north a slanted field of basalt steps, hexagonally fractured. To the south an undulating scoriaceous plain. Footprints here would leave marks for all eternity. But the prairie lay smooth as lamb's-fleece for miles.

He explored valleys and clefts, landed the hopper on razor-keen mountain crests, looking down into the black, black-pink and gray-pink tumble. Nowhere did he find a trace of the vanished men.

He studied stations C and D with eyes that saw each square inch as a discreet area, alone and individual. And beyond the disappearance of the glass leaves, he found no circumstance which could be considered suggestive.

The fourth day arrived. At breakfast Thifer engaged Magnus Ridolph in jovial conversation, plied him with questions about his ill-fated zoo, remarked several times at the surprising expense of feeding the exotic animals. Magnus Ridolph replied curtly. The mystery had eaten at his sheath of equanimity. And in spite of a distaste for using himself as bait he could conceive no other method by which the puzzle might be resolved.

He loaded the hopper with such equipment as he considered might be useful—plastron rope, a grenade-rifle, a case of condensed provisions, tanks of water, brandy, an infra-red viewer, binoculars, a high-pressure atomizer which he loaded with fluorescent dye, thinking that if invisible creatures manifested themselves, he could discern that nature by spraying them with dye. Also included was a portable TV transmitter by means of which he planned to keep in touch with Thifer.

Thifer watched the preparations with detached amusement. At last Magnus Ridolph was ready to depart. As if by sudden thought he looked ingenuously toward Thifer. "Perhaps you'd like to accompany me? You must be curious."

Thifer snorted his mastodonic snort. "Not *that* curious! I was curious to the extent of a hundred thirty-two thousand munits, that's enough."

Magnus Ridolph nodded regretfully. "Well, goodby."

"Goodby," said Thifer. "Turn on the transmitter as soon as you arrive. I want to see what happens."

The hopper rose on its four cross-arms. The propulsive jets took hold, the little platform slid off across the waste.

Thifer watched the hopper become a pink mote, then returned inside the dome. He removed his air-suit, brewed a gallon of tea, sat beside the telescreen.

Two hours later the call-light glowed. Thifer pushed the switch. A view of C appeared on the screen and he heard Magnus Ridolph's voice.

"Everything is about as usual. No sign of anything strange. I'm hovering at twenty feet. Trip lines are threaded entirely around the oasis. A snake could not approach without signaling its presence. The sun is setting, as you see."

"I think I'll turn on the flood-lights." Thifer saw a sudden increase of illumination. "At intervals I plan to spray the area with the fluorescent dye. If anything more solid than the vacuum is present it should show up."

Magnus Ridolph's voice faded off. And Thifer, watching intently, saw the view on his screen change as Magnus Ridolph slid the hopper here and there around the oasis.

Darkness came, dead black sightlessness beyond the reach of the floodlights. On Thifer's screen the oasis showed in harsh black and white contrast, the glass leaves on the trees glinting and twinkling like spray. Several hours passed, during which, at intervals Magnus Ridolph made terse reports.

"Nothing unusual. No disturbance of any sort."

Then Thifer heard him say, in a tone of puzzlement, "There's a peculiar feeling—indescribable. A presence of—"

The words broke off, the view in the screen gave a tremendous blurring swing.

Thifer was gazing into blackness. He slowly arose. "Mmph," he muttered. "Looks like the old goat earned his money the hard way."

The following day when he made a cautious survey of C, there was no sign of Magnus Ridolph, his hopper or any of his equipment. Magnus Ridolph had disappeared as completely as if Destiny had reached back in time and erased the fact of his birth.

Thifer shrugged. It was a mystery. Evidently it would remain a mystery as he intended to spend no more money and endanger no more men towards its solution. Farm C and D eighty days out of the year, abandon them during the dangerous nights. The only sensible thing to do.

Two days passed. On the night of the second day Thifer sat with Smitz the mine foreman and Edson the chief engineer at the long dining table. Dinner had been cleared away. The three were discussing a small refining plant at the mouth of the centaurium mine. A model stood on the table before them, mugs of beer were at hand.

The door opened, Magnus Ridolph entered quietly, nodded. "Good evening, gentlemen. Busy, I see. Go right ahead. Don't let me interrupt."

"Ridolph!" bellowed Thifer. "Where have you been?"

Magnus Ridolph raised his eyebrows. "Why, pursuing my mission, of course."

"But—you disappeared!"

Magnus Ridolph stroked his beard complacently. "In a sense, yes. But only temporarily as you see."

Thifer frowned and his red-brown eyes bored at Magnus Ridolph. Suddenly they glowed, became dangerously hot. "Do you mean to tell me you sneaked off the station?"

Magnus Ridolph made a brusque angry gesture. "Silence, man, silence! How in thunder can I talk while you bleat like a sheep?"

Thifer's face took on the maroon tinge of near-hysteria. In the lowest of voices he said, "Go ahead. It had better be good."

Said Magnus Ridolph, "I disappeared—just as all your other men disappeared. I was taken by the same agency that took them."

"And what is this agency?"

Magnus Ridolph settled into a chair. "It is a large black object. It exerts a tremendous urgency. It will brook no contrary will."

"Get to the point, Ridolph!"

"It is the dark star Noir—the world which you erroneously believe revolves around the white sun."

170

"But it does!" cried Thifer blankly. "You can see it in opposition and it eclipses"—his voice became a murmur—"every eighty-four days."

"The dark star follows a very peculiar orbit," said Magnus Ridolph. "An orbit in the shape of a figure-eight—around Blanche, across, around Rouge. The orbit brings it only a few thousand miles outside the orbit of Jexjeka. Close enough for its gravity to sweep the face of Jexjeka clean."

"Nonsense," snapped Thifer. "Impossible. If it came close enough to counter the gravitational field of Jexjeka it would pull the whole planet after it."

Magnus Ridolph shook his head. "Jexjeka is nine thousand miles in diameter. At the surface Noir's gravity is stronger than that of Rouge combined with the gravity of Jexjeka. At the center of the planet, forty-five hundred miles away, Rouge's gravity is dominant and Jexjeka continues in its orbit, though there are perturbations."

"Jexjeka's year is eighty-two days. Noir's cycle is eighty-four days, so that every year it passes Jexjeka at a different spot in the orbit. In ten or fifteen more years, Jexjeka should be far enough around so that when Noir swings around in back of Rouge, the effect should no longer be dangerous."

Thifer frowned, drummed on the table. He looked up at Magnus Ridolph. "What happened to you?"

"Well, first I felt a peculiar visceral sensation of lightness, which increased with amazing speed. Noir approached, passed very swiftly. Then I felt as if I were falling head downward. So I was—falling away from Jexjeka to Noir. The support-jets of the hopper, which had been turned against Jexjeka, were adding to the acceleration.

"I suppose a half-minute passed before I grasped what was occurring. And then I was out in space, falling against a great black sphere."

"Why can't we see it," said Thifer sharply. "Why is it not visible, like a moon?"

Magnus Ridolph considered. "Noir probably is composed of cold star-stuff—dovetailed protons, incredibly heavy, surrounded by an envelope of compacted gas which absorbs most of the incident light."

"Well," grumbled Thifer, "that may or may not be. Go on with your story."

"There's not much more to it. I righted the hopper, turned on all the power at hand. It was just barely enough to edge me back toward Jexjeka. It took two days to return."

"I suppose all the other men are dead?"

171

"I don't see how they could possibly have survived."

For a few moments there was silence in the room. Then Thifer pounded on the table with a fist like a small tub. "Well, if so, that's that. We know what it is and we can be careful."

"Such being the case," said Magnus Ridolph, "I have fulfilled my obligation to you. I have given you your money's worth. Now I would appreciate your returning me either to Azul or to one of the Gamma Scorpionis planets, whichever is more convenient to you."

Thifer growled. "There's an ore ship leaving pretty soon. You can stow aboard that."

Magnus Ridolph's eyebrows leveled. "How soon is pretty soon?"

"Depends on how fast we load her, how the ore runs. A month or two, maybe a little longer if we don't bring in a new vein."

"And where does this ore-ship unload?"

"At our plant on Hephaestos."

Magnus Ridolph said mildly, "That would be as inconvenient for me as Jexjeka."

"Sorry," said Thifer. "Right now I can't take time off to send you back. I've got other things to think of. That dark star—"

The engineer spoke. "Just what are you thinking of, chief?"

Thifer said slowly, "I don't know. I don't see that there's much we can do except leave and take everything movable with us every time the dark star comes around." He thudded his fist thoughtfully on the table. "Damned nuisance."

Magnus Ridolph said, "An orbit such as Noir's—a figure-eight—must be in the most exquisite balance. A comparatively slight force might have the effect of changing the orbit completely. It's very rare, the figure-eight—in fact I've never seen anything like it before."

Thifer looked at him woodenly and then comprehension dawned. "If Noir were slowed just a trifle while approaching Blanche it might change its orbit from a parabolic-type curve to an ellipse." He looked at his engineer. "What do you think, Edson?"

"Sounds reasonable," said Edson blinking rapidly.

"Maybe a big atomic explosion?" suggested Thifer. "Think there'd be enough jolt?"

Edson grimaced. He disliked being put on the spot.

172

"Well—the system must certainly be in delicate adjustment. Like a big boulder balanced on its end. Blow it, it falls over."

Thifer stood up with excitement in every deep line of his face. "We'll try it! Think of it! Think of the headlines! 'Howard Thifer changes star's orbit to protect men.' Sounds good, hey, men? Good publicity.

"By golly, Ridolph"—and he thumped Magnus Ridolph's thinly-fleshed back—"you *do* come up with an idea once in a while!" He turned to the foreman. "We got lots of atomite around, haven't we?"

Smitz nodded. "Lots of centaurium too. There's about five hundred tons waiting to be shipped."

"Crate it up. All of it. We'll use the atomite as a primer. We'll drop it on the front side of Noir. A two-billion-ton kick in the teeth for Noir."

He thought, added "Best time to drop the bomb is right now while it's leaving Rouge, approaching Blanche. Get her after the swing-around, she might start circling Rouge, and that would be bad. Yep, we'll drop her right now. Get busy, boys, this is something I want to do."

The explosion! A horrible rending blast, whiter than the heart of Blanche—Thifer and Magnus Ridolph witnessed it on the telescreen, from an image transmitted by Edson in the ore-ship.

Thifer in his excitement thumped Magnus Ridolph on the back. Magnus Ridolph moved away. Thifer bellowed into the mesh, "Did it do any good? Can you tell yet?"

"Hard to say," came Edson's voice. "We'd have to wait awhile—a few hours at least. Say chief." His voice took on a peculiar note. "The explosion is spreading—spreading fast. It's like the whole star's caught fire."

And in the screen Thifer and Magnus Ridolph saw the face of Noir glowing, glistening, blasting out in white lambent gouts.

"What's going on?" road Thifer. "What did you do?"

"Nothing, chief!" came Edson's remote voice. "Looks like we've got a little nova."

Thifer turned his boar's head toward Magnus Ridolph. His voice was low, quiet. "What's going on out there, Ridolph?"

Magnus Ridolph scratched his beard thoughtfully. "Evidently the energy of the explosion has jarred loose some of the protons of the star-matter and they're escaping with a great deal of kinetic energy. No doubt some of the energy has been molded—by the tremendous positive charge—into

173

free electrons. I wouldn't be surprised if the entire star flares up. I don't imagine the blast has appreciably affected the orbit."

"How so?"

"If you slowed it it would fall toward Blanche in a steeper parabola, snap back at a steeper angle. I'm afraid all that you could possibly do was disturb the balance of the system. On its next time around it might even collide with Jexjeka. In any event it will singe us rather thoroughly.

"Of course there's no need for alarm. A nova of this time should die down to nothing in a few years more or less. And then your mines can be operated again as good as new." He rose to his feet. "Right now I think I'll pack my baggage. The sooner we leave Jexjeka the better."

"Ridolph," whispered Thifer, "was this one of your tricks? If so I'll kill you with my two hands."

Magnus Ridolph raised his eyebrows. "Trick? The explosion was your idea."

"By your suggestion."

"Pooh!" said Magnus Ridolph. "I came out to Jexjeka for one purpose, to find where your men were disappearing. I did so. Thereupon you refused to return me to a civilized center, electing instead to drop bombs on a dark star."

"At your suggestion," repeated Thifer meaningfully.

Magnus Ridolph smiled thinly. "That statement has no legal foundation of truth. However, I suggest that instead of bickering with me you commence evacuating your crew. If Noir becomes a nova in actuality—even a small one— Jexjeka will be uncomfortably warm the next time it passes." He turned toward the door, paused.

"It might be wise to keep the publicity at a minimum. The new agencies would be apt to ridicule you mercilessly." Magnus Ridolph half-closed his eyes. " 'Dark star fights fire with fire! Thifer smokes self out.' "

"Shut up," said Thifer. "Get out."

" 'Thifer gives self cosmic hotfoot. Thought it was dark star, says miner,' " said Magnus Ridolph, passing through the doorway.

"Get out!" yelled Thifer. *"Get out!"*

Outstanding science fiction and fantasy

To order these titles,

see coupon on the

last page of this book.

Presenting JACK VANCE in DAW editions:

The "Demon Princes" Novels

STAR KING	#UE1402—$1.75
THE KILLING MACHINE	#UE1409—$1.75
THE PALACE OF LOVE	#UE1442—$1.75
THE FACE	#UJ1498—$1.95

The "Tschai" Novels

CITY OF THE CHASCH	#UE1461—$1.75
SERVANTS OF THE WANKH	#UE1467—$1.75
THE DIRDIR	#UE1478—$1.75
THE PNUME	#UE1484—$1.75

Others

WYST: ALASTOR 1716	#UJ1413—$1.95
SPACE OPERA	#UE1457—$1.75
EMPHYRIO	#UE1502—$2.25
THE FIVE GOLD BANDS	#UJ1518—$1.95
THE MANY WORLDS OF MAGNUS RIDOLPH	#UE1531—$1.75
THE LANGUAGES OF PAO	#UE1541—$1.75